CW01464536

About the Author

After working for an auctioneer and running a furniture shop, the arrival of her daughter gave her time to start developing what had been a great love since her early teens, dressmaking. The idea was a success and she produced many beautiful garments to her clients delight. In her fifties, she developed arthritis so unable to sew; she started thinking and returned to another love, dreaming up stories.

Only When the Moon is Big

Ann Kenyon

Only When the Moon is Big

Olympia Publishers
London

www.olympiapublishers.com
OLYMPIA PAPERBACK EDITION

Copyright © Ann Kenyon 2024

The right of Ann Kenyon to be identified as author of
this work has been asserted in accordance with sections 77 and 78 of
the Copyright, Designs and Patents Act 1988.

A CIP catalogue record for this title is
available from the British Library.

ISBN: 978-1-80439-374-1

This is a work of fiction.
Names, characters, places and incidents originate from the writer's
imagination. Any resemblance to actual persons, living or dead, is
purely coincidental.

First Published in 2024

Olympia Publishers
Tallis House
2 Tallis Street
London
EC4Y 0AB

Printed in Great Britain

Dedication

I dedicate this book to two people, my grandmother who told wonderful stories and my friend Sue without whom I would never have had the nerve to try to get it published.

Acknowledgements

Thanks Nancy and John for sorting out the paperwork.

Set in the later half of the nineteenth century: a time when the water board are buying up all available land on the Yorkshire Moors for water collection and building reservoirs to supply the booming cotton towns of North-West England. Jonas Bailey is a farmworker with aspirations to be a tenant farmer in his own right. Not afraid of hard work he agrees to longer hours in exchange for land to work as his own, but this places him very much at a disadvantage in dealings with his farmer landlord. Life is made more complicated still when his landlord's would be gentleman son takes a fancy for Jonas's beautiful daughter Gracie. Jonas carries on with his farming plans while his steady wife Agnes tries to steer the family along a calm path, but she is thwarted because even when Gracie marries Jonas's loyal workman Tom the problems with the landlord's son do not end. Tom met Gracie on a chance moonlight walk on the moors before he started working for her father, and he is captivated by her from first sight. Gracie and her new husband soon have to endure hardship with the fear of the workhouse always in sight, but rescued by an offer of a better job and place but this does not last and again life is a struggle until a final heartache out of which springs hope for the future.

A story of a family's hardships, sorrow, happiness, joy, and great love.

CHAPTER 1

Agnes Bailey stood in the dark low ceilinged passage, which she was sure would have been lighter if it were not boarded off just beyond the foot of the stairs. She glanced at the cold stone flags under her feet and then her gaze slowly travelled up the narrow steep stairs, she put her hand and forearm across her body to lightly press her swollen stomach. Her attention moved for a moment as she caught sight that one of the cane stair rods holding back the cocoa mat stair runner was badly scuffed. 'Need to change that,' she told herself almost relieved at the distraction, then, determinedly pulling back her shoulders, firmly grasped the smooth wooden rail that ran up the side of the brown painted wall. Hauling her bulkier than normal self-up step by step by pulling on the rail, pausing only once momentarily to ease her quickened breathing as the pain throbbed through her lower body. These stairs had been hard work for a while, really since her knees started to ache some years ago, but now carrying this child inside her she always seemed more weary and her knees more painful, so she dreaded the climb and avoided it when possible, but today and now the climb was essential and urgent.

As she reached the top step she turned sideways in the direction of the landing, and as she turned, she glanced at the boarded off passageway to the other side of the stair head, she thought as she often had that there was likely an easier wider staircase beyond the boarded partition, sighed then slowly walked a few steps along the creaking boards of the whitewashed upper landing and stopping leaned against the cold plaster for a steadying pause and as always glanced through the small deep set window. For that brief moment a smile passed over her usually sombre face. The sight of the distant high moor with its sparse wind bent trees and lower down the small irregular shaped fields sloping towards her with the stream a sparkling silver ribbon cutting a line down the hillside, all of this well-loved sight calmed her racing thoughts. Then the next pain came, this child inside her was strong, she knew that by the way it kicked. Nellie always said that when they kick like that they are kicking to get out and start life, well this one certainly was eager. The pain eased and sure enough the child kicked again. 'Have to get a move on,' she muttered to herself, but again her gaze wandered out though the window and to the moor beyond and still she lingered, for a moment of spirit freedom, for a moment, although she really didn't acknowledge it, when normal life and strife ceased to exist. There was a special fresh new intense bright green all round at this time of year, she mused, almost like a leafy haze you could wander into and be lost. At this time of early summer with the new grass and freshly emerging leaves beautiful and clean before the dust of the quarry covered all that freshness with its dulling fine grey film. 'Aye but that quarry dust will soon ruin that green, like everything else in life it soon loses its newness and becomes dull and sullied,' she muttered to herself.

Then again sighing she turned away from the window and continued slowly along the passage to the second door and entered a room with a bright beam of sunlight streaming through its deep set casement window, as she did, a smile again passed briefly over her face. This room was on the front of the house which faced the big cobbled central farmyard, and every time she entered it she counted herself a very lucky woman to have such a grand bedroom, even having a mantle shelf over an iron fireplace which housed a vase of dried flowers. She liked to see the dried flowers for she had seen them in better class bedrooms when she worked in service and was pleased she had a fireplace in which to put some, she knew some people lit a fire in bedrooms in winter but Agnes was of the opinion that was a waste of good coal when you were asleep in a warm bed. For a moment she stood in the doorway, her mind wandering back to when she and Jonas had first come to work at Hall Farm, then they had been desperate to find somewhere to live, so when they were offered half of the old unused farm manager's quarters at Beckersley Hall they had been overjoyed and very grateful to the gentleman farmer at the house. She never had understood why the farmer hadn't let then have the whole of the house but he had boarded half off, probably though that would be too generous, not want them having ideas above their station. Anyway it would only be more cleaning. Aye, yes, she thought, her mind still wandering, we had been young and eager and daft then and had spent weeks cleaning and whitewashing the rooms until the sickly smell of the rats, mice and birds who had taken up residence in the quarters had been completely cleaned away. They had come here when Jonas had been offered the job of head herdsman at the big house farm, for although there was no mention of a cottage with the job it was too good an opportunity to miss, Jonas had said. Aye, she thought, Jonas was always one for taking a chance and he always seemed to drop on his feet, whereas she would never have dared, been too scared of it going wrong. The job offer had been made to Jonas out of the blue by the farmer at Manchester market and as at the time Jonas was itching to move from where he was just an under herdsman, they took the risk and the farmer at his word. And we hadn't even known that farmer from Adam then. Still,

15

they had no children then to worry about and although the first few weeks were hard going, when they had to sleep on the floor of one of the upper rooms, they managed. 'Couldn't sleep o' floor now,' she muttered out loud. 'I'd ner' manage t' geet up agin.'

Now, again, the pain shot through her and she grabbed the bed foot as she instinctively bent forward, her knuckles white with the pressure of her hold on the hard cold iron as she gulped air and blew out slowly. Agnes knew from past experience that if you breathed deep and held it a while until the pain lessened it made it better to bear and she also knew that would be what she would soon be doing bearing down to birth this latest child. 'Please let it be a boy, a live boy,' she prayed silently. Then again her mind wandered. Jonas so wanted a boy. Oh he never said anything when the girls were born early in the marriage because they both thought boys would come but when they did they all died in birthing or soon after. The solitary tears and the quiet lonely disappointment over the years and the five little low mounds at the bottom of the old orchard where her babies lay sleeping together by a wall, sadness never spoken of but always there. She knew their loss grieved Jonas but he would never speak of it. There would have been some comfort if they had been laid in the churchyard, she silently lamented, not like animals buried in a field, but the church would not allow that, unchristened they said. 'Unchristian I say of those church people,' she muttered. Agnes shrugged away her sadness. She knew she was getting too old for this, but this time please God.

The pain eased and Agnes stirred, chiding herself for being 'soft' and began pulling the covers from the bed. She stripped it down to the striped mattress, folding each cover, blanket and sheet as she removed it. She placed all these neatly in a pile on top of a pine chest on the far side of the door. Then she padded around to the other side of the bed and lifted the hinged lid of a large wooden box which sat under the window, but before she could do any more the pain once more coursed down through her. Again, she leaned and gabbed hard, this time on the edge of the washstand by the bed side but as she bent over the stand her face was close to the pot soap dish and the strong sharp carbolic smell of the soap filled her nose and caused her to cough as she inhaled deeply, this fired the pain like an arrow through her body at which she gave out a low cry. Then she grabbed the edge of the washstand, her body weight pushing against the hard cold marble top. Finally the pain eased but she knew they were coming too close together and she had to get a move on. Then in panic she frantically pulled a pile of items from the wooden box, first a dark coloured thick waxed sheet which she laid on the bed, then several old patched and faded covers some of different fabrics stitched together until she had three layers over the waxed sheet. Then calming herself she paused this time crossing her arms across her swollen middle, nodding to herself, for Agnes was very proud of her blue and white stripe flock mattress and was always sure to keep it safe from staining. Lastly now she spread on top of the layers a patched and turned sheet, finally replacing the pillows. Now she carefully lifted from the box a worn patched pillowcase from which she drew a very neat stiff starched pile of two sheets and two lace edged pillowcases all of matching fine linen. As she drew the fabric out from the pillowcase tiny seeds of lavender, placed there by Agnes to keep away the moths, spilled from between the layers their faint delicate scent filling the air. These sheets had been given to her by Mrs Bellows in whose employ she had been when she and Jonas were wed. They were too grand to even consider for everyday use so Agnes had saved them for after lying in after the... and eventually, she mused, they would be used for lying me out, but not yet for a while I have no intention of going just yet. 'Please God.' These words escaping her lips. She placed the neat pile on the furthest side of the washstand to be to hand, next to the rose decorated jug and basin, for Nellie would change the bed after the... Even in her head she did not say the word, no point in tempting fate, she thought, as she proudly and appreciatively smoothed the folded sheets with wide spread red work rough fingers and straightened the lace edging before turning back to the bed.

The pain struck again and it was lower now. Waiting until it had eased she moved slowly across the smooth polished old floorboards towards the sunny window, taking care not to trip on the thick multi-coloured peg rug, she carried the recently removed bed covers from the top of the chest and slowly leaning over she now placed them in the box then closed the lid. Then leaning further over the box slid one side of the casement window sideways over to allow her head out to look towards the yard on the left below. Jonas was sweeping the cobbles as she knew he would be close by. He had known her time was near when he came in for breakfast and she asked him to stay close to the house for the rest of the morning. 'Joo—' was all she got out before her hands tightly gripped the window frame as again she froze at the pain. The pain eased so she turned to sit on the side of the bed. She was starting to sweat now. She felt her hair with a hand; it felt damp.

Jonas, hearing the strangled cry, dropped the brush and headed for the house instantly muttering, 'Damn that woman for being so awkard and 'ard on hersel.' She had promised that she would be careful and let him know in good time for this one, but he knew it would be the usual 'but I had to make the bed ready'. He hurried across the yard and through the house back door, for

18

once not stopping to clean his clogs on the old brown cloth sack laid for that purpose on the flags just inside the door. He halted at the foot of the stairs and shouted anxiously up to his wife, 'Agnes you alrite, would a' go for Nellie now?'

Agnes, quietly rocking herself on the the edge of the bed, could only manage one sharp short word, 'Aye.' Jonas needed no more, he was back out of the door and then he ran, not a thing he did often these days. For a big man past his prime he could still move fast when he had to, and now was such a time. Along the length of the yard and around the corner of the sandstone barn at the yard end, his clog irons skidded on the stone cobbles as the tall lean frame rushed down the side of the barn and continued the short distance along the lane which led to the row of low stone cottages where Nellie Hardcastle lived. The lane was cobbled with four foot high ivy draped walls running along its sides once it left the confines of the barn and the buildings around the yard. Long gone the days when it was the service road to the great house, now it was no longer swept by farm servants but left to nature to encroach with grass and weeds so only leaving tracks cleared by cart wheels and farm workers' footsteps.

The old cottages were home to some of the farm workers at Hall Farm and although Nellie was a widow she still lived there in the farthest one in the row. When her farm labourer husband had died a few years back she had assumed with dread that she would be destined for the workhouse, but Mrs Dixon the farmer's wife had unexpectedly insisted to Nellie's great relief that she remain in the cottage. Mrs Dixon was no fool and knew when a person was worth some 'charity' and she also ensured that the charity was justified. She made sure Nellie earned the cottage as she knew about herbs and how to use them, and she was well skilled in how to make preserves and wines so was twice weekly pressed into service in the farm kitchen in return for the cottage rent. Most importantly Nellie, taught by her mother, knew how to treat the sick and birth babies. These skills provided her with her food and fuel from the local folk. Nellie was never hungry or cold because she was always in demand, from a cure for tooth ache to laying out the deceased. Nellie Hardcastle was the one they all called on, so her cupboard was always filled and her fire fuelled. The story went locally that Nellie's mother had been a witch, but Nellie strongly disputed this always claiming, 'She had been a wise woman.' this statement usually followed by a smile and advice to, 'Teke care when speaking ill o' t' dead in case they hears and tekes exception.'

Now she heard someone was hammering loudly on her door so when she opened it to see Jonas Bailey standing there stiffly ashen faced she knew the reason. Only saying one word, 'Reet', she turned and picked up a laden basket placed ready just inside the door, slammed the door shut behind her and followed him back down the lane to the yard. The little woman trotted along the length of the barn trying to keep pace behind the hurrying man and then along the yard and through Agnes's doorway pausing only to tell Jonas, 'Stop yer panicking, man do, go back t'what yer wer doin.' As she reached the stair foot she stopped, caught her breath for moment then shouted up, 'I'm yer lass.' Before slipping off her clogs and hurrying upstairs. In the room above Agnes had taken of her skirt and bodice. White faced, she, now with the help and reassurance of Nellie, undressed, donned a nightdress and laid down on the bed to prepare to once more face the inevitable.

It was three hours later when Nellie, muscles stiff after sitting for all that time, was starting to feel tired, and despite the hard seat of the chair was beginning to doze. It seemed a long time since she had told Jonas to stoke up the kitchen fire and push the kettle over onto the hotplate to warm near the fire. A worried Jonas, leaving the house to continue with his jobs, had come back at dinnertime and brought up some bread and cheese and enamel mugs of tea, but neither woman had hunger for the food but the tea was welcome. Now Nellie heard Jonas again slowly mounting the stairs and the door slowly partly opened. His head poking carefully around the door edge, Jonas looked questioningly at Nellie and whispered, 'How is lass?' For he could see Agnes was dozing, her eyes closed.

Nellie shook her head, momentarily closing her eyes, but out loud said in a low voice, 'She's it bit tired, Jonas, but that's t' be expected, she'll be reet ner feer.' All the time wishing and hoping her words were going to prove to be right.

'Weel am off back te' farm now fer milking, al bi back later, a soon as a can geet away, a at ter go,' said Jonas quietly.

'Reet, lad, off yer go, not te worry it'll bi reet,' said Nellie trying to sound cheerful. But the concerned Nellie had barely stirred from Agnes's side for she was worried about her friend this time. Agnes was old to be giving birth but she would not be told, she wanted a boy for Jonas, for Nellie knew that was what Agnes was thinking. Aye, thought Nellie, neither of us are getting any younger, for Nellie was older than people knew. It was her small neat body that belied her years, even her hair was still the frizzy ginger mop of her youth and no babies had ever come to tire her body, which, while she had regretted that when she was young, now she knew the peace of no demanding family and she was content with what life had given her. She had almost nodded off herself as she sat beside an even more tired and weary Agnes when the mother had moaned again. Nellie roused herself and checked the patient. It had to be soon or she would be going down to tell Jonas the same sad words again. Nellie sighed, paused a moment in consideration, then slowly bent and lifted a small cork stoppered bottle from her basket then looked once more at Agnes. This was the last resort. She shrugged her shoulders, took a deep breath and took herself off down the stairs to the fireplace where the kettle still pushed to one side of the hotplate was still warm when she felt the metal side. She poured some dark coloured liquid from the bottle into an enamel cup, and then added warm water and a teaspoon of sugar from a tin in Agnes's food cupboard, and gave the brew a good stir with the spoon. Now cup in hand she trudged back up the steep stairs. Touching the shoulder of the dozing woman, said, 'Here, Agnes, drink this, it's not a good taste but it might hurry 'job along like.' Persuaded Nellie as she offered her friend the cup of brown murky looking fluid.

Without question Agnes sipped the liquid and her face crumpled as she swallowed. 'By 'eck, Nellie that's foul it 'ad better be worth it, tastes like weeds.'

'Thy'r not far off reet, Agnes.' A sad smile passed over Nellie's face, as she fondly remembered her mother's voice saying, 'Ony use that as a last resort lass, it's a kill or cure for the child.' For Nellie had decided she had to do something and that fearful herb was the only way she knew, and this time she had brought some to be prepared for the worst. Why, she pondered, could some women spit them out like a dog wi' pups while others died in the trying? Then, what seemed only a few minutes later, she jumped up as Agnes grabbed her arm.

'Now,' Agnes cried and she was right the baby was coming, whether it had decided by itself to face the world or been hurried along by the terrible leaf she would never know. Even Nellie who was normally detached found that she was willing the child to be a boy but more than that alive.

The child slid into the world and protested loudly and hard at the shock. It was healthy and bonny and as Nellie offered a quiet 'Thank God' to nobody but herself, to Agnes she smiled and offered, 'Well done, lass, a bonny strong babe.' Nellie busied herself with first the new arrival and then with the very weary and exhausted but elated Agnes who was bleeding badly. Agnes turned to look at the infant beside her, then uttered softly, 'Another lass, Nellie, it's not ter be is it.'

Nellie was quick to reply because she was expecting this. 'Now yer not to tek on so, Agnes, it's a fine little soul, lads only bring trouble anyhow.'

'But Jonas so hoped this time a know e did.'

'Well a'm sure he'll love it just the same.'

'Aye be sure e' will.' was the reply.

Nellie shouted down the stairs to Jonas, who she had just heard come into the house, and he came slowly, warily, up the stairs. As she wrapped the child in a piece of cotton cloth over which she then wrapped a small cream crochet blanket she looked at the small pinched face and for a moment had a strange feeling of affinity with this little scrap of life, then she shrugged away the silliness and thrust the child into Jonas's arms. 'Tek her downsteers for now, while a see t' lass,' was the brisk instruction. He had heard the word her. So no boy but it was alive.

'Please God Agnes is alreet,' he prayed quietly as he did as he was bid and clutching it silently took the child downstairs, to sit babe in arms in the spindle rocking chair in front of the warm fireplace. Not a man used to holding a child, he marvelled at its smallness and then watched facinated as a tiny fist struggled free from the cotton wrap and thrust itself at the tiny sucking mouth. Sitting quietly rocking back and forth it was now Jonas who began to muse on life, for it was, he decided, not a bad life. He had been denied sons of that he was now sure but Agnes would soon be up and about and he was still strong and they still had years to look forward to ye never knew what opportunity was around the corner, and here he was holding a bonny child of his makin.

Upstairs Nellie turned to Agnes looked her straight in the eye and demanded in mock sternness, 'Now, lass, weer is them fancy sheets and pillowcases a know tha'l want 'em on, let's be changing this eer bed. Then I'll be off downstairs to make some bread and milk pobs fer thee, help the milk come in the' do'. Now, lass, can yer manage to geet outa bed fer a few minutes while I change it, just sit here 'al be as quick as 'a can.' Directed by a sleepy Agnes to the pile of linen on the wash stand, Nellie soon had the job done and, with the final blanket and bedspread replaced, helped her friend back into bed.

Just for now Agnes was forbidden by Nellie to go downstairs, so she promised her friend that for a few days she would lie quietly in between her prized linen sheets. As always, as she knew it pleased Agnes, Nellie had admired them as she made up the bed. 'Quality they is, Agnes, thy'r a lucky woman te own em.' Nellie although smiling spoke sternly to her friend. 'And now, Agnes Bailey, I know theer chear in the coener is a commode an' make sure you use it, no cummin' downsteers, a'll empty it.' First fretting at the inactivity but tired so soon, enjoying the rest and Nellie's attention, Agnes dozed, the child now in the cradle at her side.

Nellie disappeared to make ready to move in with the family to help for a while. Nellie often followed this routine when a local woman had a child. She became a member of the family for a time to allow the new mother to recover and she looked after

24

older children and did the household work including making the meals. Nellie liked it when the woman's home was like Agnes's, big and clean with light rooms and a big fire in a cooking range in the living kitchen. The four rooms which comprised Agnes's home were part of what had been the home of the farm steward and his wife when the ruins behind the farm had been a great hall. So the house had been supplied with better cooking facilities which included a side oven and hot water tank, which had the added benefit of keeping the rooms warm, and were a delight for any woman. Nellie had no such luxurious cooking facilities in her own small cottage so intended enjoying Agnes's while she was there.

Nellie busied herself going back to her cottage and returning along the yard length laden with a truckle bed, sheets, a pillow and several blankets. Jonas still dallying around the house and yard saw her as she struggled carrying such a load. 'Cum 'ere, woman let me tek sum of thee clutter.'

'Aye alreet, but less o' the "clutter", non o' yer cheek, yer can leave them at' back door, Jonas Bailey.' Was all the thanks he got.

Agnes, woken from her snooze by the sound of Nellie dragging the folding bed upstairs, smiled fondly as she thought to herself, that's right, Nellie, never ask for help, always do it yourself. The little woman set up the bed in the other bedroom which was where the Baileys' two daughters slept, for it was a big enough room and there was extra space as she had moved out the cradle which was normally there in the corner. Agnes being unwilling to move the cradle into her bedroom before the birth so as not to tempt ill fate, the job then had fallen to the more than willing if struggling Nellie. 'Gradly cradle this, Agnes,' the little woman had informed her friend between puffs, 'must be solid oak, weighs a ton.' As she had struggled to drag the cradle along the landing into the bedroom.

The two Bailey girls were at the school for the morning, Jonas had told her, and then, after they had eaten their bite of dinner which they took with them, they would go to the mill for the afternoon so all would be quiet until later. Nellie wasn't sure whether the girls had any inkling about the new addition to the family. Sometimes older children were aware when a woman was expecting but if she was stout like Agnes it often went unnoticed for certainly nobody would talk about it. Well, she thought to herself. They are going to know when they come home.

The afternoon passed quietly with Agnes and her child asleep upstairs, his work at the hall farm finished until later in the day, Jonas and his relieved thoughts were in a lower field digging out a ditch which cattle had pushed in, Nellie was enjoying her new position in the kitchen. First job was to rescue the dried out half risen dough she had found, which Agnes had abandoned at the first pain, but left covered with wet cloths. A damping with a fresh very wet cloth and more kneading, into the tins, and a quick rise on the fire front then into the oven. She eyed the loaves as she put them in the oven. 'Weel yer look a bit rum but waste not want not.' After looking in the little meat safe she knew was on a stone slab in the narrow pantry partitioned off the back of the back kitchen she returned to the slopstone sink with some fat marled beef, potatoes, onions and carrots and prepared a hotpot, saving some of the beef to make beef tea in another pot for the new mother. Having managed to fit both of the cooking pots in the fireside oven after taking out the two rather flat loaves, she gave the fire a poke to stir it up, put on some coal and topped it with some slack coal dust to damp it down, then busied herself around the kitchen. For what was left of the afternoon Nellie was intending to enjoy this chance to rule her friend's household, dusting a shelf here or straightening an ornament there. The time soon passed until the two girls could be heard clogs chattering coming across the yard. When they came through the doorway they stopped surprised to see Nellie in their mother's kitchen. 'Oh well,' she said to herself at the sight of their confused faces, I've had to explain this one before and will again after this time. 'Reet now, girls, some good news yer have a new little babby sister.'

The girls looked surprised but took in the news quietly without argument and then hesitantly asked where was their mother and if they could see her and the new sister. Nellie readily agreed, relieved that not too many questions had been forthcoming and followed them up the stairs to the still light bedroom. The two young girls crept timidly into the room and saw their mother sleeping and the wooden cradle, the one that was normally in the corner of their bedroom, and was now at their mother's bedside. Confused at the strangeness of their mother being in bed at this time of day and after Nellie seemingly in charge in the kitchen they were both relieved when, as they slowly edged towards the bed, Agnes awoke and smiled as she saw them trying to peer into the cradle from a distance. 'Come 'ere an look at our new babby,' she encouraged.

Just at that moment Jonas, who had seen the girls arrive home, and had walked quietly upstairs in his stocking feet, also entered the bedroom behind them, at which Nellie stood back, turned and disappeared downstairs, hearing as she left, Jonas's soft, 'Now, Agnes, it's a bonny babe just what wer needed fer a little sister fer't lasses.'

Agnes was as Nellie had said 'all right' but it took a while and after she came to terms with another girl she delighted in the happy baby. The child was as Nellie had first seen bonny with black curls long enough for a year old child and she was strong, soon reaching out for the offered breast and feeding greedily. This was a child born to thrive but Agnes was weakened and although she slowly regained her strength she and Nellie both knew there would be no boy child coming to her house.

CHAPTER 2

Agnes named the baby Grace because she felt that God in his goodness had sent her as consolation and to give her peace after the loss of all her sons. Grace was a good baby seldom crying always happy and smiling. Gracie as she became known grew stronger and prettier and was more loved by the day. Her mother, her initial disappointment past, spoilt her as only later life children can be spoilt, allowing her licence she had never given to the older girls, her sisters played with her, their wooden dolls and other amusements abandoned as they staggeringly carried her about, and to her father she was 'His little lass'. The unexpected late sunshine of his life, the delighted child always running to 'Dada's' arms as soon as he returned home. 'Little Gracie' was the darling of the house, and being so treated, only understood kindness and being loved, so in turn she so treated all she knew and met with the same innocent kindness.

It was Gracie's birthday, she was three and for her birthday Mammy and Dada had given her a wooden doll. Gracie was very pleased because the doll had a painted face, a pink dress and bonnet, and underneath the dress it had a petticoat and bloomers. It was now afternoon, she knew that because she had had her dinner and Mammy had said that when she was three she could play outside on her own. 'Mammy can dolly an' me go out now, pleas?' said Gracie tugging at the side of her mother's apron.

Agnes who was standing by the stone sink washing dinner pots looked down at the child. 'Out, out, lass, wheer d' ye want te go?'

'Out, Mammy, ye sed.' Agnes still not understanding frowned. 'Mammy ye said when a' wer three 'a could go outside on mi own.'

Suddenly understanding as she remembered her promise the woman smiled. 'Oh, so ye remembered that then. Well alreet but ye stop near backdoor. No wandering off now.'

The child looked up at her mother. 'Aye, Mammy a'll stay near backdoor, an' so will dolly.'

'All reet then but yer leave backdoor open.'

This was all Gracie needed. Both she and dolly disappeared speedily outside. A little time later Agnes, having stuck her head out of the door to check on why the child was chattering so, cried out in near terror. Her heart was racing at the sight of the large yellow and brown dog the child was hugging. Instantly grabbing the yard brush, luckily leaning near the back door, she made to fend off the animal and at the same time shouting at Gracie to 'Get away from that dog, lass.'

Gracie shocked at her mother's harsh tone quickly did as she was told and grabbing her doll ran towards the house door, but the dog obviously still a pup reacted more in fun than fight and lunged to grab the brush and then jumped on spring like feet more to enjoy the game. Agnes soon saw there was little danger from this amiable animal but unknown stray dogs were not welcome, and this one obviously did not understand it was not wanted as it rolled over on its back and wagged its tail to show it wanted to be friends. Gracie now recovered from the shock of her mother's shouting was edging once more towards the dog her face beaming as she shrieked with delight . 'Good doggie, nice doggie. Mammy dolly likes doggie.' As the dog then licked her bare leg.

Agnes again tried to chase off the animal shouting for it to,

'Clear off, you clear off dog.' But the dog had decided it was staying as it shuffled itself closer to the child, and Gracie it seemed had a new found friend.

The dog was still sitting hanging around outside the house door at dusk when Jonas arrived home for his evening meal, a protesting Gracie having earlier been carried indoors by Agnes to be given a serious talking to about how not every animal or person was nice and kind even if they seemed it. 'That theer dog could a' bitten thee.'

'Agnes, do yer know there's a stray dog outside back door?' Jonas asked.

'Aye a' do that,' replied Agnes. 'It just appeared, near frit'nred me ter death; our Gracie was theer we her arms round it. That child does not seem to understand not every one or thing is friendly and good, an it'll geet her in trouble yet. An' another thing it's only a pup an' size it is now, grown it'll bi near size of a donkey.'

Before Jonas could reply, Gracie ran to throw her little chubby arms around his knees and plead as only a small determined child can, for the dog to be allowed stay. Agnes had insisted that the only way the dog could stay was if their father approved, which she had informed the girls, she considered to be very unlikely. Jonas was at first unmoved by the sudden onslaught from the pleading child, thinking it just the usual passing fancy, as only cow or sheep dogs were wanted on farms not dogs as pets, but he soon saw from the, 'Pleess, Dada. Pleess, Dada', that this was a most heartfelt request. Jonas looked at the child's face, how could he refuse a plea from Gracie? And so further enlightened about the dog's good behaviour by a begrudging Agnes and an enthusiastic Dora and Sarah his older daughters, both adding their equally ardent voices to the cause of

31

adopting the lucky dog, he admitted defeat.

Jonas was reluctant for untrained dogs could be a nuisance around farm animals but after such great pleading from the three girls he agreed . 'Al' reet, dog can stay so long as it doesn't cause trouble and nobody comes looking for it, an' if they do no crying it'll have to go wi' 'em, it stays tied up outside an' any trouble from it it goes. Y'll ha' ter check wi yer mam that she will provide it wi' food. And it stays an' sleeps outside i' barn, no cumin inside' house.'

All three girls stood silently with nodding heads and barely suppressed smiles, and then all scurried out to the dog who was still sitting waiting patiently outside the door. Jonas turned to sit down at the table to eat his supper. As he sat he turned to Agnes with a smile and with mock severity announced that he was having his food ruined and that she 'had better get them childer in here NOW, or ther'd be no dog stayin at this eer' house'.

Called to eat their 'tae' the girls unwillingly came back into the kitchen to eat a very hurried meal under Agnes's disapproving face, which became a hidden unseen smile as she turned away. Their tea disposed of much quicker than usual all three asked to be allowed out to make the dog's straw bed. Agnes's reply was, 'Aye but be quick about it. It's your bedtime soon, Gracie.'

Three various 'Yes Mam's' floated through the open door before it banged closed. The playful pup was tied up later by Jonas and quickly settled with the Baileys and was soon allowed loose for it always came running at the shout of 'Big Lad' and it seemed to have no interest in leaving the house and yard area. When faced with a cow the dog simply walked away so it seemed it was not a problem around farm animals. Jonas's rules were usually abided by, mainly because he did not issue many so when he did they were seen to be serious, so the girls made the dog a warm bed in the corner of the barn near the doors, and did not encourage the animal to follow them indoors. Big Lad only occasionally sneaked into the kitchen when following Gracie but soon retreated on seeing Agnes for although Agnes always fed him generously in a tin dish outside the back door, he knew there was a limit to her welcome and that limit was the doorstep. No one ever called looking for the dog so Big Lad became a permanent member of the family.

Big Lad thought Gracie was very special, her hand always gentle as it stroked his head then slipped around his neck to hug him, and he in return became her guardian shadow for he decided he had to protect the child from all real or imagined evil. As Gracie eventually grew to stand higher than the dog's head so the two became inseparable. If Gracie wandered off around the orchard or amongst the old ruins in the field behind the house so did Big Lad and if Gracie went to sit in the old walled garden Big Lad would always be found close by. Big Lad liked the walled garden because of the rabbits. The back part of the garden, on the far side of the stream, was riddled with rabbit holes out of which the occasional furry head or tail could be seen. Big Lad was convinced that soon he would catch one, but he was no terrier and the rabbits remained unharmed in their big burrow under the mostly fallen back length of garden wall, all this to both Gracie's and the rabbits' relief. Gracie was fully aware that she sometimes ate a stew made from the rabbits that Jonas occasionally brought home but they were not her garden rabbits so that was 'all reet'.

CHAPTER 3

Gracie was tall for twelve, a slim girl with a gentle smile which often spread into her eyes as their gaze wandered, and a riot of striking black curls that Agnes insisted she tie tightly back 'lest she look like a wild gypsy child'. She had what her father called 'a sunny way wi er'. Her mother said that, 'Our Gracie's soft in head about animals and waifs and strays and those in need of help and it'll get her into trouble before she's finished, she needs to harden up.' For Agnes worried about Gracie, she was a 'dreamer' she said. As her older sisters had done she attended the church school in the morning and after slowly wandering home along the lanes, she would often arrive home late to a frustrated Agnes who was driven one day to cry. 'Were'v you bin Gracie? Yo're late agin yer got to 'elp me in afternoons yer goin' to have to get home quicker or yer fer mill like yer sisters.'

But Gracie would smile, say, 'sorry, Mam', present her with a bunch of wild flowers and Agnes's disapproval was gone until the next time, which was most likely the following day or sooner.

One afternoon a few days later Agnes had other thoughts to worry her, for as soon as she returned to the house from again telling Gracie to mend her ways, Jonas arrived in the kitchen with a beaming face and an air of such excitement that Agnes was 'mystified' as she later told Nellie. 'Agnes a've got it, land, a've got it. Mister Dixon says a' can 'ave that other twenty acre. We'll 'ave a reet good proper farm now, not just one cow now a'll get two more at least. Not all at once mind but gradual like, I've werked it out. We'll werk it out so all not'all cows are dry at' same time. No more buying milk like.'

Jonas's excitement was infectious and as he hugged his wife in a silly jumping dance his normally sombre face grinning and his eyes glittering even the staid Agnes was laughing until almost crying at her husband's unheard of madness. 'Calm down, man, are yer going daft?' she gasped as she plumped down on a chair. 'Let mi get mi wind back yer making me maisy wi' yer dancing about.' Jonas had wanted some extra land to work for himself for so many years so that he would have his 'real farm' as he called it, but it had always been an impossible dream until today. 'Why 'as Mister Dixon changed 'is mind an' offered thee this?' Agnes queried slowly. Practical Agnes wisely always felt that good things came at a price in some way or other.

'Weel he sez that he 'as been watching me and thinks that a' deserve it, the way 'a werk.' The last two words said with great pride and a chest slightly puffed out. Finally calm he moved to sit in his usual fireside rocker chair with a most satisfied smile on his face.

Agnes was pleased for him but the sense of uneasiness persisted, Mister Dixon was not a man to be generous without good reason in fact he was known for quite the opposite and Agnes was of the opinion that the reason would somehow be for his own benefit. So Agnes was not at all convinced about this new arrangement but eventually unable to find justification for her doubts she had to put such thoughts into the back of her mind and was happy for Jonas. 'Maybe a' have te suspicious a mind,' she told herself.

Over the next few days Jonas was to be seen chasing about quickly finishing his work up at the main Dixon farm, then rushing home to become gleefully engrossed in checking the fencing and walls around his new land and cleaning out the extra buildings that came with the land. Jonas felt three inches taller walking with his head held higher, his stride longer and firmer for now he had a real shippon with standings, not just the loose box that had served for one up to now, and he had a stable for which he decided he needed a carthorse. He had two pigsties for which he might even have pigs one day and even a small collecting yard for cattle when needed, along with a portion of space in the barn to store hay for winter feed. What Mr Dixon had also agreed to was Jonas using the old empty farm buildings arranged around the yard opposite the Baileys' home. Mr Dixon had acquired them when he had bought the land years before but hardly used them as they were dilapidated and too far from his main farm, unlike the barn and cottages alongside the buildings for they were very useful for storage and workers accommodation, and kept therefore well maintained. That yard and buildings had been part of the home farm to the old long gone hall lost to fire, only the foundations and some larger stones now remained in the fields beyond the orchard, the main part of the building had provided material for many of the farms and their buildings in the nearby area. Jonas had for years had the use of a couple of the yard buildings near his home but now, with almost a yard full of shippons, stys, looseboxes and sheds he was happy, very happy, because now he was going 'to show 'em all he was not just a cowman worker with a few animals, he was a real farmer'. He could hardly wait for the next market day when he would be able, 'just in passing like', to make sure his new venture was widely known. What Jonas had not told Agnes though was that Mr Dixon had offered him the extra land and buildings in exchange for extra work, and Jonas did not intend telling anyone that, least of all Agnes as she didn't have any great liking for 'Mr

Hoytitoty Dixon' as she called him, so if she knew the true details of the arrangement she was not going to like that either, so best for all she didn't know. 'At least for a while, until she found out.'

Jonas knew he really had already all the work he could cope with but the temptation of 'that extra land and buildings' and the prestige it would bring was too much to refuse, he knew he would manage. 'A'll geet up a bit sooner early, an werk a bit longer at nite I'll manage.'

It was a few days later before it finally dawned on Agnes what Jonas was up to and then she rounded on him. 'What time is this to be comin in? Thy are g'ing to kill thysell then how will we manage? We'll all be out in street wi' no home. A' knew there were a catch te this generosity bi Dixon,' she cried at him.

But Jonas was not going to let anything stop him, he had a plan. He said, 'I'm going to get 'elp, thur arr lots of lads werking 'on reses' that'll work for near nowt if they get a decent roof ore' ther head an' food, a a heerd a mon say other day at market, an then I'll mek some money.'

Agnes looked hard at the so enthusiastic sincere face, then forced herself to walk away stiff backed, for Jonas, once he had decided, that was it, but she was worried for his hair seemed greyer recently and his always spare frame seemed even leaner of late. Why had he to upset the 'applecart' when all was secure and life was settled. Agnes walked away from her husband as she knew there was no point in arguing. 'He will just suit his sen,' she muttered under her breath.

What Jonas did not know was that Mr Dixon's supposedly generous offer was because he was looking for ways to economise on his costs for labour and his eye had let upon Jonas, and because he knew all about Jonas's ambitions to be seen as a farmer in his own right. The reason for the economising was Mr

Dixon's only son who his wife idolised, and who was costing far more to keep at that damn fancy London college than he ever expected. Richard Dixon had never experienced London society, but he was becoming very aware of how much it cost. What with rent for lodgings, and they had to be in the right part of town, the expensive part, and new clothes seemingly every few weeks, not to even mention the cost of 'being out in society' as his son called it, and he wouldn't do a hand's turn when he came home. Not that his mother would have let him for he was a 'gentleman' she said. Well, had thought Richard, that Jonas Bailey is keen to have that boggy twenty acres beyond the brook and I can do with his labour for an extra fourteen hours a week which means a bit less farmhand's wages, so we are both to get what we want. 'So,' Dixon muttered to himself, 'if Mrs Dixon has more to squander on her beloved Edward she will be happy, and she will then leave me alone so I'm happy and into the bargain Jonas was also made a happy man. Everybody is happy.'

CHAPTER 4

Nellie had watched Gracie over the years and had decided that her 'special girl', for the feeling of closeness with the child had strengthened as she watched Gracie grow, should not go into the mill with her sisters, and be put into way of temptation with the village lads as her sister Dora had. Dora now had a girl child of three years and the shame had nearly killed Agnes with the shunning, jibes and subtle insults from acquaintances and friends alike, and then the lectures of damnation from the vicar who had presented himself at Agnes's door. The thin elderly man had sat in Jonas's rocking chair by the kitchen range, all the while lamenting the fate of sinners and the weakness of the flesh, for an hour only regularly pausing to wipe his long thin red nose on a piece of soiled cotton rag. Finally Agnes had 'remembered' that she had promised to take some hot soup to an elderly sick neighbour, at which the vicar had no alternative but to bid her 'good day' but with a final warning about any lack of church attendance. Nellie understood why Agnes had not sent Gracie halftime to the mill after school, she had just allowed her to come home because she too thought the girl would struggle with the hardness of the mill and the women employed there, but now Gracie had reached the end of her school days and something had to be done with her. So Nellie had persuaded Agnes that Gracie be put in a better way of things if the girl were be kept at home to 'learn the dairy and kitchen' from Agnes and herself because then she could join Nellie working at the big farm and learn the ways of the 'gentry', also she would not 'come across the likes of the rough village girls and boys'. Agnes was not completely sure of the wisdom of this plan, but with the memory of the vicar's barbed words and the whole sorry matter being yet again brought to mind, and Nellie was adamant and as usual very persuasive. 'Agnes the lass is te bonny te b' sent down theer t'mill, yer know what'al likely happen.' Agnes knew she was probably right, as and as she had no better idea, it was agreed between the women over several cups of tea at Agnes's kitchen table.

One thing Agnes did think was that if Gracie ever had to work in the mill her soft nature would be taken advantage of by some of the hardnosed women who worked there. She had come across mill workers over the years and never met one she liked. When at Nellie's words Agnes remembered how she had had cause to worry about Dora and Sarah for when Dora had her child she and Nellie had pondered long if they could pass it off as Agnes's but decided that at Agnes's age no one would believe it, so the shame had to be borne, but that matter had calmed down now and both her older daughters now seemed happy to go to work and to church and be content at home. Yes, Agnes thought, I worried about the two older ones but Gracie with the way she looks will attract lads like 'wasps to a jam pot', so with these thoughts in mind she had convinced herself to agree to Nellie's suggestion for Gracie. Jonas, when asked if he agreed with the arrangement, simply absently replied, 'Aye grand.' Without any consideration, being too busy and work distracted to concern himself with the affairs of the women.

It was a bright sunny Tuesday morning in early summer and on Tuesday mornings, Nellie went to work in the big farm kitchen at Hall Farm, and as it was June and the elderflowers were just in full bloom she was, as she had informed Mrs Dixon the previous week, going to make a start on the elderflower wine and cordial. So she put on her stoutest boots and set off up the lane to the farmhouse. She sniffed the fresh morning air and saw the dew on the grass along the lane side was just starting to dry by the time she arrived at the farmhouse. When she reached the house back kitchen door she found two of the farm labourers lounging against a wall waiting, so they informed her, for her to give them her orders and that Nellie relished, she enjoyed having the 'sayso over these great lumps o' men'.

'Reet, yo two shape yersels.' Her ginger mop of hair bobbing as her bonnet slipped backwards as she briskly waved her arms to affirm her instructions, 'Get them ther baskets from back' kitchen and wee'll get goin.'

When the two men had picked up the waiting large, deep oblong wicker baskets, she shooed them out in the direction of the lower fields were she knew the best elderflowers were to be found. There, branches of the Elderberry trees spaced along the field side hedges carried great clouds of the tiny headily fragrant cream blossom were to be seen as though decorating the high hedgerows of the lower fields. The two men set off at a good pace with Nellie struggling to keep up, in the too large boots which had originally belonged to her late husband, but aided by using a long handled stick like a shepherd's crook as a walking stick, although its real purpose was for pulling down elder branches to get the flowers. The little woman, puffing loudly, chased behind determined not to admit to the men that they were going too fast for her. 'Can't thee keep up, Nellie, getting t'long I' tooth fer running?' asked the older man.

'No.' Was the sharp denial. 'This elder scent is getting t' mi chest. Bill Watson ye mind yer own business, tek that silly grin of thee face and get going we need te geet on wi' picking them ther flowers afor the sun geets high, ye'll be all ruddy day at this rate.'

Later that morning after arriving back the men, then Nellie trailing behind, with creaking baskets full of thin branches loaded with the tiny highly scented cream flowers, a still puffing Nellie ordered the two men to leave them in the outer back kitchen while she went on into the house kitchen to find 'The Mrs' as she always called Mrs Dixon. Mrs Dixon's kitchen was large and airy but warm from the big black and shiny steel fire ranges with their side ovens. The house kitchen always had a good smell either from cooking food or simply from the bunches of dried herbs, hams and bags of oatcakes dotted among the pans and gadgets which hung from the beam crossed ceiling, and today was no different. Immediately Nellie walked into the kitchen she sniffed the warm welcoming smell appreciatively, then crossed to where the lady of the house was standing beside the central large scrubbed top table. Mrs Dixon was closely supervising a young girl who was making flat pastry currant cakes, her rolling pin moving swiftly back and forth as she flattened the pastry.

Nellie did not hesitate but straight away approached the subject of Gracie. 'Morning, Mrs Dixon, I've been thinking, Mrs Dixon, I could do with a bit of help these days, a' can't get mi puff, mi knees and legs give mi pain and I don't get thu werk like I us't ter. I can't lift the pans and kettles like a' cud. A' need some 'elp and anyroad a' need to be teeching sombuddy what a' know. If a' goes and kicks the bucket afore a' do then thal be i' bother, tha'l struggle wi wine an' jams like.' Nellie was really in her stride as the words tumbled out, and Mrs Dixon stood quite taken back at this sudden outburst.

'Well, Nellie, I am truly sorry for I did not realise how you were suffering.' At this she turned to Sally, who had stopped rolling but was just standing watching and listenening to the animated Nellie. 'Carry on, Sally, you seem to be managing very well, and make sure you grease the baking tin or they will stick. Please follow me, Nellie, and we will discuss this matter further.' This spoken in a most 'I am in charge manner' as she led the way into the back outer kitchen. 'You are quite right, if that is the case it is time we found you some help. We shall have to find a suitable girl or *perhaps* you have someone in mind?'

Mrs Dixon was fully aware that Nellie, good and able worker that she was, could be inclined to try to manoeuvre people for her own ends and Mrs Dixon was not about to be persuaded into any arrangement not of her own making or liking. "Perhaps we should give the matter some consideration with regard to what a new girl's duties would be, before we make any inquiries into looking to who might be suitable.'

Nellie stood looking serious for a moment for she knew she had to convince the Mrs that, for her part, this was a plea of desperation for help and not a planned and premeditated plan otherwise she knew Mrs Dixon would not be convinced or persuaded. Now with a little birdlike movement she bent her head to one side as though considering, all the while absently pushing escaped ginger curls back under her cap, and then slowly said, 'Weel there ain't that meny girls as wud do. A wont one as won't gi' cheek. Al' think wile a' werk.' At which point she smiled as she turned and with boots clunking moved across the room to return to the waiting baskets of elderflowers. Mrs Dixon watched the clunking boots leave a trail of mud as the little woman walked away from her and made a mental note to find a pair of her old shoes and insist that Nellie wear them when indoors at the farm.

An hour or so later Nellie returned to the kitchen pleased to find that Mrs Dixon was still there, as she had yet more convincing to do. 'Weel that's that done. A've stipped all flowers we'd better get mugs but a' can't lift em, so can Sally cum and elp mi and then she can carry watter in't buckets?' Mrs Dixon was a little puzzled at Nellie's very sudden lack of strength but agreed to allowing the kitchen maid to go and help the supposed struggling Nellie. So a quietly triumphant Nellie, a little more sprightly of step, with a surprised and curious Sally the kitchen maid following, moved off in the direction of the back kitchen to carry on dealing with the elderflowers, while a disgruntled Mrs Dixon was left to finish the the remainder of the baking herself.

Mrs Dixon, considering as she rolled the pastry, decided she had a choice, let Nellie have a girl to help her or accept that she was going to have considerably less help in her own kitchen, so Nellie had won the day. Mrs Dixon had a strong suspicion that she had been coerced and an even stronger suspicion that Nellie probably had someone already in mind.

It was therefore no surprise to Mrs Dixon when Nellie immediately after arriving for work the next day called in the kitchen to say she had found 'Just the lass fer what a' need, she's quiet and will do as her's told, an wi no cheek. Al' brung her wi' mi her next time a'm in Mrs'. Then without waiting for a reply was out through the door into the outer back kitchen before the frustrated and defeated woman could argue. Mrs Dixon was not pleased as lips pursed she stared at the closing door but she was not a woman to shout at any retreating back in case it did not respond, so decided it best to appear unconcerned and wait and see. Sally who had been witness to all this made a great show of peering into and clattering the contents of a cupboard in order to hide her amused face.

The next week when Nellie arrived as usual on Tuesday for work at the farmhouse she was accompanied by an a very anxious

Gracie who was immediately disconcerted by the vastness of the kitchen. Poor Gracie felt she had walked into a great cave filled with tempting strange smells, unknown sounds, enormous cupboards reaching high above her head and great hot open fires in two hearths set at different levels at either end of the kitchen. She was used to the highness and size of church but the church was quiet and cool and calm while this place was warm, noisy and quite overpowering. Mrs Dixon was a rather solemn tall thin woman who always dressed in grey and wore her black grey streaked hair pulled back in a tight bun, and who at the time Nellie and Gracie arrived was standing in the middle of her kitchen issuing orders for the day to Sally the kitchen maid. At the sound of the door opening the mistress had turned her head in their direction, sniffed briefly as the two new arrivals approached and then looked down at the quaking girl. 'Now, Gracie, do you think you are going be able to work helping Nellie and be clever enough to learn her ways and skills? I understand you are Jonas Bailey's daughter, who my husband says is a good worker, and I believe your mother is a good if somewhat plain cook.'

Poor Gracie already overawed by all around her was startled and taken back by the lady's severe appearance and these sternly asked questions, but, remembering the orders and instructions she had been given by Nellie during the walk to the farm, bobbed in a quick curtsy as she had been shown by Nellie and answered in a low voice, 'Aye Mrs.' Mrs Dixon was sufficiently satisfied by the girl's timid reply to consider that she might be bidable, so all was settled and Gracie had a job.

It was agreed, and in this Mrs Dixon made sure she had the say in the matter, that while Gracie was new to the work, when Nellie was not at the farm, she would work with and under the instruction of young Sally, who having worked for Mrs Dixon for two years was quite well acquainted with the workings of the kitchen. So for two days Gracie dutifully ran and carried at Nellie's instruction but come the Thursday morning she found herself under the care and direction of Sally. Sally had never had the power to issue orders before so except for ensuring that any dirty jobs were done by Gracie she soon grew tired of the forethought required and suggested that they simply share most jobs. Being together so much the two soon became firm friends as they chatted as they worked in the kitchen, dairy and the other domestic buildings arranged along the yard. Sally was a little older than Gracie, so Gracie was greatly impressed by Sally's colourful stories of life in and around the farm and the people who lived and worked there. Gracie thought Sally very clever and worldly wise, admired her, and listened to her every word in the hope of gaining some of the older girl's knowledge. Weeks passed and Gracie had learned many of the workings of the kitchen and the domestic buildings which were attached to the farmhouse but arranged along the house end edge of the farmyard. They consisted of the dairy, outside cold store, wash house, and coal house. Gracie was very impressed by the size and quantity of equipment in the dairy and wash house. The washing boiler was easily four times the size of her mother's and after she saw the size of the butter churn she spent the rest of the day worrying how she was going to manage to turn the handle, only for her fears to be allayed the next day when Sally informed her that Mrs Dixon was 'not a reet slave driver' and always got one of the stable lads to do it. 'All thy'll atta do is see ter cream going in and butter cummin' out.'

The coal house was not the girls' concern as it was also the stable lads' job to fill the coal buckets, but the girls had to put the coal on the fires in the kitchen and Sally did not like this dirty job, so was glad to consign it to Gracie. 'You bein' the young 'en yer have ter tek over coal job, Gracie,' she informed the younger girl. 'Ony these two fires, the 'ousemaid Mavis does the 'ouse ens, an mek sure yer don't get any coal on yer pinny, ye gotta put a canvas pinny orer top o' yer good en when yer do' coal, or Mrs 'al play pop if yer get mucky. Use them long tungs to put on the big cobs o' coal and then use' shovel for the smaller bits.' The girl at first struggled with the heavy overfilled buckets and coal hods, often fearing she might spill the contents, but as ever in her good natured way did as she was told just telling herself it was all part of the job.

Gracie was just beginning to feel settled and confident in her new position when she arrived at the farm kitchen one Monday morning a few months later to find that Sally was not in the kitchen and not evident in the yard area outside that back door or in the wash house, and when she called her name there was no answer. Monday was washing day and even out in the yard she could smell the strong smell of soap scented steam coming from the water in the wash boiler in the wash house. She guessed Sally must have filled it up as usual and one of the stable boys had lit the fire under it. Sally lived in at the farm so was always there when Gracie arrived, usually just finishing her breakfast, so this morning she must have finished early, decided Gracie. At a loss as to what to do, as she still took her instructions from Sally so she was not sure what her work order for the morning should be, Gracie decided to look in the other nearby buildings in the hope of finding her. The first door was the wash house and through the thick cloud of steam she could see the room was empty. Next she opened the dairy door, and as she peered around it she stopped dead in her tracks at the sight that greeted her. Eyes startled wide

47

in shock and a sharp cry escaped her lips as she quickly slapped her had over her mouth to quell the sound. A seemingly unprotesting Sally was being pressed up against the back wall, one shoulder of her bodice dropped down to reveal her bare shoulder and her skirt being held up on her other side by a tall blonde haired fancily dressed man who was kissing Sally's neck. Suddenly Gracie shockingly thought Sally seemed quite happy at being kissed. Horrified at the girl's disarray and the gleam of white skin, Gracie stood for a moment in panic. At the small cry from Gracie the man turned to look over his shoulder in her direction. 'Well, Well what have we here, another new pretty little bird, welcome new little bird?" Gracie, incapable of any further speech, turned in an instant and bolted in the direction of the kitchen leaving an equally panicked Sally and a laughing very much amused man. She slammed the heavy back kitchen outer door behind her and ran through to the kitchen proper and over to the sink frantically starting to scrape off the breakfast plates stacked ready for washing.

A flustered Sally burst into the kitchen moments later. Grabbing her cap from the hook on the wall, where she had hung it only minutes before, she stuck it on her head, her blonde hair escaping on all sides. Hurriedly struggling into her cross back apron the ties twisting causing more trouble than usual and dislodging her cap for it to fall to the floor. Sally bent retrieving the cap from the floor and rising with a red face crossed the kitchen quickly to Gracie and grasping her left hand, even though it was wet and held a plate, with both of hers. The embarrassed girl burst out in a panic of words, 'Gracie thou wan't say nowt will yer? I'll get sack fer sure. Master Dixon said it were alrite cus' it wer' 'im an' he ony cum 'ome last nite and he brung me summat too. But a' durst' think Mrs Dixon will not like it if she

48

finds out.' Sally now reached into her pocket and held out her hand, in the palm, a small metal pin broach in the shape of a flower with a green glass centre stone. 'See, reel jewellery, he bought it fer me special like, I ain't never had any before,' she said with an air of pride.

Gracie stared in silent horror at the other girl's work worn hand with at its hollow palm nestling the glittering metal and sparkling green stone but quietly said, 'I'll sey nowt.' And turned away to carry on scraping the plates, her hands shaking all the while.

The girls new friendship was strained for a few days as neither spoke of the incident, yet it was never far from both their minds, but after a week the awkwardness faded as Gracie good natured as ever dismissed the incident as 'a bit of silliness'. As for Sally she just hoped that the matter would be forgotten. Sally's still somewhat subdued chatter indicated that 'the man' was obviously still around but as Gracie never saw him again, she put the incident out of her mind. All was well until one Monday morning two weeks later when Gracie was hanging out washing in the orchard behind the farm. When the weather was fine the girls hung a thin rope between several of the apple and pear trees.

Unwilling, being too embarrassed, to tell her Mother that her bodice was getting tight across her chest she had taken to leaving the bodice middle buttons undone. For if even very carefully fastened the little pearl buttons slipped back free with movement as she worked, and under her full bibbed apron she was secure in the knowledge that no one could see through the wide thick starched cotton apron bib. Now as she stretched arms high in the air, hands full of wet sheet and wooden dolly pegs she was suddenly mind and body in shock, she gave out a short sharp scream, dropped the sheet and pegs and clasped her hands to her chest to try to stop the progress of hands which had reached inside the bib and pulled her backwards with a jolt to a solid stop against what she guessed was a chest. Dazed for a moment then she twisted and turned trying to hit out but the man behind her just laughed. 'Come on, don't be a silly girl, Sally likes it, and it's only a bit of fun, and I always buy a present in return. You really shouldn't leave your bodice open you know it's very inviting.' Gracie now suddenly again experienced the motion stopping effect of shock as she felt his hand touch her bare skin. The young man grinned at her back, amused at Gracie's discomfort and stood back. Gracie in her panic, flushed and dizzy, saw the gates of Hell open before her. The sheet was left abandoned on the grass along with the other washing in the basket as a now released Gracie dashed across the yard for the wash house door as though those hounds of hell had really come through the gates to get her. She slammed the door behind her and stumbled to the darkest corner listening to the laughter outside. She quickly became aware that she was leaning against the brick outside of the still very hot washing boiler. Confused in her distress she moved sideways behind the big iron mangle in the opposite corner where there was a seat made by a low stone slab. She sat on the cold stone terrified by what had just happened, all the while trying to persuade the buttons of her bodice to stay fastened, but her fingers fumbled and the smoothness of little pearl buttons caused them to slip straight out of the cloth again. Now with her arms hugging her chest she sat as she rocked back and forth in silence, until the laughter lessened into the distance. Her thoughts were in turmoil but as the shock eased Gracie reluctantly decided that contact with the man was not that unpleasant and she liked his soft voice and the clean scented smell of him, and her face flamed in shame at this realisation. A long half an hour later a self-chastened girl slowly opened the door and peeked out, for she knew she could not stay there in the wash house any longer or someone would come looking for her thinking she was shirking and then she really would be in trouble. There was no one in sight so she scurried into the orchard and frantically started to hang the rest of the washing on the line, all the time listening and looking about frightened he would return. She then inspected the abandoned sheet which had gained mud from its time lying on the ground but luckily no grass stains so a quick soaking in the slopstone sink in the wash house and then a brisk action with the laundry scrubbing brush and the sheet was rescued and then hung along with the other washing on the line. When she returned to the kitchen to find Sally, a tide of relief passed over her to still her racing heart, for it was apparent by her friend's lack of comment, that easy going Sally had not even missed her or noticed how long she had been outside.

Silly little bird was exactly how Edward Dixon would have described Gracie had he had cause to comment but Edward seldom concerned himself with his actions, they were all just little 'birds' were the young girls who worked in and around the farm, and as such he considered that they were his to amuse himself with if he fancied and nobody bothered if you didn't go too far. 'Life in the country was so boring,' he had informed his college friend George only a few weeks before, 'one had to have a little entertainment or one would go quite off ones head.' Oh he always gave them a trinket, something shiny always pleased best, he thought. He was sure that the next time he approached that one she would have thought about it and changed her mind and be more obliging, and she was worth a second try with a face and hair like that, and she was clean unlike some of the girls who

51

worked on the farm. Yes, he mused, those black curls which escaped the cap were enough to imagine a tumble of jet black delight if all were released, and a smile crossed his face in eager anticipation.

Gracie worked through the day, her hands doing the jobs, her mind in turmoil, she had asked Sally who the man was after the morning she had walked unwittingly into the dairy so she knew he was the Dixons' son and he only came home occasionally as he was studying in London which was a long way away, because he was going to be a gentleman. Gracie knew that because Mrs Dixon had told her so, and she also knew her new job would be uncertain if she complained about him, and anyway Mrs Dixon would probably not believe her. Mrs Dixon was very proud of her son, Sally had said, and she always told everyone about him. Well, decided Gracie, I for one do not want to know any more about him, and I hope I never see him again, but she knew that was not really a possibility.

Meantime a bored Edward Dixon had decided that he needed a little further entertainment, and the pretty face and dark curls had intrigued him and the more he thought about them the keener he became to continue their pursuit. She was certainly better than the usual housemaid, and so as he had nothing else to do that afternoon he stopped Sally as she crossed the yard and asked her for the name of the new girl and then where Gracie lived and the direction in which she went home. Sally was reluctant to tell him as she did not want to share his attentions with Gracie but he would not take no for an answer. So a duly informed Edward Dixon made it his business to be waiting for Gracie as she started down the lane for home. He positioned himself leaning against the side wall beyond the curve half way along the lane, far enough along so that she would not see him when she started for home, but only when she was well along the lane. Edward as he stood waiting picturing her face was again entranced as he had been on first seeing her in the dairy doorway. Oh, the beauty of the girl, oh, how he wanted to kiss those lips and touch the black ripple of her hair. Now hearing the sound of clogs on the cobbles he sauntered into the middle of the path. 'Hello again, Gracie, see I know your name now. You are very pretty. How about a kiss, now that we know each other?'

Gracie, the moment she saw him, stopped dead, he was speaking to her but the words did not register all she knew was she was unable to pass the man and unsure of what to do stood transfixed for a moment, then need for flight rushed in and came to her aid. Grasping her skirt to lift it slightly away from the ground she unwittingly drew his attention to her feet and legs so as she saw his gaze move downwards she quickly dodged around him, his outstretched hand to late to catch her, and she fled for home again leaving the laughter behind her and with 'I'll catch you yet little bird' ringing in her ears.

CHAPTER 5

'Gracie, Gracie, oh where ar yer, Gracie?' shouted Agnes leaning her head and shoulders round the back door in order to see through to the into the old walled garden which ran down the side of the house and orchard at the rear of the yard. 'Weer is that giddy lass?' she said to herself as she turned back towards the kitchen and her baking, then when after a few minutes there was no answer and no Gracie she rubbed her floured hands down her apron and hurried out in the direction she had been looking. Again she shouted as she hurried through the arched opening in the stone wall which led to the garden, 'Gracie just yer cum 'ere now. I know yer' in here dreeming agin I saw you cum 'ome afor.'

Agnes knew she was right and she also knew just where Gracie would be. Where the little steam that tumbled down the fell side just beyond the far wall entered the old enclosed garden. Although most of the back section of the stone wall had long collapsed, the tunnelled gap through which some long dead builder had directed the stream to enter the garden still remained. The stream trickled steadily through the waist high tunnel with its arched top to run its course along the length of the overgrown garden, between the ancient neglected fruit bushes and alongside the ruined side sluice, which had once been used to extract water, until it left the garden by another similar tunnel to carry on to flow into the cattle troughs in the farmyard. Gracie was just where Agnes expected her to be, sitting on a stone at the side of the stream. The girl was almost bent double, her head bowed and her arms hugging around her bent legs. Agnes sensed straight away that there was some problem, but was at a loss to fathom the cause. 'Lass you've got to stop doin this now, yer te big te be just sitin' here ther's werk te be done,' Agnes cried in despair.

Gracie looked up from the ground where her gaze had been resting. 'Sorry, Mam, cuming now.'

Agnes turned and returned to her kitchen shaking her head unable to be angry with the girl but knowing this silliness had to stop, but now it seemed that there was some problem probably at the house as she had been nowhere else, oh the lass was such a dreamer her head often in the clouds, and not always on her work. If she mentioned it to Jonas he would just smile and say 'the lass will grow up soon' he just did not see she already had.

Gracie slowly followed Agnes into the cool dark entry passage and then into the brighter warmer kitchen where Agnes had set about finishing the potato pie she had been making. 'Mam, I don't like it at the house, Mrs Dixon's always finding folt wi me,' Gracie muttered slowly and in a low voice.

Agnes turned and lifted her eyes sharply to look at the girl's face but Gracie was looking at the floor, her foot tracing the line of a join in the flag stones. 'Weel yer must be doin summat wrong then, she's a fair lady.'

'No she's not, she's mean, she shouts, and she's not fair and a' don't want to go back.'

Agnes sighed, she had thought the girl was happy and settled at the house and she thought it unlikely that a lady like Mrs Dixon would be in the habit of shouting at anybody. 'Weel 'al go and 'ave a word wi' Nellie.'

'No,' the girl cried desperately, 'yer can't do that.'

'An' why not?' demanded Agnes. Gracie dropped down onto a stool as the sobs burst from her.

Half an hour later Agnes knew the whole sorry story and she was angry. Angry at the way that 'them folk' always thought they could do what they wanted, well she was not having it, not with her daughter, why this was the very reason the child had gone to the farm to avoid this kind of trouble. 'Tek Big Lad an' go for a walk around the orchard an' t'ruins it'll calm thee down, lass. Don't worry we'll sort this out,' she told the girl hoping a walk with the dog might 'do her good' although it would not solve the problem for how to do that she was completely at a loss. Seems, she thought to herself, these gentry are not the righteous folk what they claim to be. Out loud but under her breath, as she banged pots and pans as she tidied the kitchen, 'We might werk as servants but we're not slaves. Why couldn't this one have been plain looking like the other two? That lovely face and hair is the problem, that and her dreamy head and soft heart. She'd as well gone inte mill.'

As usual Jonas was late in from working that night, he was always late home now, thought Agnes to herself as she 'turned over' what she was going to say to him. She knew he was not going to be happy about Gracie not going to the Dixons' any more, because they might not like it, and they were not in a good position to upset the Dixons being so dependent on their good will for job, home and farm, but Agnes was not going to be moved. She had already had an argument with Nellie because Nellie said it was her who was going to 'be ' bother' and be blamed if Gracie didn't go to the farm any more after she, Nellie, had recommended Gracie and as she was doing so well, but Agnes was sure that when Nellie calmed down she would see sense. Agnes had practised her words so many times before Jonas came home, she knew them by heart. Why, she thought to herself, had there always to be bother, life was difficult enough without more problems. One part of life might be straight forward in itself but it always intertwined itself into a knot with another part.

Jonas eventually came in from the buildings and Agnes could see from his slow gait as he walked across the kitchen towards the fire that he was tired and as she looked she thought, Aye, Jonas, your clothes are starting to hang on you, skin and bone ye are, man. And as he slumped into the old low rush seat chair at the fireside to unlace his clogs she hesitated, but even as she did she knew it had to be faced. Agnes's words, 'Jonas our Gracie is in bother', instantly brought dread to the man's face until Agnes quickly waved and shook her hands about. 'No it's not that Jonas but it might as well be if we don't do summat.' He listened quietly to what Agnes had to say, and she could see the torment in his face as he listened. He was distressed at what had happened to his bonny daughter, but, like Agnes had already considered, he feared for his home and his livelihood, because as he rented home and land from Mister Dixon as well as working for him, he could not afford to upset him.

They both sat desperately talking, tired and sighing seeking any possible solution, looking for an answer by the dying embers of the fire until long into the night, into the hours when they should have been having much needed sleep. Finally Jonas sighed yet again. 'There's only one answer, Gracie as t' be ill like she has a sudden fever an then she can't go te werk,' was the final decision from him.

Agnes looked aghast at her husband who she had never known to lie. 'Jonas Bailey we can't do that an' still go ter church on Sabeth.'

Jonas looked back at his wife and said quietly, 'God will understand.' And that was the end of the matter. All Agnes had to do, he went on, was explain and instruct Nellie to take the message that Gracie was ill and unfit for work.

Agnes sighed at the thought. 'I allus get the good jobs.' But as she could think of nothing better, simply said, 'Let's away te bed.'

Early the following morning Agnes ensured that she was at Nellie's long before the old woman left for the farmhouse. 'So I ata tell em she has a fever.'

'Aye that's it, Nellie. Tell 'em it cum on reet quick. Aye an tell em she has spots an scabs, that'll put em off wanting her up there.'

'Weel that's all well 'an good, but I've just lost me helper. An the Mrs is not banna be reet appy about loosin' her maid. She'll ner believe it came on or'neet.'

'Say as she were not feelin' reet weel yesterday. An' a'm reet sorry as it as te be you, Nellie te do it but it 'as te look normal like an' you're going there anyhow. A'm reet sorry, Nellie but it's fer best, that lad is a wrongen and no mistake. Our Gracie looks t' good for her own sake an she's t' soft. It has t' be done.'

Nellie was resigned and reluctantly agreed to convey the story, then walking up the lane, a little later, cursed out loud and blamed that spoilt Dixon lad for her own now increased work load, for the fact was added to that she could not think of another girl who would be a suitable replacement. 'Curse him, nasty piece a' werk he is, even if he is his mother's darling.'

Gracie was forbidden to wander outside the house for the next month during her 'illness', and then after a few weeks the neighbours were told that she was only recovering slowly from the sudden attack of fever and was still weak so was going to work at home for the time being. She was relieved at her father's 'rescue' but soon began longing for the outdoors, the hills and fresh air, for she was still denied trips away from the house in case someone saw her with no evidence of the terrible spots. The carefree walks on the moor with Big Lad, that she was sure he was missing as much as her, were desperately longed for. She helped Agnes with the house cleaning, and cooking and was even allowed to help with the washing but not allowed to hang it out for fear of being seen, although this was no sorrow as the thought of hanging washing still brought a bright red blush to her face. Being two of them the housework was soon done, and as Gracie was not allowed out beyond the dairy or other buildings then she was often left to sit indoors. Even Big Lad was begrudgingly allowed, by a reluctant Agnes, to sit beside the 'invalid'.

'Gracie why don't yer hav a read of those books that Mrs Dixon sent for Sarah? She said they were very suitable for girls reading when she sent 'em.' Agnes tried to occupy the girl.

'I don't want owt to do wi' owt from them Dixons,' protested Gracie. Agnes despaired but she couldn't help but sympathise with her daughter.

'Well what about 'aving a go at meking a few more pinnies yer still havn't mastered that there sewing machine. We were very lucky to get if from Mrs Worthington, it's like new she only had only it a few months. A' still don't know why she chose to give it te us. She just likes spendin' old man Worthington's money if yer ask me. Nellie said she heard tell she doesn't even like the new one she got instead. There's some strong white cotton in't bottom left dresser drawer, yer could cut that up fer em.' This said, Agnes left her unhappy daughter warily eyeing the treadle sewing machine sitting in the corner of the room, and went to go and hang out the washing.

It was a stifling warm August night, and Gracie had been 'ill' for five weeks when after lying awake for what seemed like hours she again turned slowly in her narrow bed, decided she had to get out of bed, so pushed back the covers and dropped her feet to the boarded floor. She was sure she had turned over ten times and her nightdress had twisted around her until she was in the middle of a knot. She just couldn't stand being in the bed any longer, it was so hot even the air in the room seemed warm to breathe. Gracie shared the room with her older sisters and Dora's little girl Elsie but did not sleep in the big bed with her sisters, as she had been so much younger, they had both objected so she and Dora's child Elsie both had small truckle beds similar to the one Nellie had brought to the house when Gracie was born. She eased herself quietly over the wooden edge of the bed and crept to the window, lured there by the shaft of moonlight that was shooting through it to strike the floor at the foot of her sisters' bed. The sliding casement was slightly ajar to one side and through the open narrow nick she breathed in the clean air so freshly sharp after the still warm air of the room. The moon was full and the sharp light hit her face and through the thick glass she could see right out to the high moor. Grateful that by the moonlight falling through the window she could see at a quick glance that the other girls were all asleep, she remained longingly gazing out. The window overlooked the walled garden where she longed to go sit and beyond she could see the stream as it sparkled trickling down the hill through the little wooded valley before it reached the tunnel in the tumbled down back wall of the garden. She stood gazing through the window and as she did she remembered that Nellie always said that people called the little valley 'the Fairy glen'. Nellie had told her years before when she was a child that the fairies could be seen just at the top of the moor near the top pit (pond), and there was a fairy queen who sometimes visited when the moon was big. Gracie didn't really believe Nellie but it was a nice story. She had once seen a picture of a fairy in a book, like a beautiful little dolly but with tiny wings on her back and a beautiful short white dress.

The longer Gracie stood there at the window the greater the longing became to see if the story could be true, although she thought it wasn't, she was sure. She also knew full well that she should not go outside the house alone at night, but then proceeded to spend the next five minutes convincing herself no one would know if she wasn't outside long, and no one was going to see her for her sisters had never stirred. Well, she told herself, she hadn't been outside for weeks, and she could take Big Lad with her and he would protect her, and it was all the fault of that Edward Dixon so nobody could really blame her if she wanted to be outside, she was suffering for something that wasn't her fault and that wasn't fair. Now very self-convinced it was quite all right, she slowly moved, one footstep at a time, across the room to the low doorway, walking close to her bed so avoiding the creaky boards she knew were there near the big bed. Now holding her breath as she lifted the door handle sneck very slowly, but it still made a soft click as it slipped free of the hook on the door frame. Gracie stood waiting perfectly still for a moment but her sisters' breathing never altered. She pulled the door open enough to slip through at which it made a low creaking sound. She hesitated for a few moments but her sisters remained still in their bed, so she then managed to pull it quietly to almost closed but leaving it slightly ajar, not risking the sneck handle again. Now outside the bedroom she could see her way by the shaft of moonlight also coming through the landing window so crept slowly along to the stair head and then on down the stairs. Almost every footstep produced a squeak or creak but the family was used to the house and its noises and no one stirred.

As she descended down the stairs into the cooler darkness of the stairwell, Gracie felt her long white nightdress trailing on the steps and dragging against the front of her ankles, so she decided she had to hitch it up or it would get soiled from the floor and her mother would know she had been wandering about and want to know why. The passageway at the stair bottom was very dark but familiar and in the blackness she felt the back door in front of her. Her hand touched on used lengths of twine her father always hung there on a hook for future use. She now separated one of these, pulled it free from the bundle and tied it around her waist and hitched up her shift above it so that she was bare from mid-calf down. The heavy latch bar of the solid door opened easily with only a dull thud and she was out in the cool moonlit air. The door pulled closed as easily and quietly as it had opened and she sighed in relief.

Almost before she had taken another step, Big Lad had silently appeared at her side, having heard the house door he had stirred from his sacking bed in the barn as the high barn doors were always left open at this time of year. The dog, one ear cocked, looked questioningly at the girl but then quite happily and willingly trotted alongside her as they walked away from the house.

Without a word spoken, the two padded barefoot along the nearest outer wall of the old garden turning at the broken down back corner where a tree had grown through the stonework, and into and up the shallow valley which cut through the higher ground on either side. Here the little steam wound its way down wriggling between moss clad stones and twisted tree roots to then pass through the gap in the wall and along the garden to its final destination: the troughs in the yard. Tonight the water whispered quietly, the only sound in the still moonlit night, as it moved constantly on its way and a short distance along the valley bottom the travellers stopped at the water's edge. Big Lad tested the water with a paw, bent his head, lapped quickly and then sat quietly at the glistening stream edge. The sound of a cow lowing in the distance caused Big Lad to lift his head listening but then all was silent again but for the murmuring water. Gracie watched the dog for a moment and then sat down beside him on the stream bank and hung her feet into the chilly water. The coldness was almost numbing but sent a welcome sense of soft tranquility through her body, far better than the hot restlessness of the bedroom. They sat there in the stillness, only the soft trickling sound of the water breaking the silence until now an owl hooted at which Big Lad became restive, and Gracie stood again saying softly, 'Well, lad I suppose we should go 'ome but that owl will do us no harm it's lovely out here. What say we'll just go't top pit for a look afor we go 'ome it won't tke us long.' At which the dog looked at the girl, head tipped to one side, looking at her face as if seeking to understand her words, then as she took a step as if agreeing, both moved off again, tracking the stream up the hill side, the girl striding along, the dog jogging along beside.

Tom Briggs had also been restless that night lying in the workers' wooden shed along with all the other navvies from the reservoir site. Unable to stand the grunts, snores and smell of many unwashed bodies in the hot close atmosphere of the low building, he decided sleep was not to be his this night, so almost relieved at the decision, he escaped silently into the cool night and seeing the unknown beckoning moors in the bright moonlight, all thought of sleep vanished completely, he set off at a brisk pace in their direction. Tom's clogs made little noise on the short soft grass of the lower fields and after half an hour's walking he heard the low gentle sound of the stream coming from where Gracie and Big Lad had just been sitting, and unwittingly heading in the same direction, he arrived just in time to see the silhouette of the girl and dog as they climbed the last steep part of the hillside and reached the ridge of the moor top, and gained the level ground at the summit, on their way to the top pit: the pool which supplied the stream.

Amazed and intrigued by this sight he also climbed slowly upward on the fell slope keeping a distance from the two adventurers, being fearful of startling them he became more careful not to make any sound, and then when he saw they had come to a standstill he too stopped to stand behind and just below a stunted bent hawthorn tree which had somehow kept its footing on the very bank of the stream. Scared that he would certainly frighten the pair if they knew of his presence, Tom remained behind the tree, were he could just look up over the ledge at the edge of the moor and beyond to its flat slightly lower vista with the glimmer of silver pool at its centre and further hills in the darkness behind. His view illuminated by the soft white light of the full moon, he gazed in wonder at this sight before him. As his head was only just above level with the ground above he was almost invisible to Gracie and Big Lad, but they were not looking in his direction as they headed for the moon bright water of the pit. Gracie spoke quietly to the dog urging him to stay close as awareness of their isolation came to her, but as the lure of the silver mirror sheen of the water drew her closer, the girl skipped towards it and as she looked into the smooth surface she saw her refection. She gasped, at first unable to believe her eyes, but yes there she was the fairy Queen, she really was, so it was true after all. Thrilled she fancied it must be the fairy queen staring back at her, for there she was in her short white dress although she couldn't see her wings but of course they would be on her back and as she was facing front they and her back were hidden from

64

sight. She was under the water but fairies were magic so they could do anything.The fairy stared back at Gracie, not moving, not smiling, just staring, which worried Gracie, for maybe the Queen was angry at her for visiting the Queen's pit. The Baileys did not have much in the way of mirrors and Gracie had certainly never seen a full length self staring back at her, so she had no inkling as to what she looked like. The fairy Queen still remained motionless, just looking back at Gracie and for a few moments the equally motionless girl was at a loss what to do, but then remembering what Nellie had taught her to do for Mrs Dixon, she tightly grasped the hem of her nightgown. She lifted the garment sides and coyly bobbed a stiff curtsy to the reflection in the water all the while watching the Queen from under her loose curls, and amazed and delighted she saw the fairy queen curtsy back at her. The delighted Gracie now dipped lower in her curtsy and at the same moment Big Lad decided to have a lay down so both she and the dog disappeared suddenly and instantly below Tom's line of view. The man started, his heart lurched and then raced, fearing the danger of the nearness of the water, but he hesitated just for a moment so just as he started to move forward towards the water both girl and dog appeared again and Tom breathed once more and stepped back again behind the tree. Laughing quietly as she spoke to Big Lad, the girl moved away from the water, and as she turned to look again at the pit, the Queen had gone, so twirling again and once more holding up the sides of her skirt she skipped towards the dog, who had moved even further away from the water. As she turned the moonlight shone fully on the smiling face and the swirling black curls, unrestrained by any binding ribbon, but stirred by the gentle breeze and the girl's spinning, and the white bare legs gleamed as she danced. Tom was captivated, moon, stars, a dancing twirling spirit of a girl and an enormous dog. He was sure he was in a living dream. 'Well, Lad we ner saw the other fairies but the queen wa theer alreet, an' she did a curtsy back, how about that!' Gracie whispered to the dog. 'Pity, but best not tell anybody or they'll know we've been up here.' Tom, still spellbound but now convinced by hearing Gracie's words that she was real, his breath held as he stood perfectly still and silent as girl and dog descended the hillside passing within reaching distance of him and the tree. Just as they passed, the dog raised its nose sniffing the air; as it turned in Tom's direction a low growl started in its throat, but the owl hooted again and Big Lad's attention moved to the bird's sound. Tom felt he could hear his heart pounding as he dared to breathe, but still he hesitated to move. Then the girl spoke again, her words carrying clearly on the gentle breeze, 'Cum on, Lad it's time to go home.'

When they had finally disappeared from his view, for he watched them as they descended into the distance the girl's white dress being the last thing he saw in the moonlight, he sat down slowly, the slope of the hillside affording a convenient and essential seat. 'Well,' he told himself, 'never seen anything like that afor' and probably won't agin, were they truly real or is the moon affecting me' head?'

CHAPTER 6

Gracie hurried down the hill towards home with the dog in front both having sensed the urgency of returning quickly as the sun was rising, its yellow tinged brightness suddenly shooting over the moor top. Ever watchful of the girl, Big Lad stood to see Gracie pass in through the back door before he headed for his bed in the barn. Getting back into the bedroom was no worse than the leaving, easier really as daylight was creeping through the small window, but Gracie stopped midway across the room and held her breath when she heard the bed ropes squeak as her father rose for the day, but he must not have heard her for he walked straight down the stairs past the door without stopping. Relieved she had not been found out of bed she let out a low sigh. Edging carefully past her sleeping sisters, she slipped into her own bed pulling the covers up to her chin, then remembered the string was still around her waist and wriggled as she removed it, thinking as she did that she must remember to put it back behind the back door or her mother would be asking questions if she saw it in her bed. Her efforts in removing the string made the little bed creak but her sisters slept on.

Tom had also finally become aware of the approaching dawn, and the equal awareness that he must get back to the site before work started or he would not get his morning bread and tea, so unwillingly leaving his perch on the brook side, he rose and set off down the hill. The food supplied by the water works for the navvies was not generous but it was better than nothing, and Tom was hungry after his eventful night time trip on the moor. The first person he encountered on nearing the site was Billy. Billy, who everyone called 'Daft Billy' for that young man who had grown to tower above others and had hands 'size a' shuffles' so everyone said, although the big man still had the thoughts of a young child, his strength assured him a job in the navvy gang, often doing others' work as well as his own. 'Weer yer bin, Tom, a knew yer'd gun out when yer planks was empty?' was Billy's greeting. Tom knew that Billy would have been worried if he knew that he was not there as Billy was lost without Tom's presence close by.

'Fer a walk, but yer alreet I'm back now.' And Billy was happy, the smile returning to his face at this assurance, his concern quickly gone.

Tom had become Billy's 'mate' when they had both been working with a canal repair gang a year before, and Tom had rescued Billy from several navvies who were using Billy for a fool by having him standing needlessly in deep water to repair the tow path. The other gangers had been enjoying the joke of Billy up to his shoulders in the cold weedy water but Tom had put a stop to the entertainment by telling Billy he had done a good job and could finish. The men disgruntled and complaining at their fun being ended soon moved off to resume their work. Billy, grateful without really understanding why, sensed relief and the security in being by Tom's side. Tom for his part was glad of Billy's company; it was undemanding and assured.

'A saved yer bread, Tom and yer can 'ave mi tay,' beamed Billy as he produced a thick wedge of bread from his coat pocket, and offered a can of tea.

'Ta, Billy, but al geet some water, yer keep yer tay,' returned a grateful Tom unwilling to deprive his friend of his morning hot tea. He knew how much thought the act of saving the bread had taken and he really was grateful as he quickly ate the thick and slightly battered wedge. 'Let's geet ter werk now.'

The two men headed down into the reservoir site where the gangs were gathering for the day digging and shovelling earth as the great deep hollow was dug for the new extra reservoir that was being built to supply water for more new cotton mills and the surrounding spreading towns of East Lancashire. Billy, his blonde head towering above those around him, as ever moving twice the amount of earth as the other men, was engrossed in his labours, his movements regular and deliberate as he concentrated, oblivious of the mocking directed towards him. Tom was also digging in a regular action more from habit than thought, but that was because his mind had transported him back up the moor to the little pool under a moonlit sky. Who was the girl? he wondered, and was she real or was this wandering hard way of life finally sending him off his head? He didn't think there could be many girls around who looked like that and acted like a spirit dancing in the moonlight, especially accompanied by a very large dog. Again the thought kept repeating in his head, 'are they real, were they real?' While all the time he just kept shovelling.

The next Sunday, the only day when the workings in the valley were quiet as the Sabbath was a day of rest for navvies, because the Water Board dictated so. So Tom and an eager Billy in tow passed the deserted site and set off for a day walking the hills. Tom was of a mind to see the moor and pond in daylight and Billy was more than eager to join him when he suggested the idea. After his evening jaunt he was unable to clear the girl and dog from his mind, he had to see the place again for he was becoming more and more convinced he had dreamt the whole thing. He was not to be disappointed when the two reached the summit, it was beautiful and the peace and tranquility of the place was a salve to his racing mind, although it did nothing to help him decide whether his experience was real or not, for it was just as he remembered except for the lack of moonlight, and the two wistfully remembered adventurers. As the two friends sat at the water's edge, and ate the bread and cheese they had managed to persuade the camp cook to give them, with cupped hands they supped from the glistening stream where it left the pit, the world around them was still except for the water's gentle murmur. That was the beginning of Tom's affinity for the moors, for these were smooth round soft hills. Oh, he knew they would still be hard in winter but they mostly hid their inner soft brown stone like treasure under the green, not displaying the steely silver grey to repel like the hills of the part of Yorkshire where Tom had been brought up.

Evenings that often lasted well into the night became peace time for Tom as he escaped, drawn to the now indispensable hills, sometimes accompanied by an eager Billy, but Billy's presence meant that the trip was usually shorter as the nights were drawing in and to the younger man the arrival of dusk was 'home time' as he was always uneasy after dark, constantly asking if they were going back to camp and the assurance of safety that came with it. Tom knew this aversion to the dark was due to Billy's childhood when he had often been shut in, it seemed, according to Billy's vague description in what must have been a cellar at the Work House where he was brought up. Billy needed the comfort of a lamp or candle nearby, for without comforting light he became angry and troubled.

It was a windy early autumn Sunday morning when Tom, walking alone for once, decided to keep to lower ground where the gusts came with reduced fierceness to cut less through his thin worn coat. He carried a rolled oilskin strapped to his back for if the rain started, but otherwise unencumbered he strode on at a good pace up the hill, keeping to the sheltered leeward side of a long stone wall where the wind was less and the late summer sun warm in its shelter. He saw he was heading towards a scattering of buildings he had seen in the distance, and as he approached the hamlet, a stone step stile in the wall led him into a narrow, cart track bounded by two stone walls. After a few moments he turned, suddenly alerted by the sound of pounding hooves, to see a wild eyed black bullock come charging through an open gate to the right not far behind him. It swerved sharply around the nearest stone gatepost and then along the track between the enclosing walls, to head wildly in Tom's direction. The racing animal a leather halter dangling wildly from its neck had obviously escaped from somewhere. Tom had spent his older childhood as a farm servant and was fully aware of the dangers of trying to stop runaway cattle and in an instant jumped to the side and half scrambled up the nearest part of the wall as the bullock passed by his feet. Sitting atop the stones he had a first-hand view as first a young lad came chasing the animal with a struggling Jonas Bailey lagging behind. Tom dropped from the wall back to the ground and without stopping joined the capture party, as he could see they were heading towards the row of buildings and cottages he had seen from the wall top, and that bullock was not going to stop on its own but more likely to do damage or harm. The beast and men emerged from the confines of the track and walls into a yard area bounded by in front of them a house, and barn with farm buildings to either side and in a momentary view Tom saw a small old woman and standing beside her a girl and dog. THE girl and dog, and in the next moment the dog barred its teeth and flew at the bullock in a fury

71

of fur and teeth. The animal stopped in an instant, its braced front legs skidding on the yard stone cobbles, then it half turned and snorted, its nostrils flaring as it bellowed, its back legs lashing out wildly hitting the dog in the head and chest. There was a sharp high pitched yelp as the dog was thrown several feet by the power of the hooves to land in a broken furry heap. There was a long moment of silence before the bullock, now standing all four braced legs, bellowed and the girl screamed. The lad grabbed the rope dangling from the halter round its head and Tom helped him corner the animal where some of the side farm buildings met a wall.

The girl was still screaming and crying 'Big Lad' which Tom assumed was the injured dog's name. The older man then moved slowly towards the still dog and seeing the damage to its head quickly lifted the animal and turned the bloodied head towards his chest. There was no movement from Big Lad and as Jonas walked towards the motionless Gracie he saw the grief in her blanched face and saw she knew without a word being spoken, the dog was dead.

Jonas carried Big Lad towards the barn where he laid him gently on his sacking bed. The lad tugged on the rope he was grasping and the bullock was taken to continue its broken journey to the holding yard to await its morning walk and fate at the local slaughter house, and even the beast seemed subdued at the carnage it had caused.

Gracie could not be persuaded to return to the house but sat on the stone barn floor beside the still dog stroking the now motionless head. Jonas signalled to Tom to accompany him into the house and they found a distressed Agnes wringing her hands sitting beside a very quiet Nellie. 'Can we 'ave a cup 'a tay, Agnes, this lad here helped mi chase bullock?' Jonas asked.

But before she could reply Nellie jumped up with a quick 'Al do it'. The room was silent but for the sound of cups, tins and spoons and then the kettle scraping the hob as Nellie made the tea. 'Shall 'a tek some te Gracie?' Nellie queried already expecting the quick 'Nay.' from Jonas.

'Nay leave 'er be.' After a time Jonas stirred and mumbled his concern for he was becoming anxious about the jobs he was not doing and it had crossed his mind there would be no church going tonight and the unattended stock were still where he left them when the chase had started.

Tom sensed his dilemma and divided concern and offered his help. 'Ave nowt 't do 't day. Can 'a elp?'

The older man immediately opened his mouth to instinctively refuse the offer, then thought better for what was the harm? He seemed a good lad, clean and tidy with a pleasant face and manner, and right at this moment Jonas felt at a loss how to deal with this mess. 'Aye yer can and welcome. We'll go 'an see 't dry cows 'a wer movin' an then cum back te see ter dog.'

When they came back a good hour or so later Gracie was still sitting by the dog in the barn and declared through her tears, as she cowered over the prostrate animal, that she was not moving 'ever'. Agnes had tried to comfort the girl with ' Gracie lass, Big Lad died saving ye from bullock.' but that did not help.

'Well it should a' killed us both, that wud a bin best.' It was the reply at which a helpless Agnes went back into the house.

Jonas and Tom returned to the house to find an anxious bustling Agnes trying to keep her mind calm by keeping her hands busy doing unnecessary tidying of anything and everything. Jonas went out to the barn to see the girl but quickly returned. 'A don't knew what 't do wi' that lass she's 'art brocken,' burst out Jonas. Tom felt for the couple for although he had never had a family, so far as he could remember, there had been an old lady in 'the House' who had been kind to him when he was small and he had been desolate when she had died and left him.

He looked at the obviously desperate couple and his mind racing said softly. 'Meybe she'll let me bury it, like an underteker.' The two looked at the lad doubtfully but Agnes glad of any possible answer to the dilemma nodded her head.

'Aye maybe, am not reet sure what tha mean but give it a try, lad, please.'

Tom walked slowly to the barn, all the while trying to work out how he was going fulfill what he had just suggested for it had been a sudden idea without any forethought. As he approached the high barn doors he heard the girl talking softly to the dead animal. He waited patiently for a break in the girl's words. 'Hello, Gracie, yer dad's ast mi to help yer gi' Big Lad a funeral, weer would yer like him to rest?'

The girl slowly turned her tear stained face up to look at the stranger, his heart lurched, she was every bit as beautiful as he remembered, no more so. 'Yer sure he sed, we don't know ye.'

'Aye,' Tom returned, 'yer mam asked 'cus yer dad's not feeling s'good after runnin' atter that bullock.' Tom knew this was not too much of a lie because he had seen Jonas struggling for his breath when he had picked up the dog. 'Aye' he repeated.

'All reet then, if Mam said. Big Lad would like to go ter far side a' garden, near rabbits,' Gracie said slowly and softly. Tom was at a loss.

'Garden?' he queried.

'Aye 'far end near wall 't'other side o' waater.'

He hadn't an inkling where the girl meant, but gently lifting the prostate dog the weight of the animal surprising him, he silently acknowledged it was a big animal and strangely he felt honoured to be carrying such a brave creature. Then, being careful to hold the blooded side of the dog's head covered by the sacking and pressed to his chest, said, 'Aye reet, 'am sure he'll like it there, yer lead the way.'

Gracie at its head, the small sombre procession slowly headed for the walled garden and on though the stone doorway. Gracie led the way along the length of the garden and over a wooden plank to the far side of the steam where she stopped close to the back wall. Tom followed, soon understanding where the girl meant when he saw the stream, then he slowly lowered the dog to the ground by the wall, gently folding the hessian sack from its bed closer around the body, and ensuring it covered the dog's bloodied head. Gracie sat quietly on a stone while Tom, telling her he would quickly be back, that he was just going to find a spade, returned to the yard to look in the buildings and to his relief quickly found a large spade. Returning he found the girl patiently waiting. Indicating the place he was going to dig with his spade, Tom looked at the girl for approval which was given by two slow nods. Silently digging the grave, a quick job for a man used to wielding a spade, when Tom gently and slowly laid the dog in the deep hole he watched Gracie from the corner of his eye, for he was uncertain of her reaction as he could not see her face for the now cap free tumble of black curls which spilled around her shoulders. She never moved until he lifted the spade to fill the grave and there was a low sharp 'wait' as the girl stood and headed out of the garden. Tom groaned under his breath having been expecting problems and he now stood beside the open grave waiting, dreading her return, but Gracie having run in the direction of the house returned quickly with a large knuckle bone. She thrust the bone into Tom's hand and then said in low voice, 'Ee adn't finished it an' he wouldn't like somebody else to 'ave it.'

Gracie stood by the graveside as Tom placed the bone in the grave moving the hessian aside and lifting one paw to place it over the bone which he had placed beside the animal, then he filled the hole and smoothed the mound, looked at the girl once more and without a further word headed for the house, leaving her standing there. He glanced back as he passed out through the stone arch to leave the garden. Gracie had settled herself on the ground close to the new mound.

'Thanks, lad, it was reet good on yer. It wer' a reet nice thing ter think o'.' Was repeated by the Baileys several times and he was asked to stay for something to eat, but Tom knew it was time to go and leave them to their own company for he knew a stranger's presence added extra strain at times like this, but before he left they made him promise to return. 'In a day er two lad when things have calmed down like.' Were Agnes's parting words.

CHAPTER 7

Billy was wandering around looking very agitated when Tom arrived back at the camp. He had heard a rumour was going round that the banking stone would be coming from the quarry soon, maybe even next week, and then the builders and stonemasons would arrive and the navvies would have to move on. 'A like it 'ere Tom an' a knows yer do,' stammered the distressed young man, 'a don'st want to leave.'

Trying to calm the young man, Tom thought quickly. 'Don't worry, Billy, they'll wont puddlers for the bottom after that, an then yer never knows what might 'appen.' Tom tried to sound confident but the news worried him for he liked it round here too, and his new found friends up at the farm gave him a good feeling of being wanted he had only previously felt about Billy. The stone blocks did start arriving on the following Thursday and, as they had only to come the short distance from the quarry over the far side of the moor where Tom had first seen Gracie, the horses drawing the heavily laden carts did not become over tired and so continued ferrying regularly every few hours from the cutting site at the quarry.

Agnes and all her neighbours firmly shut all their windows for now it was sand, far worse than the usual wind carried quarry dust, that was blowing from the passing ferried stone. Carried on even the lightest breeze and covering not just the green of the surroundings but entering every house and building through every nick in a door or window. Nellie cursed when she found a fine coating of sand on wild herbs and leaves she was collecting one morning, and then cursed even louder when she went, on one of her now still regular days, up to the Hall Farm and found every dish and bowl in the dairy was covered in the same fine layer, someone had left the dairy door open. At the end of her patience she stormed into the kitchen to loudly heap the blame onto poor Sally. 'Girl, just you stop leaving that dairy door open, the'll be the devil to pay if the Mrs finds sand in the butter. 'Ave you nothing but daftness i' that brainless head o' thine?'

Sally, about to reply in kind, thought better of it as she had already had a warning from the Mrs about leaving doors open, so instead gave a loud 'umh' and left the kitchen banging the door behind her, leaving a fuming Nellie behind.

The ferrying increased and the banks of the reservoir and all the outer enclosing walls, run off channels and sluices began to take shape. Some of the navvies now became involved in helping to move the thousands of stone blocks onto the banks for the builders to place in position. While others still worked in the bottom of the site puddling the vast flat bottom with brought in blue clay. They stamped around the great stone sided amphitheatre, their feet flattening the grey sticky mess, like ragged warriors welding tamping tools in a war dance. Wheel barrows and horses were now prohibited from the site as they roughed the surface. The sooner they finished that blasted reservoir the better for all was the general feeling by all the locals, and on days that it rained folk welcomed the damp as never before. 'Nowt better thana bit o' rain te settle t' dust.' Was heard from many a mouth. The wiser commented that it would be months before 'We get rid o' the dam grit'.

Sunday saw Tom up early and eager to retrace his steps to the farm, but Billy had seen him rise from his pallet and quickly followed. 'Off up't hills agin, Tom, can 'a cum wi' yer?'

Tom groaned because he wanted to go alone and was about to refuse when the sight of the eager expression on the normally placid face stopped him. Billy was unsettled by the prospect of a the future change. Billy did not like change it made him afraid of the unknown. 'Ye ner know what could 'appen next,' he kept telling all who would listen. The future could be bad, as the past had often been, so Billy needed to be near Tom as Tom was safe and solid.

'Al'rite but yer do as 'a says.'

'Oh 'a will, Tom ner fear.' Was the quick reply.

So the two strapped on rolled oilskins, again convinced the camp cook to give them some bread, cheese and an onion, and carrying these strode out briskly and soon came in sight of the farm and cottages. Once over the stile at the bottom of the lane, Tom told Billy to wait until he came back, so the lad promptly plumped down and settled himself on the grass verge to patiently wait. Tom approached the farm with a certain amount of trepidation unsure how his return would be greeted, after the sadness of the previous meeting. He knocked softly on the back door and stood waiting until it was opened by an unfamiliar young woman. 'Yes what de yer want?' she asked her face blank and unsmiling.

Tom's heart sank but in the next moment the very welcoming face of Agnes appeared around the door edge. 'Cum in, lad, thy's welcum. Sarah, this is Tom, thy knows we said, who burid Big Lad for us.'

Sarah's expression changed instantly as she opened the door wide. 'Oh sorry, cum in.'

Tom, who had never before enjoyed such a friendly reception and invitation into a house and home, was quite overwhelmed. Embarrassed at all the attention, he blushed as he pulled off his cap and absently twisting the garment in his hands stuttered, 'It were nowt, anybody wud 'ave done same.'

'Wel 'a don't see it that way, lad, it wer reet clever on yer te think on it, our Gracie could a bin sitting there yet but fer thee,' insisted Agnes. 'Now yer mun stay for th' tay.'

Tom was so pleased and quite overwhelmed to be asked and was about to happily reply, but then his smile faded and his heart sunk as he remembered Billy at the bottom of the lane. 'A can't, Mrs Bailey, mi mate's waiting down the road, a' just called to say t'ra as I'll be movin' on soon. The diggin's near ended, ther stonin' banks and puddling now then it'll bi pitch an' all 'll bi finished.'

'Jonas's not here right now an' yerv, got ter see im,' was Agnes's quick reply.

'A'll mebe see 'im afore a go, but a can't wait now, sorry. Good bye,' Tom insisted sadly, and at that turned to the door as Sarah opened it for him. Making his way along the lane he saw Agnes standing at the open door waving as he glanced back. He waved in return, then determinedly made his back down the lane to the waiting Billy all the time cursing a cruel fate which had made the wrong girl open the Baileys' door.

Later that evening Tom was sitting, dejectedly pondering his future, perched on a wooden stool outside the navvy shed, when Jonas still dressed in his Sunday church going best clothes, appeared striding across the field above the reservoir site. Tom watched, pleased but curious at his arrival at the site, as the farmer approached heading purposefully towards Tom for he with had come with a proposition. For some time as he had said to Agnes he had been looking for a good farm hand, and although he had looked around none had really suited, but this lad seemed just right if he would agree. The thought of him moving on as

Agnes had said he was going to be doing had pushed Jonas to come down to see the chap, before he left the area. Tom, after his initial surprise, was flattered by the offer; in fact he was proud that someone had come looking for his services, but then Billy's face visualised before his eyes. The same feeling of despair as at the Baileys' cottage overcame happiness as he remembered the lost hopelessness again in Billy's eyes, just as it had been when he first met the young man. He couldn't just abandon Billy, the lad just could not manage on his own. Slowly, defeated by his own conscience, he explained the problem of Billy to Jonas. 'So am really reet sorry, Mr Bailey, but a' can't a'll ata go wi' navvies to keep Billy company, he'll ner manage on his own.'

Jonas queried Billy being Tom's responsibility but when the situation was explained the fact of it only raised Tom in Jonas's opinion. But Jonas had decided what he wanted, and not being one to let one little drawback stand in his way, his mind quickly sought a solution to the problem. He was not going to let this chance slip, so after a few minutes consideration, standing deliberating chin in hand, he had the answer. 'I know just the anser, lad. Mr Dixon up at big farm is alus lookin' fer a strong digger fer ditches an' such, we'll sort 'im out theer.'

Tom was dubious. 'Are ye sure as this Mr Dixon will want Billy, not everybody is comfortable wi Billy he's such a big strongen just t' look on' 'im frighten's some folk? He can be 'ard werk to explain to at times, he don't allus get what he's supposed te do.'

'Don't yer wory, lad, 'al have a word an Mr Dixon'l be grand. There's a lot o' farm labourers don't know theer right from theer left. He'll bi fine,' said Jonas with more confidence than he felt, but he was sure that Mr Dixon would see the benefit of the arrangement when he saw what Tom had assured him was the size and strength of Billy and the potential for heavy work that somebody that size would have. The future fate of many was settled in that half an hour and as Tom knew the water board only needed short notice it was agreed that the two lads would start work on the farm the following week Monday.

CHAPTER 8

Jonas was in high glee complimenting himself on his 'sorting out' of the situation as he cheerfully made his way up the sloping road to home, so even when a shortage of breath caused him to give up on the happy whistling, his enthusiasm was not dampened.

Arriving home he was as ever eager to convey his plans and news to Agnes, but again as usual, his wife greeted any change with reservation. ' A hope yer know what yer doin', Jonas Bailey, yer don't reetly know these lads from Adam, and weere is they supposed live and sleep?'

Jonas, who was not to be daunted so quickly, replied, 'Oh 'av thought o that on way back, ther's a single cottage near 'end a row, next t'Nellie, that's empty an' yer always meke t' much food fer us, we'el be grand.'

'Jonas Bailey that theer cottage is not thine te b' letting out, an' anyhow it's a real mess, nobody's lived in it fer years.'

'I a' know that but w'l soon fettle it up.' Was the quick reply.

At which Agnes came back again, 'An' a'll ata b'meking a lot more food fer two grown men.'

'The way thy provide, lass thy'l never notice, just stick a few more spuds' i' pan.'

Agnes defeated by a lack of argument to Jonas's answers retreated into her back scullery uttering loudly over her shoulder, 'Umf, well I hope the big and mighty Mr Dixon agrees to all your organising else ye'll be in a reet mess.'

Jonas was never satisfied, which Agnes acknowledged was

often a good thing, and although she knew he could do with the help, she just wondered if he understood he would have to find wages for one and maybe even both if Mr Dixon did not agree to take on this other lad, and he certainly could not afford that. What also really worried her was Jonas had admitted he had not even seen this other chap, he could be a troublemaker or any kind of wrongen. Oh, Jonas, she silently pleaded, please watch what you are doing, you an yer big ideas, they'll get yer inter bother yet.

Agnes need not have worried on the subject of Billy, as after his first immediate instinctive reaction to object at Jonas's interference, Mr Dixon relented when he was informed that by all accounts Billy would do the work of two men for the wage of a lad, and that would be a good move in the cause of saving money. He was quite happy for the two new workers to live in the empty cottage as nobody else wanted to as it was so rough, and he fleetingly thought if the arrangement doesn't last I've got the cottage done up for nought, and let Agnes provide their meals at a pleasing no cost to himself which seemed most satisfactory as the farm food bill was not increased. Mrs Dixon was never happy when the live-in workers increased in number as they had to be fed and male farm labourers seemed to 'expect to eat so much' she was always saying. Mr Dixon was still looking to economise as that 'son of Satan' as he was beginning to mentally call his son was costing even more brass of late, so this seemed like quite a lucrative arrangement.

Tom soon became a trusted member of the Bailey household. Jonas, after an initial uneasiness at also being the a boss instead of just head cowman, quickly settled into the new routine for their relationship soon became more of workmates and confidants. Tom was hardworking, obliging and a quick learner and he had experience with helping with the the horses on the reservoir site, and soon recalled his knowledge of other animals from when he had worked on a farm when younger. Mr Dixon soon saw that Billy was not only a good worker, especially when it came to hard physical labour, but also potentially a very useful source of extra income by way of hiring his services to neighbours. Men who could keep on digging for hours were hard to find, mainly because most of them had the sense to give up when they were tired, but Billy never seemed to tire. So Mr Dixon set his moneymaking plan in motion by sending out word by all he met that he was offering a special digging service. Then he bought Billy the biggest spade he could find, making a great issue of assuring a delighted Billy that it was a special gift just for him, and informing him that he must take great care of it as it would increase his reputation as a 'great digger'. Billy, unused to such attention and never having received a gift before, took great exception to anyone else even touching the spade, clutching it closely if anyone came near it, and dug all the faster when using it, and never failed to wash and polish it with a sacking rag before taking it home to the cottage every night. Mr Dixon was very pleased with his investment.

The two men reported to the Baileys' back door at breakfast and evening meal times and were provided with food by Agnes, which they ate in the downstairs room of the little cottage and then Billy always insisted on returning the enamel mugs and plates to Agnes's back door in the hope that he would see and be able to stroke the cats who sat around the door. Each evening the two men climbed the short ladder to the upper floor where Tom had constructed two rough sleeping platforms. He had added some pegs to the walls for coats and other clothes and in time after several visits from passing pedlars the two had acquired blankets and some new clothing, for they still had some of the dwindling final payment from the waterboard. By the time winter arrived they were comfortable and for the first time ever both men were beginning to feel settled. They had a home. Billy left the cottage early each morning, cloth wrapped bread and cheese under his arm, to report at the Hall Farm for orders, only returning late in time for his meal, but he was happy. One night sitting in front of the dying embers of the fire in the grate just before going to bed, Billy stuttered then announced, 'Tom, ain't we just foun' t' best place e'er? I an't been so appy afor an' t' cats like mi.'

Tom, surprised at such a lengthy statement from the usually tongue-tied man, was relieved that he and the lad had found such happiness and security, but it did worry him that that happiness was a liability dependent upon himself. Still, he told himself why worry about what might happen tomorrow? It's today, and we have no way of knowing what tomorrow will bring.

While Tom had decided just to think himself lucky to have found such a job and home he was uneasy about the meals being provided by Mrs Bailey. They were always good and wholesome and provided cheerfully at the door by Agnes or one of the older daughters. But Tom felt he and Billy were imposing on Agnes's generosity especially as Gracie made a point of avoiding him although he knew she was often around the yard area when she worked in the kitchen or dairy. He was sure Gracie did not like him around although she seemed happy to talk to Billy, for Tom had seen the two speak when they were not aware he was in the yard. Tom was at a loss as to what he had done but thought it could only be because it was he who buried the dog, for it was the only contact he had ever had with Gracie.

Tom and Billy had been in their new employment about two months and the weather was turning colder and the days shortening when Tom decided that they must make some steps towards providing their own food if only so that Agnes had just to provide a daily evening meal. He had repaired the broken fireplace in the small cottage soon after they moved in so they were enjoying a fire's warmth in the evenings and were assured some winter warmth when the really cold weather set in, so he was sure that the he could mend the fire front bar stand to take a kettle and pan. The cottage was becoming a proper home, which brought a new and comforting experience to both men.

When Tom quietly suggested to Agnes that he and Billy become more self sufficient as he had mended the fire to take cooking pots she was quietly relieved because, much as she liked the two lads, the extra work of their meals was becoming tiring. So she bustled round searching the backs of cupboards and with a few contributions from a willing Nellie the men were provided with kettle, pans, and tin plates, dishes and cups, and also a few knives and spoons. Agnes assured Tom that she was more than willing to provide them with dry goods and bacon and eggs and informed them they must ask Grace in the dairy for their milk and cheese. Tom was not sure about this arrangement as he was now quite convinced that Gracie was avoiding him, so he decided that the only thing to do was confess the problem to Jonas. Jonas quick thinking as ever soon deduced the situation, and after pausing for a moment's thoughtful hesitation, explained what had happened to Gracie at the Hall Farm. Tom listened without speaking, while his mind registered a strong dislike for the unseen Edward Dixon, and then asked Jonas what he thought was the best way to get the milk and occasional butter from the dairy without upsetting Gracie. Jonas as ever sharp and confident at working out a situation assured Tom that if he called in the dairy just before dinner time he would be sure to be there himself and act as a go between for them for the first time or two.

Tom was not so sure, he had seen the look on Gracie's face when she glanced at him, in fact the idea of forcing Gracie to speak to him made him very uncomfortable, but just as instructed, Tom presented himself outside the dairy at the suggested time. As he waited warily outside the door he heard Gracie softly singing a hymn as she worked, and the peace of the moment was a balm to his tensed nerves which steadied slightly until the arrival of a bustling Jonas who appeared around the building corner with a cheery greeting. 'Weel now, Tom lets get yer some milk.' Gracie's singing stopped abruptly as the door opened and her smile of greeting disappeared instantly when she turned and saw Jonas was not alone. 'Now, Gracie, Tom needs some milk for themselves because he is doing more for themselves to relieve yer mother of meking all their food.' Was Jonas's carefully worded explanation. There was total cold silence in the dairy as without speaking a word Gracie dipped a long handled measure into a milk kit, filled the small can that Tom had brought and then turned away to return to the bucket she had been scrubbing. Tom uneasy at continuing standing there turned with a quick nod to Jonas and low 'thanks' over his shoulder and quickly disappeared out of the door. 'Gracie that was rude, he's a grand lad. Yer can't be like that to every lad because of that Dixon devil.' Was Jonas's quick reprimand. 'And he's goin' t' come fer milk ev'ry day so yer might as weel get used t' it.' There was no reply from Gracie so Jonas abruptly turned and determinedly walked away from his daughter, frustrated at her attitude, but he knew he could hardly reprimand her for her fear. He strode to Tom's cottage, knocked on the door, opened it slightly and shouted in, 'Teke no heed o' lass, Tom, she'll soon get used to thee,' he shouted hoping he was right.

Tom was very uneasy the next day when he called for the milk, and for many a day after that but there was no option. He always knocked on the dairy door to warn her of his entering the building and stood silently while she equally silently filled his can with milk, all the while avoiding looking at him directly. He always turned away to leave with just a lowly voiced 'ta'.

Slowly Gracie became less scared, until one day about two weeks later, when she smiled and quietly murmured, 'D' yer like it here?' And in doing so looked up fully into his face.

Tom was stunned, for he had never seen her eyes before. They were the most beautiful shade of rich dark brown and for a moment he seemed unable to breath as he gazed into their depth, but realising he was absently spilling the milk he recovered enough to stammer 'aye' and then hurry away from the dairy with a happy grin on his face. Maybe it was just as Jonas had said, it needed time for her to get over the fright that Dixon had given her.

Tom's joy at Gracie finally speaking to him was nothing to his delight about a week later when she also presented him with a cotton cloth wrapped piece of cheese, holding it out towards him with the explanation that, 'She had not had chance to take any into Mam yet te give ye, ye cheese.' Tom was a happy man for the rest of the day.

A few weeks later, by which time Tom had spoken to Gracie at least three dozen times by his reckoning, on entering the barn by the small side door looking for a rake, he almost stumbled over Gracie as she crouched over a pile of sacks close behind the door. Panicking at first thinking that she was hurt he saw at a proper look his mistake, as he saw curled on the sacks a cat and six kittens. 'Eee there's a bonny sight, we need a few more mouse catchers even if they can't see owt yet,' he softly joked but even as he said it he thought Jonas might have a different opinion on the kittens' future.

'Shhh—' Gracie quickly returned. 'Father musn't know or they'll be in t'barrel. I'm teking em up on scaffert out o' way. Faather wain't drown 'em if they get big enough wi their eyess open afore he sees em.'

Tom knew she was probably right about the kittens' fate, and while he also knew he shouldn't help her, he did. Jonas was always moaning about how many 'blasted' cats ran around the place. 'Breed like rappits they do.' Then, still knowing full well he shouldn't , he gathered up the four corners of the top two sacks and grasping them together with cat and kittens securely in the sacking sling he climbed the ladder which was strapped to the wall side and deposited them on the scaffert loft floor.

An anxious Gracie followed him up the ladder. 'Oh thanks, Tom, a' think a' would a' struggled. Th'as a kind man.' She placed her hand on his arm as she looked straight into his eyes, at which he felt the heat of a blush travel up his neck to his brow as he quickly turned away.

'Reet you'd better sort em out now, Gracie, an' please don't tell thee father who browt em up eer.'

And with that he disappeared down the ladder and out through the big front barn doors. Just as he passed through the doors he heard her voice, 'Thanks again, Tom, that really wer very kind.' So a very smiling and very elated man crossed the cobbled yard without even knowing where he was going.

CHAPTER 9

The cool weather of golden autumn turned to winter's bitter sharp winds and shorter daylight hours but the two young men were comfortable in the warm firelight of the cottage after the day's work, and still told each other how lucky they were. One evening a few days after the cat rescue Billy seemed very excited and finally burst out, 'Ee, Tom a' want te tell ye how much a' think yer are a reet good mon fer saving them kitties. Gracie showed em te me an' she sed yer saved em. She wer pleased as punch, sez ye ave a good hart.'

Tom stared amazed at Billy who, to Tom's certain knowledge, had never spoken so many words together before. 'Gracie told yer that then.'

'Aye, Tom she did.' Tom hardly slept a wink that night, his head in a spin and his heart so light he was sure it was floating out of his chest. Tired but happy, the morning brought a Tom convinced he was the luckiest man in the world.

Tom worked well with Jonas, carrying on Jonas's work when his boss was working up at Hall Farm, as he now knew the animal stock, and it became clear to both men he had a natural knack with animals especially with horses, so the two began to plan for a busy following year. Jonas had sold enough surplus stock at market to pay Tom and have a bit extra left, as he was quick to inform Agnes, proud as she was at her husband's prospering, she was still wary of him being overconfident and with a withering 'One swallow doesn't mek a summer tha knows' denied him the

91

expected compliment.

Billy felt wanted for the first time in his life, because Mr Dixon had assured him that he was the best 'digger he had ever known' and so Billy worked all the harder, especially when hired out, so as to show strangers his prowess with his spade. Billy was taken to farmers far and wide, as he could not be trusted to find his way alone as he often got lost, but once he had arrived in the care of another farm worker he was left to make quick work of ditches and any other digging the farmer required so with well satisfied customers Mr Dixon was very happy making more money for his wife to spend on her son.

Christmas was a time of celebration even in the normally staid Bailey household, so this year the two newcomers were invited along with Nellie to share the family's Christmas dinner, with everyone eagerly anticipating the day. It was only about mid December when Billy found out about the forthcoming party and their invitation to join the celebration. From that day every morning he asked Tom how many days to Christmas day, till Tom in desperation found a small hard piece of limestone and drew on the cottage wall a line for each remaining day telling the excited Billy to mark off one line each morning. On the morning when they rose and Billy crossed out the last line his excitement was visible on his face and his jumping about caused Tom to greatly regret that he had not drawn a line for Christmas Day. During the entire day of Christmas Eve Billy spent it continually asking everyone he met if they knew it was Christmas Day the next day and that 'there was only one more night before it was here'. Like the child he still was, he wanted to go to bed early so that it would come sooner.

The following morning the lad was excited to a point where Tom had to shout, 'Billy ye need to calm down, lad, get yersel a pail o' water from 'trough and wash yer hands and face an' flatten yer hair wi' some water too ter mek thee sel smart. An when thy's done that get the'sel up' ladder and put on them new clothes we bought. An' when thy's done that go an' sit in yer chair by' hearth and don't move til I say so. D' hear me Billy?'

Billy nodded enthusiastically at which Tom left him for he had to finish his morning's work for much was still awaiting his attention as animals still had to be fed, cleaned out and cows milked regardless of the day. Tom's instructions to Billy carried out with great deliberation had the desired effect and a much quieter Billy was found sitting quietly in a chair by the hearth waiting to accompany Tom to the Baileys' house. 'Can we really go now, Tom?'

Billy's excitement was very evident although he dare not rise from the chair until Tom said so. 'Aye, Billy, we can go now.'

At which Billy jumped up from the chair in such a rush that the chair toppled over backwards. Tom started to speak but Billy was almost out of the cottage door, so he just sighed and followed the lad out. He caught up with Billy just before he reached the Baileys' door. 'Billy stop, tek a deep breath. Now when yer go into the Baileys' house yer stand still and say te Mr an' Mrs Bailey, "Thank you for havin' us for Christmas Dinner".'

'Aye, Tom, reet, Tom.' Was Billy's eager reply.

On entering the Baileys' Tom quickly grapped Billy's cap from his head, and Billy standing still visibly concentrating on his words said, 'Thank you for having our Christmas dinner, Mrs Bailey.' At which great merriment and laughter followed.

Jonas saw the look of uncertainty on Billy's face, grasped his arm and said, 'Ee, lad thy's welcome, now cum an' sit down 'ere at table.'

The Bailey family and the three guests gathered in an air of great excitement around Agnes's large kitchen table. The room was very warm from the orange glowing fire and aroma filled the room with the rich smell of roasting fowl. A temporarily sombre Jonas tapped the table with the flat of a knife and offered a thankful prayer of grace. The food was rich and plentiful with boiled vegetables and the sage and onion stuffed roast goose carved with great ceremony by Jonas. With a great flourish he held aloft spiked on a long two prong fork a large slice of the fowl. 'Now, yer two big lads another 'elping o' this grand bird?' To which the two eagerly agreed.

Billy later shyly delighted in the extra helping of currant rich pudding pressed upon him by Agnes. All sat replete as Tom gazed contentedly around the table at the happy faces and as his eyes met those of Gracie he smiled and she smiled back before quickly looking away, but the smile lingered around her mouth as her finger traced the pattern on Agnes's best white damask cotton tablecloth. Nellie had brought a bottle of blackberry port which she now drew from the basket she had brought with her and presented it with great ceremony to a waiting Jonas who, after pretending great surprise because he had known all about the treat, proceeded, with much ado, to draw the cork with the help of a knife, while at the same time instructing Agnes to hurry along with finding some glasses. Agnes flustered, because she had not been privy to the secret of Nellie bringing port, was soon spurred to action. First at a high top shelf to reach for the required wine glasses then at the slopstone sink ensuring the little used vessels were rinsed so not dusty before bringing them to the table. Dora and Sarah seeing and sharing their mother's embarrassment, at having to wash the glasses, rushed to help with drying rags. An oblivious Jonas proclaimed a few minutes later as he rose to his feet, 'Now if you'll lift yer glasses in a toast. First t' our friend

Nellie for bringing this eer wonderful wine and then to all our joint future prosperity and happiness on our farm.'

From that Christmas day, Gracie and Tom began an easiness of manner which soon became apparent to all who bothered to notice and which delighted Jonas and Agnes. Gracie no longer avoided Tom, and Tom for his part made sure that he crossed the yard several times a day about the time he knew Gracie would be crossing to the outbuildings. A wave or a nod from Gracie, and Tom was happy for the rest of the day. Agnes worried about all her girls but the two older sisters seemed still to have no interest other than work at the mill, where both were now respected full time weavers, and church. She was happy to see Gracie becoming close to Tom because she felt the girl needed the protection of a good man as she still had that air of unworldliness which worried Agnes, the girl seemed to drift like a gentle breeze, only occasionally being caught up in an eddy to the reality of life. Gracie also became a friend and champion of Billy, who she saw as needing looking after and protecting from the people who would 'Mek the fool outa him, ee's a nice lad just a bit slow, but he means well.' And so she encouraged Tom to 'be sure that poor Billy' was not used too badly by Mr Dixon. Tom was more than happy to agree to this although dubious as to his sway with Mr Dixon he felt he could rely on Jonas if need be. He was pleased at her confidence in him for he thought she was probably right to worry about Billy.

The spring and summer had passed happily in the Bailey household and now a last few flowers of the autumn still survived in the shelter of the old walled garden so Gracie, who had seen them when visiting Big Lad's grave, was just picking a bunch to take to Nellie who had done something unheard of for she had lately taken to her bed with a chill. Agnes, who was bothered about Nellie because she had never seen her old friend so 'downed' by a simple chill, had insisted that Gracie also take Nellie hot food and drinks although, as she informed Gracie, the flowers would not help a chill but the food might. Gracie still thought that flowers would cheer Nellie, so few of the late blooms in an old jam pot were also going into the basket of food from Agnes's kitchen. Gracie was concerned when she found Nellie weak and shivering in the bed in the cold upstairs room of the small cottage, and after a few cheery words of encouragement to Nellie to try her Mother's food, quickly returned to Agnes to tell her mother of Nellie's plight. 'Mam, Nellie looks real ill an' it's very cold upstairs' in cottage', soon spurred Agnes into action.

Not being one to delay, as soon as Jonas returned home from the farm she had him and Tom employed in bringing Nellie's bed downstairs while Nellie sat close to the warmth of the fire newly lit in the cottage hearth. 'It's a good job old Bob med that staircase afor he died,' Agnes' commented to Jonas. 'We'd 'ave 'ad such a job wi both Nellie an' the bed if it wer still 'owd ladder.'

Jonas nodded his agreement. 'Aye but who's reet now.'

Nellie soon rallied with all the attention but was not going to be in any state to report for work for Mrs Dixon as she was due to do the next day. 'Now d'yer feel a bit better now, lass? Just get a day or two and y'll be right as rain agen, an back t' work,' Pronounced Agnes. But she was not able to convince a morose Nellie who was fretting about her inability to go to the farm, and getting herself into such a state of distress, as she feared for her free cottage.

'O Agnes a'll atta go t'farm yer know me work's me rent payment,' croaked Nellie between coughs.

Agnes looked sternly at her friend. 'Yer in no fit state ter go anyplace, an' anyway Mrs Dixon won't want thee theer if yer coughing and spluttering all orer' place.'

But an unconviced Nellie was now was weakly weeping. 'I'll atta or all be out of house an' 'ome an i' workhouse.'

'Now, stop that Nellie our Gracie can go in yer stead, tight and mighty Mrs Dixon should be appy wi' that,' announced Agnes in desperation as she volunteered Gracie's services as a substitute.

Later, as she left a now sleeping Nellie, Agnes started to realise just what she had said and done for now her concern was how she was going to persuade Gracie to take the old woman's place. Gracie was well capable of the Christmas food preparations which Nellie should be doing, but convincing her to go up to the farm was another thing altogether, as she had not been near the place since the day of the Edward Dixon problem, and to be honest to herself, Agnes knew what she was asking was not really fair.

CHAPTER 10

Gracie started, her face creased in horror at her mother's suggestion of temporarily replacing Nellie at the farm, and reacted quickly with, 'No, I'll ner go that place agin.' But after an hour of first asking, and then in despair, outright bullying, Gracie buckled and agreed.

The incident with the Dixon son had not diminished or mellowed in Gracie's mind even after all this time, in fact it had become worse the more she thought about it, which she did a lot when simple tasks allowed her mind to wander. But Gracie, being Gracie, felt she had a duty to her mother and to Nellie, and that duty was more important than her own fear. The next morning with great trepidation, a pair of house shoes under her arm and her shawl pulled tightly around her head and shoulders, she set off in the still dark early morning along the walled lane in the direction of the big farmhouse. She had not walked the path to the farm since she had run home in distress so every step was forced, the last steps across the cobbled yard even more so, and after almost turning around at the sight of the back door, she stiffened her back, drew a deep breath and knocked hard with whitened knuckles.

Mrs Dixon, not a woman to display dismay, was quickly over her surprise at being informed by Sally that Gracie was waiting in her kitchen. Anxiously waiting to explain that she was there only as a temporary replacement for a sick Nellie, the girl stood motionless dreading the lady of the house's reaction but

Mrs Dixon was quite happy to accept the change as she remembered how useful Gracie had been. With her previous knowledge of the kitchen she thought she would be well capable of getting through the waiting jobs probably more quickly than the aging Nellie. She also was aware that Gracie's sudden leaving probably had another reason apart from the one that was offered at the time, but she considered it best not to inquire to deeply into the affairs of servants. Her cheerful, 'Well Gracie we really are quite pleased to have you working in the kitchen again, just like old times', did nothing to dispel Gracie's concern or calm her churning insides, so she listened silently as the woman informed her of the jobs to be done during the day.

Immediately Mrs Dixon left the kitchen and disappeared to the privacy of her parlour, Gracie quickly turned to the curious Sally, who had been hovering in the far end of the kitchen pretending to be busy. 'Sal, that Edward Dixon i'nt here at 'ome is he?' Gracie quickly questioned the other girl.

'No he's cumming 'ome next week. The Mrs told me.' Was the reply which brought a flood of relief to the anxious Gracie. Relieved at the other girl's answer she set about the allotted tasks.

The day passed quickly as the two girls worked together making puddings and mincemeat for the forthcoming celebrations and Gracie began to enjoy her outing safe in the knowledge that nothing disturbing would happen. As she was putting on her heavy clogs and shawl to make the journey home, Mrs Dixon returned to the kitchen to thank her and ask if she could return the next day, instead of 'poor' Nellie to give her another rest day to help her get better. Straining wine and checking bottled fruit and cheeses were the jobs for the next day, she informed Gracie, and as Mrs Dixon had seen the amount of work that Gracie had 'got through' and considered that if she could gain another day of Gracie instead of the much slower Nellie it would be quite a bargain. The idea of working with all that wonderful food, much of it of a kind far beyond the more frugal fare of the Bailey household, was such a temptation that Gracie happily agreed. The darkness was falling fast as she walked down the lane to home and as Gracie turned the corner in the lane her heart skipped a beat and her foot hesitated for a moment, but she chided herself for being foolish, tomorrow would be another good day and there would be more lovely food to deal with and Sally to chat to. Yes, she decided, tomorrow would be another nice day to look forward to.

Nellie although still coughing was feeling much better by the end of the day, but was greatly relieved when Gracie informed her it would not be necessary for her to brave the weather the next day as she was going to the farm again, for as she explained to Nellie, it would be best for her not to go out as it was growing colder by the hour. So next morning Gracie, after putting on an extra shawl, for the weather was worsening as odd flakes of snow floated down, walked the lane to Hall Farm, all the while feeling happy anticipation at the thought of an enjoyable day to come. She duly presented herself again in Mrs Dixon's kitchen only to be greeted by an excited Sally who could hardly wait to inform her friend that, 'Master Dixon's cumming 'ome sooner, cus of the snow cumming, could be t'day.' Gracie's usual pale complexion blanched even whiter, as her heart thumped in her chest. Instantly descending from happiness to distress, she thought, Serve yourself right yer stupid fool for enjoying being here. The desire to flee was so great that in her panic she turned quickly instinctively looking behind herself that she knocked a large white enamel kit of milk from the table for it to clatter to the floor and the contents become a spreading lake of white on the scrupulously clean scrubbed flagstones. Horrified at seeing the milk starting to disappear down the cracks between the flags, Gracie instantly threw aside her shawl to grasp drying cloths from the table to try to stem the spreading flood. Sally quickly joined her on her knees on the floor, when the connecting house door opened suddenly and the son of the house entered the kitchen.

'Well, well what have we here two pussy cats lapping milk?' As the two girls both received a slap on their behinds, and with his usual mocking laugh convinced that he had made a very witty quip, the young man scooped up from the table a plate containing a large jam tart, then turned to pass back through the door throwing the words, 'I'll be back later when you've drunk up', over his shoulder.

Gracie's face flamed red as she rose from the floor, straightened her milk stained skirt, and demanded of Sally where she could find a mop and bucket. Sally who had never seen Gracie angry before was quick to find the cleaning items before offering vainly to do the mopping. 'No, I'll clean my own mess.' Was all the thanks Sally received. Unable to leave the kitchen without fulfilling the required tasks, especially as she thought Mrs Dixon might well notice the loss of the milk, Gracie suffered a long day of dread, often glancing at the wooden case, glass fronted wall clock which seemed to be going very slowly, before considering she had done sufficient to ease her conscience, after which she quickly donned her shawl leaving the farmhouse swearing that this time she really would never ever cross its threshold again. Edward Dixon had not returned to the kitchen that day but Gracie had endured the day expecting that he might so it was a very different minded and troubled young woman who marched back down the lane to home that evening.

Agnes knew there was something wrong as soon as Gracie walked through the door without speaking a word and by the way she flung off her good shawl, regardless of scattering the clinging flakes of snow, and her better apron was quickly replaced with the heavier shabby one she wore in the dairy, then she hurriedly flung on an old shawl, crossed it over her chest and tied it behind her back. Agnes looked at her daughter's set face and saw not a flicker of emotion. She held back the temptation to speak for she knew it would do no good. She watched silently as Gracie took another shawl to throw over her head and shoulders, picked up a covered storm lamp which she lit with a taper fired at the kitchen hearth and left her Mother's kitchen without a word. The last thick shawl she held pulled close over her head and crossed the now snow scattered yard to the dairy carrying the lamp aloft. A worried Agnes watched from the window as the girl crossed the yard, the lamp's glow giving her a halo of bright snow swirled lamplight as she walked. Gracie entered onto the cold dark dairy, set the lamp on a high shelf and set to scrubbing the already clean kits, buckets and bowls, the numbing chill of the ice cold water feeling like a welcome penance. Her mind was in a confused turmoil. 'Why?' she muttered to the silent kits and bowls. 'Why does he bother mi s' much? A hate him but he bothers mi, he troubles mi head. Tom doesn't bother mi like that. Tom's kind. Tom's safe. Tom doesn't bother mi head. Aye Tom's kind an' safe.' Her speech to the kits finished, she turned to lift another bucket of water but, finding it almost empty, and as she now felt calmer she sat exhausted on the old wooden stool at her side. Sitting still on the stool she gazed absently at her breath as it formed a cloud of damp air in the dull lamplight.

Agnes suspected what kind of event must have happened because earlier Billy had called at her door looking for Tom and informed her with great pride that Mr Edward had come home and was taking him to 'Owd Dan's' as a reward for being a great digger. Agnes had tried to dissuade the lad but he was not to be convinced that the trip was unwise, for innocently, the big young man saw Edward Dixon's offer as a great treat, not understanding that he was again to be the butt of the local drinkers' jokes once a single glass of beer had reduced him to foolishness, as it surely would. Agnes stood deep in thought, after Gracie had rushed out to the dairy, as usual musing to herself how her life could become so complicated without a single effort to make it so, at least by herself. But then she thought, I don't need to do anything, Jonas can manage to make a tangled mess for everybody without any help.

Agnes knew she was being a bit harsh because Jonas was not really to blame for this day, but someone had to bear the blame, for her mind was in a whirl and she wondered what was going to go wrong next. That Edward Dixon was trouble and 'newt were surer,' she whispered to herself. 'He wanted to tempt Gracie and her bonny face, aye he wanted Gracie she was sure of that, for a bit of passing fun. 'His kind don't wed a worker's daughter,' she muttered to herself.

Gracie, her frantic scrubbing in the dairy now long finished, her body had calmed but she had far greater troubled thoughts than Agnes could ever have contemplated, for much as she disliked the attention of Edward Dixon, he had stirred feelings within her that she knew were wrong. She now decided that was why he bothered her head. Very wrong, they were the kind of feelings that the minister shouted about on Sundays as 'the sins of the flesh', the kind of feelings that she knew she was not supposed to know about. Sally knew about such feelings, and often was quite happy to elaborate when they had shared tasks up at the farm. Gracie's face flamed again as she remembered the feel of his hand on her behind, so she splashed the little icy cold water left in the bucket up to her hot face. The water cooled the heat but the feeling of shame remained. She still sat on the stool, still unable to face her mother, her mind in turmoil, and still seated on the stool was how Tom found her when coming in from the shippon, for he had seen the glowing light in the dairy window and opened the door to investigate.

On peering around the door, Tom at first thought the dairy was empty until he saw the motionless Gracie seated in the darkest corner. 'You alreet, Gracie?' Was his immediate reaction for the girl looked distraught and there was no reason for her to be there at this time of night.

At first she didn't answer but keeping her head lowered she then answered in a low voice. 'Aye am reet, I'll cum in soon.' Which left Tom no alternative but to unwillingly leave her sitting there.

Tom went straight in to Agnes to voice his concern over Gracie only to be prevented from doing so by being greeted with a sharp, 'D'yer know where Billy is? A' think he gone drinking with that Edward Dixon.'

Tom's face hardened instantly, all concern for Gracie pushed aside at this news, for he knew that one single drink could reduce Billy to silliness enough to land him in all kinds of trouble, so he turned on his heel and, regardless of his lack of a thick coat, headed straight back out into the bleak dark night and down the now snow scattered lane at a run. Agnes shouted as she opened the door Tom had just closed behind him, a big empty sack in her hands for his shoulders, but the man was already too far away to hear.

When Jonas came in only minutes later the weariness in his

104

face vanished in an instant to be replaced by exasperation at Agnes's tale of Gracie's mood and Billy's disappearance, and Tom's chasing after Billy. 'Reet I'll go after them, that Tom is like to kill that Dixon lad if he finds him plying Billy with drink. Mind if he did that would solve the problem with him chasing our Gracie, but then it would get Tom hung for sure.' At which he also disappeared down the lane after Tom. Agnes closed the door behind Jonas and returned to her chair by the fire. She sat considering whether to go and talk to Gracie, decided she was best left to come in when she was ready, so she poked the fire and sat back down, put a cushion to her aching back to be a bit more comfortable, and waited.

Tom heard the laughter and cheers long before he reached the alehouse door, and as he neared the entrance, two men emerged who had obviously been enjoying the entertainment for their conversation as they walked away from the door was clear. 'That Daft Billy really is, I ain't never seen a mon take a spade for a drink afore. An' ee's well an' truly kettled, an he's daft as a brush he is.'

Tom tried to look through the alehouse windows but inside the thick glass was running with water and steam, he opened the door slowly to peer through the heavy smoke laden air of the low and beamed ceilinged room. Billy was standing near the bar, with who Tom suspected was the young Dixon standing next to him. The man was too well dressed to be a local, almost dandified. Billy had a tankard in front of him on the bar but was not drinking but standing clutching his spade in front of himself against his chest, his face showing his distress. Tom stood for a moment to assess the situation and at a loss for the best course to take was about to simply grab Billy and drag him out when Jonas arrived quietly at his elbow. Motioning to Tom they both moved towards the bar. 'Now, Billy, we were getting worried about you, Mrs Bailey sent us to bring you home safely.' Jonas's softly spoken words calmed the fear in the lad's face.

Billy turned to Jonas. 'I want t' go 'ome, Mr Bailey.'

'Aye, lad, let's go home that's best.' Jonas repeated the words, grasped Billy's arm and directed him to the door, and doing so glanced at the face of Dixon who was patently annoyed at having his entertainment ended.

Edward looked condescendingly at Jonas who was steering Billy towards the door. 'Never mind, Billy, there's always another day,' he directed at their retreating backs. Then he glanced at Tom his eyes narrowed and his face darkened in anger for he had seen Tom enter the alehouse first and attributed the main of the blame for the interruption at him. For his part Tom looked Edward straight in the face dislike clearly etched for this was the man who had hurt Gracie if not in body but in mind.

Agnes again plumped down wearily in the chair after a look out of the window to see the light still in the dairy window, then rose again to add some more coal to the fire for, she thought, someone is going to be chilled before this night is over. She could hear the wind starting to whistle outside and muttered to herself, 'That theer wind sounds like it's coming from east, an' that'll mean more darn snow.' She was greatly relieved when half an hour later a shivering Gracie entered the kitchen. 'Sit down, lass, I'll meke thee some tay,' was all Agnes said, thinking less said soonest mended. The lass was obviously unharmed in body if troubled in her head.

Jonas, Tom and a very subdued Billy arrived home nearly an hour later, Jonas going into his home and the two younger men straight to their own cottage and cold hearth, which Tom glanced at then thought the better, told Billy that he was tired, and leaving the sorry figure downstairs alone in the feared dark, Tom sought his own cold bed up the ladder in the icy chill of the bedroom.

Next morning Tom awoke to the sound of scraping as Billy with his precious spade was clearing a path through the new knee deep white snow to the buildings and beyond. Purposely ignoring the urge to go and help with the snow clearing, Tom set about lighting the fire, using the usually reserved fir cones to make a quick job, checked the kettle which still had water in it, and fetching bread from the cupboard he struggled to spread the very hard dripping onto the two thick slices he had cut. When Billy finally came indoors there was a heavy silence between the two men until Billy no longer able to stand it any longer blurted out, 'I'm sorry, Tom, yer know I'm daft. Mr Edward said it would be a 'treat for me, an' a believed him and he did buy me some beer, an' it were reet good, but they all laughed a' me cuss a took me spade. They don't know I ata look ater it proper, Mr Dixon said so.'

Tom gave in, defeated by Billy's naivety with, 'Weel don't do it agin.' And passed the lad an enamel can of tea.

Crossing the yard a little later, cursing Edward Dixon with every step he took, Tom swore the man was just trouble. First Gracie now Billy, who next? As he walked he told himself, 'Darn good job Jonas wer theer last nite, what wi' with the clever look on his face I could happily have downed him theer and then.'

CHAPTER 11

Christmas this year was not to be the happy occasion of the previous year for Nellie died two days before the day, never really recovering from the bout of chill and fever her spirit seemed 'damped down', Agnes said, and nothing would cheer her. So the day of celebration arrived without the usual preparations and all went about their jobs and Christmas dinner was a very quiet meal after which all dispersed to continue work outside in Jonas and Tom's case, while Agnes and the girls occupied themselves in the house.

Agnes was just glad when finally the weather started to turn warmer and so less cold and wet penetrated the house with less mud on the men's clothes and clogs. Signs of new growth were starting to show on the trees and the snowdrops started to peep through the ground in Big Lad's garden as the walled garden was now called by all. Gracie went there every day to the dog's grave even though he had been dead for nearly two years his loss was still felt by all, most of all by Gracie on her still frequent but now solitary wanders on the hills. Tom often saw her head out around the garden wall and remembered that night on the moonlit moor. Then one evening when the nights were lengthening he saw her leave in the direction of the moor and summoned up the courage to quickly follow, calling, 'Hey wait fer me, Gracie, I could do wi a walk.'

Gracie pretended to not hear the shout but, when after a quick spurt of speed he caught up with the striding girl, she feigned surprise but did not reject his offer of accompaniment for the walk. This was the first of many such walks, always unarranged and as if by coincidence and so that the gentle companionship grew greater between them as they walked and talked along the way. Gracie was happy that Tom never made any attempt to touch her, not even her hand or arm even if he might have on the grounds of helping her up the hill at a steep slope. Their friendship was respectful of each other and often seated on a stone wall or on the grass on a warm evening, each giving rein to their own thoughts, but to each the other's nearness was tangible.

One late summer evening, Gracie and Tom had climbed beyond the top quarry to a high vantage point they often sought to gaze over the valley. To the left in the distance was the small town's smoke rising into the sky, its now many tall mill chimneys standing high above the general buildings. Straight in front to the right was the pond where Gracie had seen the fairy queen, and where Tom now knew he had fallen in love with Gracie. The farm and buildings and the cottages were there lower down the valley with the sparkling expanse of the water of the new reservoir beyond with the backdrop of the further hill beyond that. Further to the right the hills reached one behind the other until the distance became too great to see beyond. They sat each with their own thoughts but unwittingly in tune. Gracie's of Big Lad and the moonlit pit and the way the dog had been so very special, Tom's a vision of a very beautiful girl and a watchful dog in the moonlight. 'What's it like over them hills, Tom, I know you cum 'ere from that way?'

Gracie's words caused Tom to ponder for a moment, during which short time he gazed at the waiting girl, his eyes taking in the fair face and shining black curls, after which the reply was a harsh sharp, 'Lonely.'

'Well I hope I never 'ave to go there then,' returned Gracie. 'Home is comfortable and safe, I don't want to leave ever.'

Tom considered these words for a few moments then, taking a deep breath, suggested quietly, 'There might be a way to mek sure o' that, Gracie.'

'What de yer mean?' was the hesitant but quick reply, as a frown crossed her face.

'That yer would ner need ter leave yer 'ome.'

'How?' Then she carried on, 'How can yer know?' Was the simple return.

Tom sat still and silent for several seconds remembering the recent conversation with Jonas when the farmer had quietly suggested that Gracie needed the support and protection of a good man 'like yourself'. Then bracing himself for disappointment blurted out without further ado, 'We could get married, I asked your father if he would mind and he said no it was a good idea and if we did we could tek over when he finished.' All of which came out in a quick stumbling hurry.

Gracie was stunned, her hands and arms drawn protectively instinctively clasped in front of her chest, for marriage to anyone had never crossed her mind as her two older sisters were both unmarried and it was normal for sisters to marry the oldest first and so on down the family. 'Are you sure Faather said that I could bi wed 'cause Sarah and Dora are still unwed, a' don't think that can be reet?' Gracie turned to look intently at the young man to see if he was joking with her, but saw the earnest expression on the strong pleasing face, and as she waited for an answer she saw his body sink down, his confidence shook.

Gracie at first completely taken back was now embarrassed, intently looked down at the grass around were she sat and saw

110

how short and springy it was after the sheep flock's grazing. Grateful for a way to change the subject she patted it with her flat hand. 'The sheep havn't left any grass to go to waste this year.'

Tom happily joined in the conversation diversion. 'No they eat their fill when they can.' Neither said another word for long minutes then Tom could stand it no longer, feeling he was a fool and should have kept his mouth shut, for now Gracie might never let him near her again. 'Should we be going back now d'yer think?' Gracie nodded her grateful assent and quickly rose to start the walk home which continued in awkward silence until they reached Agnes's back door where Tom offered an embarrassed quick 'G'nite' and headed quickly for his own cottage.

Tom slowly closed the door behind him and leaned back against as if for support. 'Well you've buggered up the job now good an' proper, Tom Briggs, have yer ever. Get yer stupid self to bed, ye'll probably be out of 'er on' morrow.' So with that fearful thought he slowly climbed the ladder to bed. Billy who was already in his bed had offered a greeting to Tom but it was ignored and poor Billy lay long awake wondering what he had done wrong now. Tom lay tossing through the night, just glad when light streaking through the small window gave justification for an early rise and the prospect of relief and distraction from hard work.

Gracie on entering her home was every bit as perturbed as Tom, as Tom's suggestion while it had shocked her did not displease her. I had just never even thought that someone would ask me to marry them let alone it be Tom, was the thought that turned Tom's words over and over in her head that troubled night and the following day until, spying her chance when Agnes was standing hands busy peeling potatoes, she quietly asked, 'Did yer and Faather know Tom wer to ask marriage ter me?'

Agnes had been waiting for this to be mentioned since Jonas had told her Tom had plucked up the courage to ask him permission several weeks before. Tom, he said, had stumbled and stuttered over his words when asking Jonas, sure as he did so that he was reaching over his station, he only being a rough labourer. Tom need not have worried so, Jonas had not hesitated in shaking Tom's hand as he said a finer man would not be found, wealth was no substitute for the strong back and true heart. The willingness and sincerity of the lad made Jonas sure Gracie would do well with him and she needed a good man's protection before her comely face and unruly curls caught another roving eye besides that menace Dixon, or, for that matter, that the devil himself managed to induce the girl. 'Aye, 'an yer Faather is pleased, and so am I.'

Still dubious, Gracie continued, 'But what about Sarah and Dora, won't they mind?' Gracie asked her mother, who only waved her hand as if to dismiss the idea.

'Ney, lass, I doubt either of 'em have any thoughts in that way. They won't be bothered,' Agnes insisted.

That next day as Tom had climbed down the ladder to face the sacking he was convinced was coming because he was sure he had upset Gracie and Mr and Mrs Bailey wouldn't want him on the place after that, but evening came and the only words Jonas had spoke to him were normal and pleasant. No calmer and still very much on edge Tom went to bed the next night having not seen anything of Gracie all day. Billy was agitated because Tom had hardly spoken a word to him and he was now convinced that he must have done something very wrong, but he could not work out what. The fire in the lads' cottage had not been lit for days and Billy was fed up with just the bread and cheese that Tom was making to feed them. The days for Tom seemed endless and many times he went over the conversation on the moor trying to see what he had said wrong but not being able to and that made him feel worse.

Tom's torment ended when Gracie followed Tom into the cow shippon one morning a few days later and as she shyly reached out her hand to touch his jacket sleeve he held his breath in dread of what was coming. Then in the best English she could muster trying to remember how Mrs Dixon spoke Gracie slowly said, 'I think I would like to marry you, Tom, an' Mam and Faather think it's a good idea too.'

Tom unable to believe his ears stood speechless for a minute then rallied his senses and smiled at the girl. 'Ee that's grand, yer are sure, Gracie, we'll meke a go of it us two, a'll werk ard an all.' Unsure what to do next, Tom made to hold Gracie's hand, thought better of it and rubbed his hands down his jacket front then grasped both of hers between his. Seconds passed, neither of them moving til releasing his grasp, Tom shook his head. 'Now I had better get that last cow, it's probably gone back te' top field while we were gabbing.'

The cow who, while she knew a feed was waiting in the shippon, was at a loss when the gate into the yard remained shut, had wandered back down the field. Tom heard her bellowing then saw her yards away with the gate between him and her. That gate was just the invitation he needed, with one hand on the top bar it was cleared in one leap with an accompanying woop. 'Hey up, cow, come on ther's werk to be done,' he informed her as he opened the gate and motioned for her to pass as he stood to attention with a salute as she passed by.

They were married ten months later with the sun shining as the family party walked to and back from the village church along the cobbled lane. Gracie with a new Sunday dress of floral print cotton and the first real bonnet she had ever owned, her black dancing curls for once allowed freedom below the bonnet edge, and Tom equally resplendent in his first ever matching jacket and trousers. Agnes had treated herself to some bottle green striped cotton sateen and the two girls each had chosen plain navy twill all of which the three had worked very long with the treadle sewing machine and patterns sent for in the post to create new dresses for the occasion. So along with Jonas in his well brushed and newly pressed best suit the entire family was splendid as befitted their new status as tenant farmers. While the ledger was signed by the happy pair the wedding guests hurried out after the service so to be ranged waiting along the sides of the church path to cheer as the newly married couple appeared, and then they followed the main party home.

Married life was all to look forward to, first sharing with the Baileys for their meals but with a separate parlour-cum-bedroom which Jonas had arranged with Mr Dixon by knocking through a doorway into a room which really belonged to the other unoccupied half of the quarters behind their own rooms. Mr Dixon had no objections to these further renovations, other than that the door from the room into the unused part of the house had to be locked from the other side and he saw to that. So, a few days of repairs, whitewash and airing with an open window saw the room habitable, and table, chairs, chest and bed from Nellie's old cottage completed the new couple's needs.

Jonas had taken on the task of explaining to Billy that he and Tom could no longer live together in their cottage after Tom and Gracie were married, and he had suggested to Mr Dixon that if Billy lived up at the farm he would be handier for sending on jobs. After a slight hesitation, again reluctant at being organised by Jonas, Mr Dixon saw the advantage in the newly renovated cottage being available for some other worker, and agreed.

The wedding celebrations duly enjoyed, the assembled company all in high spirits, partly due to some homemade dandelion and fruit wine, and the remains of Agnes's spread of food cleared to the meatsafe in the pantry for the morrow, the new couple retired to their room. Tom was uneasy at the tentative suggestions and smirks from the wedding guests, so much so that when all the joking had quietened down he suggested that the two of them take a breath of fresh air up on the moor, stopping at the garden to tell Big Lad their news. Gracie's relief at the suggestion was great, but their leaving of the house which had to be though Agnes's kitchen in which the wedding guests were still socialising caused great merriment, so much so that it was a very red faced Gracie who passed through her mother's back door. Tom clasped her hand. 'Don't fret, Gracie, it's only a bit of fun, we'll not cum back 'til they've all gone 'ome.' So after calling at the garden and telling Big Lad of their new happiness, the two roamed the hills until dusk when taking a moment's rest Tom as he was standing behind her reached his arms around her waist to hold her close. Instantly she stiffened like a statue and he could feel her tremble. 'What is it, Gracie, what is it, love?' Was his desperate plea as he sensed her distress and immediately released her, but comforted at the sound of his voice, he sensed her become calm. Tom, unaware of the stirred memories of a dropped sheet that his actions had caused, stood back unsure what to do, but regretted his gesture, greatly upset at her reaction. Then the past receded, this was Tom, her new husband who she knew she loved. Tom stood back waiting, she turned and reached out her hands, he hesitantly grasped the offered hands and stepping one step towards her gently fleetingly kissed her lips. 'A love yer, Gracie, a alus will.' Hand in hand they returned down the hill to begin the new routine of sharing a bed.

Gracie was sixteen years old when she married and she was seventeen years old when her first child came easily and quickly into the world, and she was content, in her marriage, with her new daughter, and with the prospect of the future living and working on her father's farm which would one day be hers and Tom's for Jonas had already started putting the idea of Tom as a future head cowman into conversations with Mr Dixon. Tom was very proud of his new wife and family, and of what he had achieved in the few short years since he had first chased the runaway bullock towards the farm. In turn Jonas and consequently Agnes were happy in the way life was settled. Tom had no worries as even Billy was happy as he had moved to quarters in Hall Farm and found even more friends for the easy going farm lads simply accepted him as another able worker. So all was well set for a happy future but sometimes alone in a field or awake in the dead of night Tom was fearful, it was all too simple, too easy, for he knew from past experience life had a habit of presenting the unexpected and as Billy said the future was not always good.

CHAPTER 12

One day Jonas looked lovingly at his new granddaughter and decided that the little family needed a house of their own, and he had just the place in mind, Nellie's old cottage which had stood empty since her death. He was sure it could soon be made presentable; with Tom's capable woodwork and building skills and a bucket of whitewash they could 'work miracles'. Jonas's enthusiasm was as ever infectious especially as he soon gained permission from Mr Dixon, on condition that the extra room from the house was closed and returned to the empty part of the house. This triumphant negotiation he quickly relayed to an ever doubtful Agnes. Richard Dixon once more happily anticipating cost free repairs to a dilapidated cottage. 'Yer sure he don't want rent for it, Jonas?'

'No, Mr Dixon said that the efforts of this family were payment enough.' Was Jonas's proud reply. Still Agnes was dubious and worried, they were becoming more and more reliant on the good nature or not of Mr Dixon, and although Jonas didn't seem to see a problem with that, Agnes definitely did and wondered what this latest move was really going to cost.

Tom closed the cottage door behind him and stepped into the cosy warmth of the room. A happy smile crossed his face lingering around his eyes, and the usual feeling of satisfaction and gratitude filled his mind as he crossed to the spindle rocking chair placed in front of the glowing fire. He slowly lowered himself into the chair, for it had been a hard day and his shoulders and back ached with the constant swing of the scythe he had been wielding all day between milking and feeding. The room was quiet except for the odd crackle from the fire and as he bent to unlace his clogs he smiled again for he heard Gracie coming down the stairs. She would have been putting the child to bed. 'Oh, Tom, I hope ye made a good job o'cleaning them clogs of thine, a just swept t' floor this at'ernoon.' Was all the greeting he received, but he was quick to reassure her.

'Now, lass, ye know a' allus do, look fer th'self.'

'Sorry, Tom, a' knows thy does, it's just as a'm ser proud of this cottage, an' how ye have made it nice.' Tom smiled again, he always seemed to be smiling these days, he was just so happy. Life was good, what more could a man ask for? A beautiful wife and heathy child and a warm and cosy cottage. 'There's waater fer a good wash, an' thee tay's nearly ready, love,' Gracie told him as she turned away to fetch a cloth and knives and forks for the table.

About a month later walking along the cart track to the village Jonas was absent mindedly gazing down the lower valley admiring the blue sparkle of the reservoir but, when hearing a horse and trap approaching from behind, stepped to the grass verge side to leave the way clear for it to pass. The trap, which Jonas then saw was driven by Mr Dixon, did not continue but stopped, the driver turning and bending down to speak to the waiting Jonas. 'Morning, Jonas.'

'Mornin, sir, Mr Dixon.' As both men nodded in acknowledgement.

'Jonas, I have been meaning to have a word about a little matter for our mutual benefit.' The farmer looked down on Jonas with a meaningful stare, at which the man standing waiting sensed trouble coming. 'My good lady wife Mrs Dixon has mentioned that since the loss of Nellie she really does struggle to get enough help in the kitchen, and as your daughter, who learnt so many of Nellie's skills, and her new husband are now using Nellie's cottage.' At which point he held up his hand to prevent Jonas protesting or offering to pay rent, which was not what Mr Dixon or rather Mrs Dixon required at all. Dixon then having gained the advantage by the element of surprise continued quickly to prevent any chance for objection, 'So we have decided that for a small but generous remuneration to your daughter, in view of her previous experience, she can offer her help in the kitchen for a couple of hours each morning. That will leave her with plenty of time to complete all her work at home. Mrs Dixon has also most kindly offered to allow Gracie to bring the child with her so that it will not prove an obstacle. Now I wish you good day, oh, and Mrs Dixon said she will allow her to start tomorrow.' At which he jerked the horse's reins and disappeared down the lane at a brisk trot.

Jonas, his face white with anger and frustration that he had cleverly been denied a chance to even voice a single word in opposition to the arrangement, turned round in the road and angrily retraced his steps to home, all the while thinking that Agnes was going to say, 'Told yer so. A knewed it.'

Agnes listened to Jonas recount the meeting with Mr Dixon, all the time thinking, It had to happen, I was right, we have slowly become more and more reliant upon the good favours of the great mighty Mr Dixon. But she kept her thoughts to herself and said out loud, 'Do we have any option?'

Jonas's reply was a quick 'No'. Then, 'The only saving is that that young Dixon is away down south agin.'

'Aye but how long fer? He's a devil fer arriving home at a moment's notice, probably when he runs outa money.' Was

Agnes' quick return.

'But anyhow, Gracie is a married lass now, wi a child,' Jonas argued.

Agnes looked at the husband in pity. 'D'yer really think that'll mek any difference, if she's up there at 'house?' Jonas, angry at his own naivety and at the way he was being bullied by Dixon to be made look a fool in his wife's eyes, tried to turn the situation to his advantage by suggesting that this was a very generous offer being made to Gracie, but Agnes was having none of it and informed Jonas that he would be the one 'To tell our Gracie where she had to go and when', and, 'God help you when you do'.

A very reluctant and rebellious Gracie and a child whimpering, because it sensed it's Mother's bad humour, made their way to Hall Farm next morning. Gracie had protested and Tom had desperately attempted to sway Jonas to objecting, but both knew that Gracie's help had not been requested, it had been demanded in the guise of generosity, and there was no way out to be seen.

As she entered the kitchen, which she had sworn never to set foot in again, she was greeted with the words 'Good morning, Gracie' by a very determinedly friendly looking Mrs Dixon for the lady of the house was fully aware that Grace and her family had been coerced, by devious means. She had suggested to her husband that if she could be persuaded Gracie would be a great help in her kitchen then, left it to him to find a way to arrange it. With a curious Sally standing behind, the older woman continued, 'It really is good to have you back, Gracie, we are so glad to see you here again, ar'n't we Sally?'

From Mrs Dixon brought an unconvinced, 'Aye, sure,' from Sally.

'I will do mi best, Mrs Dixon,' was Gracie's short and deliberate reply. 'If yer will show me weer to put me child am ready to start werk.' And so Gracie's reemployment at the farm began.

Edward Dixon was now employed in London so his visits home were somewhat curtailed, so after an initial feeling of strange wariness, Gracie finally stopped looking behind herself and became settled in her new employment, beginning to enjoy the change of scenery and renewing her friendship with Sally. Gracie was, though, concerned when Sally informed her that she had struck up a friendship with Billy when he had moved up to the farm when Tom and Gracie married. Gracie felt that such a friendship must in some way be more beneficial to Sally than Billy for Sally to entertain such a relationship. Mr Dixon, concerned that he might lose the profitable lad, had offered Billy accommodation with the unmarried hands and groom who slept in a loft over the stables and store and were supplied with meals from the kitchen. Sally was responsible for seeing to their food and always ensured that Billy got plenty to eat so his loyalty was guaranteed. Sally in return it seemed, so Gracie learnt, was the cheerful recipient of ribbons, trinkets and other cheap odds that Billy was persuaded to buy from calling passing pedlars or from the market stalls on the odd occasion he visited the local town. Gracie having seen Billy offering gifts on several occasions was minded to caution Sally on the wisdom of allowing Billy to buy her gifts suggesting that Billy might be expecting favours in return but, as on the occasion years earlier with Edward Dixon, Sally was adamant that it was quite all right informing Gracie that Billy, 'Is harmless like a little lad, he don't know owt else.'

Gracie, with her Mother's keen foresight, saw trouble in the arrangement but could not see a way to alter the situation as she knew Billy could not be able to understand her concern. So she kept her thoughts to herself, her hands busy with her allotted jobs. She considered sharing her worries with Tom but knew this probably was not wise, he worried enough about Billy as it was, maybe with a bit of luck Sally would tire of Billy's attention if she found another to buy her gifts. A few days later on seeing Billy in the yard Gracie, although she knew she really shouldn't, attempted to caution him that Sally's attention could be fickle but Billy was having none of it. 'Ney Sal likes me, sez a'm her special lad.'

Gracie knew it was no good trying further but she was really worried for Billy now, he was going to be let down, and when that happened he was going to be distraught.

Gracie knew she was expecting again before her daughter was six months old, but she kept her own counsel as she knew the first thing her Mother or Tom would say was she must finish at the farm, but she didn't want to do that as the small extra payment Mrs Dixon gave her though meagre was very useful, and truth to tell, she enjoyed her hours there in the warm busy kitchen and the spacious storerooms and dairy; they being a pleasant change from the routine of daily life. The other consideration which no one else seemed to appreciate was that they lived in the cottage at Mr Dixon's generosity, a generosity that did not come with a guarantee.

Gracie pushed the heavy tin tray of loaf tins into the hot oven, feeling the rush of heat coming from its black interior, she straightened and closed the heavy door shut, turned the lever handle, then stepped back and turned around, her face flushed as she pushed a loose curl under her white cap. She reached behind her back, loosened her apron in readiness for reaching for the wakened child in the basket on the back window bottom. She took the first step in its direction continuing to remove her apron, when the house door opened, but expecting Mrs Dixon she ignored the sound until a well-remembered voice said, 'Hello, Gracie, I heard you were back.' She stopped, stood stock still and then unwillingly but without choice she turned to face Edward Dixon. Without a word she stared at the now mature, even more confident man. He took two steps to come closer to her, his face smiled, his eyes searching hers. Her mind in a whirl, while her body refused to take action Gracie was motionless, her eyes unable to move away from his face. His hand reached out to touch her face, then a gentle finger traced a line slowly from her temple to chin. 'Even more beautiful I see, I have often thought of you, you know.' Gracie stopped breathing, her body still motionless, as the finger travelled down the length of her neck and then further down her bodice to rest at the breast point, where it rested for a moment, then nature surged and a moist dark spot stained the bodice. Edward Dixon's eyes suddenly glazed, his lips smiled and in his mind's eye the face he was gazing at blurred to become that of his mother.

The back door of the kitchen opened noisily and the hand instantly drew back and the face assumed its usual cynical expression. 'Quite the mother aren't we? Mothers are wonderful things, always the source of life and nourishment. My mother always supplies my every needs. Always has, always will.' With that strange statement he turned to a curious Sally who had come through the open doorway and stopped suddenly as she realised she had walked into a strained situation. Edward quickly moved across the room to her side and put his arm around her shoulders and doing so turned both her and himself away from the silent Gracie, and softy uttered, 'Well here's my favourite girl.'

The two then left the kitchen leaving a shocked and

trembling Gracie who stood still, motionless for a moment, after which she stirred herself to attend to the child. Gracie's mind was in a whirl of desperation and her body a quiver at the shock, why, she thought, every time I meet that man, does he manage to upset me and my life? Some time later, trying to concentrate on the required jobs, her face still red with shame, she was confronted by an annoyed Mrs Dixon asking why a batch of loaves was being burnt as surely they must be as she could tell the smell in her sitting room. The rest of the morning passed in a haze of work and troubled thoughts for there was no way in which Gracie was willingly coming back here again. 'For I never should have come back this time,' she whispered out loud. But her father was going to 'go mad' and then there was the cottage to consider; if they lost that they would be back in the single room again, and anyway, Mr Dixon might not even allow that. 'We're in terrible trouble, I know we are,' she muttered.

Her mind in turmoil, it was a very unhappy Gracie who later trudged child in her arms down the lane home, thinking as she walked that she always seemed to be fleeing down this lane away from that man and the reasons were getting worse and bothering her head even more. She was a happily married woman, she told herself, how was it he still had that effect? But she could not find an answer her conscience would let her accept. Her silence and obvious air of distress soon became apparent to Tom, who after failing to elicit the cause of the problem, resorted to asking the help of Agnes. Agnes also failed to find out the truth although, she had her suspicions for she had heard that Edward Dixon had arrived home again and that usually meant trouble for Gracie and everybody else for that matter, and with this information in mind informed Tom that, 'Gracie was for sure expectin' again and best way for all was she finished at the farm.' While a convenient excuse, she thought it probable that Gracie was pregnant again as she had had 'that' look about her for a few weeks, and anyway that was the best end to the problem. The question of Gracie's ceasing the work in return for the cottage, Jonas would just have to solve in some way or other, he was usually good at sorting out things like that, she thought bitterly.

Jonas did not have to consider how to solve the problem as Tom was sure he had the answer in the form of an exchange arrangement where he would offer his labour for a few hours a week at the farm, in exchange for the loss of Gracie's efforts. So he duly presented himself at the farm back door later that day to make the offer to Mr Dixon along with an explanation of the situation, confident that, when explained, the farmer would agree to the new arrangement. When Sally opened the house back hall door, she was surprised to see Gracie's husband standing there as he was not in the habit of coming anywhere near the farm, but at his request to see Mr Dixon she soon scurried away leaving Tom standing in the yard outside the closed door. The door reopened a few minutes later to reveal not the older Mr Dixon who Tom was expecting but the son. 'Yes, my good man, what do you want?' was the opening gibe in a very condescending manner.

Edward Dixon had instantly recognised Tom as being the man who had ruined his fun at Openshaw's beerhouse with the idiot Big Billy, and he was not about to be pleasant towards him. Standing at advantage as he was two steps higher than Tom standing in the yard below, Edward now simply stared down his nose at Tom who was determined not to be easily aggravated but quietly questioned where the senior Dixon was. 'Resting, so I will deal with you.' Still out to placate, desperate to resolve the problem rather than cause trouble Tom ignored the sneering tone and words, just quietly explaining the difficulty with Gracie's

125

further employment. Edward purposely failed to understand and instead sought to demean so replied, 'Expecting another child you say, becoming quite the breeding cow, what?' Tom clenched his hands into fists, considered putting them in his pockets but knew this would be considered insolence, so moved them behind his back. 'So you will be helping in the kitchen then, you aren't quite as decorative as your wife you know.' Was the next insulting verbal poke.

Again Tom tried to explain, 'No, Mr Dixon, sir, I am offering te do werk outside on' farm, to make up fer Gracie not bein' able te werk, to pay rent fer the cottage like. It at' be outside werk.'

'Well that is not quite what we need, you see, my man.' Was the airy reply. 'You don't quite have the attributes that we require!' Followed with a snigger and sarcastic smile as he tipped his head to one side. Tom starred in disbelief at these words, but the insults to his wife and the aloof look proved too much for the normally calm man. He remained standing for a long few seconds accepting the fact that nothing he offered was going to resolve the problem. Like an arrow at release his arms came from behind his back as he jumped onto the upper doorstep and in one fluid movement his right fist hit the other man square in the face knocking him backwards into the house. Tom hovered for a moment on the step, long enough to see the blood trickle from the nose of the fallen man who had risen to his knees. Then jumping down to the stoneset surface of the yard, shaking in shock at what he had just done, did not speak a word but turned on his heel and walked away from the injured man, who was loudly sending threats at his assailant's retreating back.

CHAPTER 13

Almost dazed at what he had done, for he knew his actions would have severe repercussions, Tom ran almost stumbling back to the lane leading to the cottages. He passed his own cottage furtively watching the window for any sign of his wife then thankful that Gracie did not see him pass, he reached the Baileys' home but still kept going. Almost senseless he turned at the old walled garden wall, headed on past the fallen wall at the tree and kept on going up towards the moor and the pit high above. Then he saw the hawthorn tree still hanging on the side of the stream, and he stopped and sat down suddenly like a man exhausted. Becoming calm at last he then began to shake as in a fever. The shaking eventually ceased to leave a man distraught, ashamed of his own actions and at a loss what to do. 'I can't g'back, how am I t'tell Gracie and the family what 'a've done?' he told himself. 'Good for nothing now, that's me. How do a' tell em?'

After much self-torment, Tom had come to a decision, he was sure that if he were to offer to go, the Dixons would allow Gracie and the child to stay with her parents, at least for the time being until he found another job and sent for her. So, fortified by his belief in what he had decided, he trudged back down the hill past the Baileys' house. He arrived back at his own cottage to find a worried Gracie, concerned over his long absence, but her concern heightened when he informed her that he had a terrible confession to make to her and her parents. 'We had better go now and tell thee faather and mam what I have done, because it could

127

be the ruination of us all, and I don't think a' can live wi that after how good they've been te me.'

'Oh what have ye done, Tom, tell me?'

But he would not tell her then saying, 'Best if I tell ye all together.' The older Baileys were shocked by the story Tom related but after their initial reaction both tried to calm the man by insisting that after everyone considered Tom's reasons, including the Dixons, they were sure it would all calm down. 'Yes, but I think I might have to leave to find another job, and then when I am fixed up I will come back for Gracie.'

'Nay, lad, let's wait and see, Dixon knows a good worker when he sees one and the old man might be prepared to take your offer, that son of his a'll be leaving soon.' Was Jonas's attempt at easing Tom's panic.

Tom might have thought he could ease the situation by offering to leave, but he was wasting his efforts, and Jonas might have thought the situation could be resolved but they were both very wrong. Edward Dixon, but more importantly Mrs Dixon, had ensured that the young man's threats were not idle, for no one was going to get away with hurting her son. So before nightfall Mr Dixon himself had arrived at the Baileys' door to inform Jonas, in his very superior not to be questioned tone, that Tom and his wife were no longer entitled to the cottage, and should be out before the end of the week. Also Mr Dixon informed Jonas, 'I am prepared to allow you and your wife and other daughters to continue with the tenancy and our working arrangement and the extra land on one strict condition. That ruffian navvy Tom Briggs is dismissed immediately never to be seen on this farm again. This, Jonas, is what comes of helping people of his common type. Your daughter Gracie can come to visit you on occasion but not him. Mind my word or you will all be out of work and home.'

For some time after Mr Dixon had left there was complete silence in the house, the reality that they could actually be facing eviction, and the further terrible acceptance that Mr Dixon could dictate to them in such a manner. Tom felt distraught beyond guilty and declared he would leave alone immediately but Gracie would have none of it, and anyway she declared with agreement from Agnes and Jonas that would solve nothing, another way must be found, as it seemed even Gracie was not to be allowed to remain with her family. Next day Tom and Jonas, up even earlier than normal for neither had slept during the night, their morning home jobs quickly started, Tom being left to finish them, so that Jonas would have no further jobs once he returned from his work at Hall Farm, Jonas left for morning milking. Immediately he returned they set off to find work and lodging for the young family. Gracie was distraught so Agnes had persuaded her to rest in Agnes's own bed, and after doing so was soon asleep, the child in a basket at her side. She was still asleep when the men returned disconsolate without success in their hunt. It seemed that either the Dixons had warned any local farmers off of employing Tom or as Agnes preferred to contend, 'There were just no places needing fillin at t' moment.'

After his afternoon work Tom set off again, this time alone as Jonas had to return to work. Cursing himself with every step he took, but in his heart he knew how great was the power of some men over men when they had money and 'the say', he knew he should have never have done what he did. This kind of situation was the lot of many a hard working man and his family if they incurred the displeasure of boss or landlord. Although getting late, Tom carried on his quest and set off again, after calling at two more farms, turned away from both without any hope of work, he reckoned he must have walked about seven or eight miles and his feet were really starting to hurt. The light was failing when sitting on the roadside for a rest, it began to rain so he moved a little further along the road so as to be under a tree for shelter, and as he sat hopelessness starting to take hold, he began to think about when he first came to the Baileys and how he had become complacent about his future. It all seemed so simple and easy, work and all would be well. Well now it was all changed. Best answer, he thought, was for him to go walk away, Gracie could stay with her family surely the Dixons couldn't really object to that, but then that Edward Dixon obviously still had thoughts about Gracie and that he could not bear the thought of. 'Dear God what are we to do?' he uttered softly in prayer.

As he sat at the road edge he gazed into the distance, higher up the fell and through the now constant drizzle of rain saw a light glimmer, but he had no recollection of seeing a farm up there. Still in desperation he rose stiffly from the ground and started to stride in the direction of the twinkling light until at a twist in the road it disappeared. Unsure what to do he carried on a little further thankful for the now increasing moonlight helping to see the narrowing lane ahead and the deep puddles starting to form in ruts in the lane surface. The wind had started as he walked higher up the hill and now it was blowing the rain straight at his face. The moon disappeared behind cloud so he was walking in almost pitch dark unsure of the direction he was taking. Tom's now wet feet were beginning to rub in his clogs and the rain had penetrated through his clothes and his teeth began to chatter, so when at a further turn some distance on where he could just see by the faint light that the road became even narrower and rougher, he turned, now without hope, to return home. Then just as he turned, the light again caught his eye as it appeared this time closer and to the left. Now again as the moon peeped through the clouds he saw close by a pair of tall carved stone gateposts at a break in the wall, one upright and standing tight to the meeting wall, the other leaning at a sharp angle back into the field behind. The remains of a battered fancy iron gate still fixed to the leaning post had half buried itself into the ground. Doubt that gate'll ever close agin. An' those once were very grand gateposts fer a farm entrance, thought Tom and then he called himself a fool for even bothering to consider such things in his present situation. So, knowing he had no alternative for there was nothing to go back to, he passed between the posts and continued down the farm lane to find what lay beyond.

Tom could now see the light was coming from a window. It was not really bright but seemed so in the darkness of the house wall, for the moon had again disappeared behind cloud, and surely a light was evidence that someone was at home. Just as he reached the large door, which looked battered even in meagre light from the window, a dog jumped out wildly barking from ramshackle kennel a little further along the house wall. Quickly looking for a stick to defend himself, Tom desperately cast about, but to his relief the animal came to a sudden choking stop as its neck chain reached its length. Now seeing that the starved looking animal could not reach the door and taking a deep breath, Tom knocked on the battered wood. As he waited to see if the door opened he gazed around, the moon, which had appeared again after hiding behind the clouds, revealing the great size of the house and heavy stone mullions to the windows and looking up Tom saw a fancy carved crest above the door. His misgivings on walking and slipping across the muddy manure and tool strewn yard were now further strengthened by the rough voice from behind the door. 'What yer want? Bugger off.'

Tom hesitated but thought that as he had walked all this way he might as well persist further, desperation brings perseverance. 'Tom Briggs, sir, looking for work.'

Silence for a moment, then the door opened slowly to reveal a thin shrivelled elderly man carrying a large oil lamp. By the light of the lamp and aided by the moonlight, Tom saw he was dressed in a dirty raggy jacket and torn trousers with unlaced clogs caked with clods of mud. In fact from what he could see by the light of the lamp the man seemed covered in mud or cow dung. 'A' towd yer clear off, anyhow what yer doin here at this time o nite?' he muttered through a toothless mouth.

'Is master about, yer luk like yer could do with help around here?' Tom tried again, his desperation now really getting the better of sense.

'Al master yer, I's master 'bout ere.'

In an attempt to right his mistake Tom tried again. 'Sorry, sir. Looking fer work, sir.'

The man seemed to consider as he eyed Tom head to foot. 'Aye well mebe a' do need 'elp but y'd have to werk ard.'

'I can do that, sir, if the'll be a cottage i' part wages.'

The farmer lifted his cap and scratched his head, then replaced the cap, stroked his chin and without further preamble muttered, 'Be 'ere termorrer soon.' With that reply the door slammed shut. Tom stood for a few moments, then finally becoming aware that the conversation was over, he walked away from the chaos of the dirty yard all the while comparing it to the one he was returning to and quaked. How could he take Gracie to that place, or indeed did he have an option? She would have to decide, he was tired beyond being able to think, all that was going through his mind was, Tom Briggs yer a fist happy fool, and no good t'yer family if this is the best yer can cum up wi'. Trudging along the road to home Tom, thinking it was further than he had thought, had time to again consider the mess he was in: 'An' am dragging Gracie down wi mi.' When he reached the lane to head for home, he stopped, looked into the darkness up the lane, and then carried on past. 'Best job a' be gone,' he muttered. A mile or so down the road his nerve failed. He needed Gracie so much, he had to go back. He turned in the road.

CHAPTER 14

When Tom related his experience to Jonas his reaction was immediate 'Ye' must a' bin up ter Windyfell, yer either brave o' daft. He's a madman is owd Shepperton, wonder he didn't turn his shotgun on ye, he's known fer it, an' he 'ates women 'cus 'is wife ran off wi' a gypsy when she coun't stand 'im any longer. An' it wer her house, her family house, but married 'im so he were boss like.'

'What choice do a' ave?' was Tom's question in reply.

'Non, lad non. Yer reet. Yer said there weer a cottage?'

'Eye,' replied Tom.

'Weel w've tried all others. God bless and help yer and our Gracie. Agnes and me al' elp yer all wi can.'

Next morning before daybreak Tom was once more knocking on the battered door of the ramshackle farm, walking back only a few short hours since he had left the previous night, he was just grateful for the early dim light of dawn to show him the way. He shivered as he stood waiting in the yard, the strengthening light also fully showing how filthy and weed and grass covered the yard was. 'It'l be ink black out ere when ther's n' moon at all,' he muttered to himself.

Then the door creaked open to reveal an inside to the house barely brighter than the light outside. 'Oh, so thee turned up then, they don't usually, thy mun b'desperate then. Well see'n as thy'r here let's see yer put yer back int' some werk.' Was the only greeting. 'A'll show thee shippon ter start milkin.' Followed and that was the start of Tom's employment at Windyfell.

It seemed that Mr Shepperton did not have to make much effort to sell his milk as he had a ready market in the form of the inhabitants of the quarry village. The largest of the local quarries was located just a bare quarter of a mile from the farm and the stone masons and their families lived on the site in hastily built wooden cottages. Tom wondered, when he saw some of them later in the day, if the women who trudged over the fell to the farm to buy the milk had any idea of the filth of the conditions in which it was produced, but then he thought the disevelled state of some of them they looked like they might not be too bothered anyway. Once the cows had been sent back outside, Tom went looking for his new boss. 'Alreet if a' clean out shippon now, sir?' Tom asked politely but the answer was certainly not what he expected.

'Don't come yer clever sir'ing at me laddy, or yer'll be down 'road quick.'

Tom was at a loss how to behave. He stood for a moment then, as he told Jonas later he never knew where the idea came from, but he looked Shepperton straight in the eye and in a rough tone said, 'Reet, what now?' He later told his father-in-law that he never knew whether the old farmer was too shocked to object or whether that was simply how he liked to be treated, either way while it did not make him any pleasanter it seemed he was prepared to accept Tom as a permanency.

The day passed without further confrontation, as Tom made further equally gruff requests for instructions. Well after dark Tom decided he was going home as it seemed he was not to be told to finish for the day. Shepperton had disappeared some time before so he knocked at the door to inform him that he was away home. He also needed to ask about the cottage because the end of the week was looming. He had seen what looked like a small cottage attached to the end of the main house. As the farmhouse door opened, he wasted no time but said bluntly, 'Reet I'm off now, be back in morrow but what about 'cottage a' need ter bring wife soon an' then we can stay here?'

The reply accompanied by a scowl was, 'End a' house theer, an get on wi' it but not i' my time.' At which the door was slammed shut. Well, thought Tom, it's a roof and that's a start. At which he wearily headed for home.

The next day proved to be very much a repeat of the first, Tom asking with the least possible words and Shepperton answering in a similar manner except for when the two men had just passed in the yard a little before dusk. Shepperton: 'Mek bloody sure ha' fasens up them hens, a'm sure a' heer'd them quarry brats trying ter get into em last nite.'

'Reet,' shouted Tom over his shoulder. He wasn't surprised at Shepperton's warning as had seen some raggily dressed children close to the farm as he arrived that morning. Aye, he thought, a few eggs or better a stolen chicken would be a real prized luxury to those skinny childer.

A little after that he decided that he had done enough for the day and went to take a look inside the cottage. What had probably once been a nice small home was a dump. Walking in through the door which was standing ajar because, as he soon discovered, it had become too swollen with damp for it to fit the door case. Even in the darkness he could see the floor was littered with dirt and rubbish, the fire grate of the small range had the remains of a long dead fire and the only pieces of furniture which seemed intact were an unlevel table and a spindle back chair. Going back into the yard to find a brush, he found Shepperton waiting for him with a belligerent smirk on his face. 'Up ter stan'ard is it, mon?'

Keeping his reply curt but polite he answered quickly, 'Aye, it'll be reet.' And headed back inside to sweep the cottage through. Thankfully, thought Tom, there were steep but proper stairs to the low ceilinged room on the first floor or Gracie would struggle carrying a child up there if it had been only a ladder. Getting a bucket of water from the yard trough he wiped the small window panes with a piece of dampened sacking. Not a good job, he decided as he really could not see much for the approaching dark, but they're better than before, at which point he decided to go home.

All of the long way home Tom's brain was desperately searching for an alternative to returning to where he had just left but in his heart he knew none existed, or at least none he could think of. Weary, he walked through the doorway of his cosy soon to be lost cottage to be faced by an overly cheerful Gracie. 'Yer alreet, Tom, how did it go?'

'He's a funny chap, Gracie fer sure. There's a cottage but it's rough.'

'Never mind, love, we will manage.' She smiled.

'We ave no option, thanks te me an me temper,' he replied but at the same time thinking thinking, Gracie ye've never seen anything like that cottage. But he said nothing further.

Gracie saw the tear forming in his eye. 'Now come on, lad. let's eat and te bed yer need yer sleep.'

CHAPTER 15

The daylight was becoming stronger as Gracie slumped down on the only chair in the cottage. She was desperately tired after the walk for she had insisted on accompanying Tom the next morning and although Tom had carried the sleeping child Gracie had the other one inside her. In the dim light which was struggling to enter the room through the small deep set windows she saw the dirt and the cobwebs which Tom had not seen in the dark the night before. Then she saw the damp walls and the disconsolate man standing in front of her and smiled at him. 'We'll manage, Tom. We'll be alrite, go an' see t' farmer now.' As he walked out of the cottage door a very large spider spun down from the ceiling to run across the dirty floor, she grasped the child to her chest and whispered, 'Oh God.' She was tired as only hopelessness, disillusionment and pregnancy can make a body, still as she looked at the child and felt the new life stir within her the urge to fight all for her family rose, she stirred herself to move to the open doorway, saw the hill rising to the moor so close from the cottage, the moor which gave her comfort as it did her mother. Her heart followed her eyes to its summit while her mind's eye travelled up a path with a dog, she whispered, 'We'll manage with God's help.'

Then came the sound of a horse and cart entering the yard and Jonas and Agnes appeared waving from the vehicle over loaded with the contents of her lost cottage. Agnes, covering her distress at the sad sight before her, chided her daughter gently,

'Now, our Gracie, don't just stand theer being mard, let's get yer sorted out wi' a new home.' They did, as they worked for hours sweeping and mopping sustained by bread and cheese and cold tea, brought by the ever practical Agnes, so that by nightfall when a deathly tired Tom appeared, he found a home with a fire in the hearth. Jonas who had returned home to see to his own day's work arrived back once more and the older couple, although loath to leave, departed promising to return soon with more food.

Just as Jonas and a struggling Agnes climbed onto the cart to leave, Shepperton marched across the yard towards them. 'Got em all cosy like ave yer? Well al' 'ave non of yer nosy visiting. If yer brung 'em owt yer leave it at yon gate. Yer welcum ter brung 'em food en like but only ter gate mind. Theer's a owd tin trunk near gate, leave owt in that.' Neither replied but both stared unflinchingly at the farmer as Jonas flicked the reins and they moved off.

Agnes sat silently for a moment then could contain herself no longer. 'What 'ave they got them sel' into Jonas?'

'I don't rightly know, lass, but we will bring 'em food because they are bana need their strength.'

Tom would always remember the time they spent at Windyfell as the worst of his life even though that year saw the birth of his son, he ever wondered how Grace and the children never took ill for regardless of her efforts at sweeping and wiping the walls remained damp so keeping clothes and bedding dry was a constant battle. Nothing could remain on the floor for fear of vermin for a rat had chewed one of Gracie's only pair of shoes one night, which meant she even had to wear her clogs inside. Rain still leaked in at windows and the roof despite Tom's countless repair efforts. At first Gracie rarely left the cottage, except to use the privy or get water from the yard pump, for fear of the old farmer with his boasted hatred of women he had, it seemed, taken exception to even the sight of her. Abusive language was his main weapon but on occasion he took to banging on the cottage door or windows usually followed by a curse on ' devils i' skirts'. He took to catching rats and fastening them in the privy for Gracie to be shocked at finding as they jumped out as she opened the door. But to keep them in the privy he had to put a board at the bottom of the door to fill the ventilation gap left below the door and Gracie soon 'twigged his tricks' as she told Tom, so the torment stopped when the old man realised he was failing to shock. Hardened to his antics Gracie simply ignored him and so seeing he was wasting his time he in turn kept away from the cottage and a truce reigned.

From when they first arrived, occasionally and always alone but for the child, Gracie would undertake the long arduous trek to her parents' home, for Tom feared for Jonas's livelihood if he was seen at the Baileys', and anyway he dare not leave Windyfell for fear of repercussions if Shepperton knew he had left the farm. Agnes always fired up a good supply of hot water for a welcome good wash when Gracie and the child arrived. Those warm water washes for her and the child were a balm to the troubled Gracie always so used to being clean. Agnes always had clean clothes for both. The dreaded return was always too soon but Jonas would take her within a short distance of the farm, but not close enough to be seen by Shepperton.

Their food supplied by Shepperton was plain and barely sufficient but often supplemented by extra brought by a willing Jonas, as Tom was never allowed to leave the farm, and if he did he had been told again in certain terms not to come back. The food brought by Jonas was left at the farm gate, in the old tin trunk that was checked by Tom every day after Shepperton had told Tom what he had instructed Jonas to do. Tom was so ashamed that his father-in-law had been so treated on his account but grateful and for Gracie's and the child's sake he accepted the charity. Jonas never came all the way up to the farm for fear of antagonising Tom's boss, who frequently resorted to threats of instant dismissal and eviction if displeased. One thing Shepperton had never thought to restrict was Tom taking milk for his family so thinking it better not to ask he made sure the child and Gracie drank plenty, and perhaps due to this the second child was born easily and healthy but with only Agnes to help its arrival. Tom had managed to send a message by way of one of the quarry women and true to her promise she had walked to the Baileys' home, to be well rewarded by a grateful Agnes. When an anxious Agnes arrived at Windyfell, Jonas having brought her on the cart and left her at the gate, she was ready to do battle with Shepperton to gain access to her daughter but he must have sensed what was afoot and kept well out of the way.

Tom's efforts through the summer began to show results as the cattle and sheep began to improve in appearance, and doors were hung straight and roofs repaired.

One morning Tom was working clearing a stable when Shepperton approached purposefully from the direction of the house. 'I've bin thinking that wife a thyn she can cum an clear up mi house, like.'

Shocked at the suggestion Tom returned to his usual polite manner. 'Sorry, sir, Mr Shepperton, but she's busy wi' childer.'

'Hey none of thee siring agin ya's bin towd. A need mi house cleaning up, like yon yard is. Now though, not tomorrow think on. Non of her shinanakins. Ner fear a' don't want her body, just mi house clean.'

Tom was at a loss what to do, but Gracie, when he braced

himself to tell her all of it half an hour later, was practical about it and simply said, 'Reet, if he leaves me alone a'll do it, we're in this t'gether, but the childer will have to cum wi' mi', tell 'im what.'

'Aw, lass, I ner thewt I'd bring thee ter this, cleanin' up ater a dirty owd farmer.'

'Ner mind, lad, weel get o'er this, ner fear.'

Tom returned to tell the farmer to expect Gracie and the children, all the time feeling shame for what he had brought them to, but at the same time proud of his wife's strength.

A little later Gracie walked over to the house and knocked on the door. It was opened immediately by the farmer. 'Reet, cum in. Clean it up. Thee seem like thee should as good at it as thee husban' at cleaning up mi farm. A've looked in at' cottage winders, ye got it clean in theer. Put thee brats in that sheep pen a' brewt in. A don't want em runnin loose in mi house.'

Gracie said nothing but thought looking around the inside of the house she was more of the opinion that the two children were probably safer inside the confines of the sheep pen rather than being able to wander about in the filth and jumbled contents of the house. So having ensured that the children were safe in the wooden pen, which she checked to make sure it was not going to fall over on them as the base really needed to be pushed into soft ground to be stable, and it looked quite out of place in the middle of the farm kitchen, then she turned her attention the house and Gracie had never seen the like of the interior of that house. There was no evidence of any food so she assumed Shepperton had hidden it all away but a large milk jug had been left in the centre of the table. Peering into it her breakfast rose to her mouth as she saw the whole surface of the milk covered by a floating layer of dead flies. The milk and flies were soon poured down the sink.

Starting by sweeping the floor she saw how much the dust was rising into the air so quickly back to the cottage to bring back an old sheet to throw over the sheep pen to protect the children from the dust cloud. Gazing about the kitchen she mused that it must have been a very grand but cosy kitchen before it became a tip. The large stone slopstone sink, located in a side back kitchen area, even had its own water pump but it also had a thick coating of hardened fat sitting on the bottom and half way up the sides. She scraped this off with a knife then lathered the stone with soft soap to good effect. There was little she could do about the dirty walls but she again returned to her own cottage and brought sticks and with coal she had seen in a bucket left by the back door lit a fire in the range and put the iron kettle to boil. She had also brought back some bread and milk pobs from the cottage and fed these to the children who both, once fed, settled for a sleep. Now with warm water and some of the soft soap she had found to clean the sink she set about wiping the furniture. The high back dresser thick with dust and greasy smears when wiped revealed a hidden shine and a large mirror back which instantly brightened the room with its reflection. The large table, its scrubbed top now wiped, gave promise of better if it were actually scrubbed and its legs with their white pot and brass castor feet gleamed when dust and linking cobwebs were removed. Five carved highback chairs randomly spread about the room were all retrieved and wiped down before being arranged around the table. The chairs all had their leather seats torn or split to varying states but once pushed under the table this could not be seen so the overall effect was quite tidy. Grace quietly pleased at the effect paused to wonder 'Now where is the sixth chair?' but it was not to be seen so she then turned her attention to the many wooden framed pictures on the walls. Dust and more cobwebs soft brushed from them, then a wipe to clear the smokey grease on the glass showed an amazing array of curiously painted cows, horned bulls and horses of different sizes and colours. Satisfied that she could do little more to the room but pleased with her efforts she then turned her attention to a deep set door leading from the back of the kitchen. This led into a back hallway with a narrow staircase. The stairs were uncarpeted so starting at the top Gracie swept down the accumulated dust and what looked like dried lumps of soil and midden muck which had obviously fallen from boots or clogs. Reaching the foot of the stairs she emptied her dustpan grimacing at the feel of grime on her face. Shrugging, for she decided there was no point in bothering about the muck for she was certain she would find more. She walked along the corridor and came to another door which opened only with a hard push after she had managed to lift the stiff latch, revealing another wider hallway. To the left another brown painted door which again opened only with a very hard push. Inside the room the air was stale and musty. At first she could see little by the dust laden shaft of light creeping between the thick half drawn curtains. Once her eyes had become accustomed to the dim light, Grace gazed in amazement at the sight of the room for she had seen the inside of Mrs Dixon's parlour and this was far grander. A long couch with a high arm at one end and two chairs: one large, one smaller and lower, all covered in black with many buttons creating a deep pattern effect. These all arranged facing a marble fireplace with a high over mantle with a large mirror centre. The walls covered with wallpaper, which damp had discoloured, but still showed faded green stripes intertwined with roses. A piano with brass candlesticks on the front and a table with many small ornaments arranged on it. Heavy gold framed pictures on the walls showed well dressed sombre-looking men and women gazing down at her.

'There must have been money and riches in this house at one time,' Gracie mused to herself. 'Shows how things can change.' Nothing was untidy about the room so she dusted every surface with a soft cotton cloth and with a long feather duster disturbed several spiders' webs, then with one last admiring glance, she closed the door. Having checked on the children in the kitchen, she retraced her steps through the first door and walked in the opposite direction to the sitting room, along the corridor to find herself in a spacious entrance hall with a second wide and carved staircase but this one was covered with a red patterned carpet. It seemed this hall must be at the front of the house for a wide door with glass panels obviously led to the outside. Beyond the staircase she could see there were further rooms but unsure where to clean next she returned to the kitchen to check on her children for she had heard a whimper, just then she heard the farmer's voice before she entered the kitchen.

Shepperton walked over to the table and gruffly asked where the milk had gone. 'Drunk it have you?'

'No I threw it down the sink, it was covered in flies it had no cover,' Gracie countered.

The farmer's face darkened in anger. 'What? Yer mad stupid bitch, yer scoop em of, it'll be reet. Throw any more good stuff, any, and you're out o' that cottage. We don't need thee fancy ways 'ere. Oh aye, I fergot to tell yer, yer only go outa 'ere up them narra' stairs an' do the two bedrooms theer, no going anywere else, don't open any other doors, no nosing anyweer else, cleer is it?'

'Aye, it's cleer,' she sharply replied and quickly picked up the sheet and both children anxious to leave before Shepperton asked any more questions about where she had been in the house.

Just as she closed the back door behind her she heard a low, 'Ta it's grand.'

145

Gracie returned several times to the house and turned her attention to the two bedrooms leading from the narrow staircase. Refusing to make the filthy beds or touch the evil smelling commode in the corner of the bigger room, she cleaned as much as possible, but always made sure she had not eaten just before a visit as otherwise the consequence was the loss of the recently eaten food. Strangely although Shepperton never acknowledged Gracie's efforts, whenever he had been for a visit to town there appeared outside her door some unexpected item of food. Gracie being Gracie decided that maybe things could get better.

The winter days as they came were worse for keeping the cottage dry and warm, and Tom just thanked God that none of them took ill. He spent any spare time searching the land about for fallen trees or boughs and sawing and chopping them for the fire so that at least they would be warm in the cottage. Gracie when she wandered outside for any reason always regretted the trip when she came indoors with a wet hem which spread half way up her skirt and a very chilled body, many a trip ended with a quiet weep and fleeting mood of dispair which Gracie quickly shook off before Tom should see. She was so aware that he blamed himself for the situation they were in but as she told herself, 'A man can only be pushed so far and Tom was a proud man and he was defending her when he did what he did.' Tom, for his part, saw with a heavy heart how Gracie struggled but never complained, even simple tasks became more difficult because of the privations of the cottage and he vowed they had to go. At night in the few hours before bedtime Tom often sat silently watching his wife torn between admiration for her hardworking determination and heartbreak at what he felt he was responsible for bringing upon her. His love was strong like hers but his guilt was constant. This had to end, he decided.

CHAPTER 16

One late winter day, Tom returned to the farmyard as the light was starting to go. He knocked on the back door because he had not seen Shepperton all afternoon and he was worried about a cow that was due to calf but kept going down on its back legs as if weak. There was no answer so he went back to the cowshed to she how she was doing when he heard a commotion in the yard.

The sight that met Tom was one of which his even wildest imagination could never have dreamed. Shepperton sitting on his heavy farm cart raced into the centre of the yard the horse skidding to a painful stop as the man pulled hard on the reins. This was shocking enough but the most amazing of all was that Shepperton was wearing a white stock, black tail coat and trousers and hard bowler hat. What was quite clear as he tried to descend from the cart was that the man was very drunk. He slipped from the bottom rail step, grabbed the brake lever and stumbled to the ground. Regaining his feet he attempted vainly to straighten his coat and hat and suddenly demanded of Tom, 'Why art thee stan'ing theer? Help me unload this damn cart.' Still totally at a loss, Tom started to unload what appeared to be leather bound boxes and heavy lidded tin cases all with locks at their fastenings. 'Tek em in'ter kitchen and pile em up tidy.' Was Shepperton's next instruction. Having finished carrying all the goods into the house, Tom stood beside the considerable pile waiting for further instruction. 'Reet get out.' Was all the thanks that came. Tom not surprised at this return to usual behaviour turned to leave. 'Ney wait, I have summat ter tell ye. Terday justice it were done. The bitch died, ah fund out where who were livin'. Legal fella said as how I 'ah te be towd. She still had most o boxes who took we' her, an I's got it all back. Seen her grave jumped onit 'a did.' Tom listened to all this, his mind racing as to what would happen how. 'When who left who nearly took it all 'cept house and cattle and stock 'cause who couldn't carry them. Went when 'a were at market, at her orders.'

Tom made no comment but began to hedge towards the door. 'All reet if 'a go now we'v a cow not good 'a need to go to her?'

'Aye bugger off.' A little later Tom leaving the cow for a moment looked out towards the house when he saw Shepperton unsteadily cross the yard and return to the house with a chisel and hammer. He went back to the cow because he was sure that any request to Shepperton for help would be refused. The shouting started a short time after the banging of hammer on metal. 'Bitch, filthy bitch, rot in hell, ye bitch.' And carried on in the same vein for over an hour.

From comments over the next few days, Tom gathered that the boxes contained not the expected money, gold and valuables but cheap trinkets and general household items of little value. It seemed his wife had had the final laugh at his expense.

Tom had had no intention of their remaining at Windyfell for the thought of another winter there turned him sick and now that Gracie was also expected to work it had to end. The trick played upon Shepperton by his dead wife had sealed his decision for the man seemed now almost insane. Again he had taken to shouting abuse at Gracie and she admitted that now he frightened her so much so she feared entering his house and so did her best to keep out of his way. Tom just had to work out how to get away and find another place and that he knew was not going to be easy as he was not allowed to leave the farm. It was Christmas he was sure of that and as his hands worked busy with the cow he was milking his thoughts wandered to another Christmas in a warm firelit kitchen with friends seated around a big table loaded with food and laughter filling the room. The winter passed and still Tom had not thought of a way to leave without it being a direct route to the workhouse. One day he pondered as he worked but was shocked to feel a tear had crept down his cheek and hovered at his chin end. He knew he was losing heart and Gracie for all her brave front was too, he knew that, she walked more slowly these days and was getting thin, her clothes beginning to hang loose on her shoulders and she had little to say even after a trip to her parents'. She was giving her food to the children, he was sure. Finally, quietly one night as they sat before the fire in the little time between work and bed, he told Gracie that they had to make plans. They decided after much deep deliberation to brave fate and to take a chance, they had to leave. They could not continue living like this, better to take the risk of being homeless than to carry on this servitude or slavery as Tom had come to consider it, for other than the meagre amount of food supplied by Shepperton they had received no money payment in nearly eighteen months and Tom was not optimistic about any future chance of wages. Their clothes that were left were becoming rags and those rags had seen little soap except some Gracie admitted to Tom she had stolen from the farmhouse. They were dying as they lived like he had seen men and women do when as a child he had lived amongst poverty and hopelessness. 'This has to end whatever the consequence,' he told Gracie one night as they sat before the fire in the little time between work and bed. 'We are becoming working beggars. We have to leave on Lady Day, the spring hiring day, which is in a few days time.'

Come the morning he told Gracie to head for her parents' home without looking back. She looked at him uncertainly at this suggestion even after all the discussing. 'Are ye sure, Tom? It might get better here, Shepperton seems a bit better lately. At least we have a roof over our heads and are together.'

Tom looked at his wife. 'Gracie ye alus see 'best in folk, he'll never change; if anything he is worse since his wife got her own back, we're goin' today.' At this Gracie looked round the cottage for one last time, dressed the children in their warmest clothes and, wrapping a shawl around herself, put another one over one shoulder, tucked the baby into it and tied it tight to hold the child in place, grasped the hand of the older child and checking the yard was empty set off up the lane to the gate and the road beyond. Tom watched her go, waited until he was sure she would be well across the first field that had a footpath to her parents' house. Then, after checking Shepperton was occupied, he ran down the lane from the farm and headed along the road for the town and its hiring market to chance finding a better place, another place, any place but this.

The risk of Shepperton's rage and revenge racing in his head, Tom hesitated even then his nerve wavering, feeling sick he stopped, almost turned, at the leaning gate post, because he knew if he failed to get a place they could be out of a job and home with nowhere to go but the workhouse, but thinking of the cruelly hard life ahead if they stayed at Windyfell, the thought of the workhouse might not be that bad. He straightened his back, looked straight ahead and marched determinedly on to town.

CHAPTER 17

Tom was standing in amongst those looking for a place, all of them positioned on the outer edge of the crowd in the market square. His eyes gazing at his leather clog upper where it was leaving the wooden sole, he raised his toes pivoting his clog on the heel and the gap between upper and sole widened. He absently considered the sight wondering how much longer the two would hold together. It was easier to think of anything other than letting his mind run wildly through the possible terrible consequences if he didn't find a new place. From his clogs his eyes now strayed up and rested on the frayed edge of the front of his jacket and it had the top button missing, he groaned, 'Man yer stanin' here in rags nobody is going to look at yer twice.' He quickly glanced at the others standing close by. There was a bent old woman who looked like another day's work would kill her, but other than that everyone else looked fit and much tidier then he did, and much more likely to find a place, in fact he thought some of them looked too well off to be standing there looking for work.

Now his legs started shaking like they would give way, he had had nothing to eat not wanting to waste time before he ran from the farm, he cursed himself for being daft for it had not occurred to him to bring an old bottle with some water so now his throat was parched after the run and walk to town. He closed his eyes in despair, the sun was becoming brighter and warmer and he felt himself sinking into a comforting almost comatose state as the sounds and sights around him began to blur and fade. From this place of peace and comfort he was was suddenly awoken by a voice calling his name. Forcing himself to look from under lowered lids he saw stopped in front of him a pair of very shiny brown boots. As Tom slowly raised his eyes he could hardly believe what he saw. Above the boots were a pair of equally gleaming brown leather gaiters. Now looking fully up he saw standing in front of him, and bestowing upon him a very warm smile, the best dressed man he had ever seen. Tan fustian cord trousers, a green checked jacket, a red spotted neckerchief in a chest pocket, a brown bowler hat and an enormous waxed moustache completed the outfit to perfection, and much to Tom's amazement, the wearer was speaking to him. Above the moustache a rather large nose, ruddy cheeks and bright blue eyes. 'Tom, I believe, latterly of Windyfell and before that of Jonas Bailey's employ.' Not sure it he was hearing right, or even if he was simply dreaming, Tom hesitated for a moment, which prompted the speaker to again ask, 'It is Tom, I am right, am I not?'

Quickly dragging his cap from his head and forcing himself to concentrate on his answer, Tom gasped. 'Yes, sir, yes, sir, that's me, Tom Briggs, sir. I'm wed to Jonas Bailey's lass Gracie, sir,' Came out in a great tumble of words.

'Well, Tom Briggs, my name is Albert Sowerbutts and I am here to offer you a place, am I not? I have been speaking to the worthy Jonas Bailey, have I not? And he assures me that you are just the man to run my yard when I am away, does he not? I am a man who buys and sells the finest of animals and I need a man of your calibre to watch over and look after my wonderful beasts while I am away abuying and aselling of same, do I not?'

Tom, even more amazed by this speech the like of which he

had never heard before, stirred himself to reply, 'Yes, sir.'

'Well, Tom Briggs, it is agreed then, or is it not?'

Was the return, to which Tom had sufficient presence of mind to confirm, 'Yes, sir.' And the matter it seemed was settled.

'Well, Tom, you and I will walk apace and work out our initial strategy for your removal, along with your family, to my estate.' At which the gentleman started to briskly stride off in the direction of the better of part of the town. Tom hesitated for a moment then realised he was supposed to be keeping pace with his new boss and stirred himself to follow in a similar manner. Amazed at the speed of movement of the elderly portly gentleman, Tom spurred himself to keep up while at the same time trying to concentrate on the information and instructions that were being directed at him. 'I have lodged my horse and carriage at the Hall Arms, where I will be partaking of a fine dinner of roast beef before returning home so if you would like go and arrange with your father-in-law to help with said future removal, and meet me here in two hours' time you and I can make our way home, can we not?' At which the speaker entered the hostelry door leaving a very stunned Tom standing outside. Tom stood for a moment at a loss what to do next as he attempted to sort out, in his totally confused mind, his given instructions, then shook his head as if to clear his thoughts and set off at a run towards Beckersley Hall.

Agnes was just throwing some grain to the hens who tended to congregate around the entrance to 'Big Lad's Garden' when she turned in alarm at the sound of running steps to see a very excited Tom Briggs waving as he ran towards her up the lane and into the farmyard. He skidded to a halt in front of his amazed mother-in-law who was still somewhat at a loss as to why Gracie and the two children had staggered into the farmyard earlier with very little explanation, and carrying nothing but a bag of clothing. One glance at her disheveled daughter struggling to carry the baby with the other child at her hand was enough for her to help them indoors without uttering a word, for fear of sobbing at the sorry sight. They were now resting in the kitchen; Agnes still no wiser as to the reason for their unexpected arrival. 'A just can't fathom why she's landed and i' such a state but she's te weary ter be quizzed,' she informed Jonas when he called in mid morning.

Regained of her near lost composure at the sudden happenings, for after taking one look at her son-in-law Agnes was shocked at his ragged and disheveled appearance for she had not seen him since the last child was born and then only fleetingly as he dare not leave his tasks. She stood momentarily aghast at his tousled uncut hair sticking out from under his cap. Then she saw the smiling face and her panic eased but still confused she shouted loudly towards the barn door, 'Jonas, you there? Come quick. Tom's here now.' Jonas emerged from the dark innards of the barn, to be quickly joined by Gracie who had heard Agnes's shout even inside the house.

Many frantic questions and answers later the whole story was told by Tom as he related the events of the morning to the delight of all. 'Aye I bumped into Albert about a month ago and he said he wer' looking for a good stock man who knew about horses, an' a' towd 'him about you but thought newt would cum of it. Just goes to show yer ner' know.' From Jonas explained how Mr Sowerbutts had come looking for Tom. But how he knew Tom would be there that day, that was a mystery but one that all were happy to accept as a coincidence or a blessing from God. Jonas knew the answer to the mystery but for once was keeping his own council for fear of Agnes accusing him of interfering again, for he had got an inkling of what Tom might do at hiring when Gracie had said on her last visit that Tom was undone at her working cleaning and had said it had to end. Certain that Tom would walk away from Windyfell, Jonas had made it his business the week prior to seek out Albert Sowerbutts at the local cattle market and mention that Tom might well be at the hiring. Jonas had given Albert a full and very glowing description of his son-in-law and hoped for the best.

Tom was getting restless. 'I need te be gone afore the Dixons find out I have called or y'll be in trouble, Jonas, an' anyhow 'A 'ave to be back at the Halls Arms in two hours,' he said, 'so I'd better be on mi way, I mustn't be late that'ad not be a good start,' he insisted, refusing the tea and food Agnes offered, his need for food and a drink forgotten and indeed gone in the rush of joy at what had happened. Jonas had explained approximately where he thought Albert lived which thankfully was only about four miles further down the valley. 'Oh and Mr Bailey what does initial strategy for moving our goods mean, for that was what he said we had to work out?'

Jonas smiled and quietly explained at the same time informing Tom that Mr Sowerbutts often had a longwinded way of saying things but he always meant well. Jonas promised to visit Tom the next day to arrange moving the family's goods and chattels over from Windyfell to their new place. Gracie anxiously asked her father if knew if there was a cottage when Tom had admitted that he had not asked, but Jonas had no close knowledge of the Sowerbutts' farm so Gracie's question went unanswered. Common comfort and relief gained by all at the seemingly resolved situation, Tom took advantage of the nearby water trough to scoop cupped hands of water first for a much needed drink and the rest rubbed around his still hot face. His eyes desperately sought those of his wife trying to convey his great

155

relief at the outcome of the day and was rewarded by a gentle smile and a softly uttered, 'Ah knew yer'd find somewheer.' Elated, his steps suddenly enlivened by this praise, Tom turned and happily waving set off at a brisk pace to meet Mr Sowerbutts.

Immediately Tom left the Bailey's home, Jonas set about working out how to remove the Briggs's goods from Windyfell to the new place, a task which he knew was not going to be easy or trouble free. Jonas as usual soon had a plan, so when his Dixon cattle work was finished till later in the day, he decided to make his way to Hall Farm yard to find Billy. Billy would, he was sure, be more than willing to help Tom and Gracie, and his size and strength would be invaluable in what Jonas knew was going to be a difficult task to claim the contents of the cottage from the premises belonging to old Shepperton who he was sure was going to object very strongly to their removal. Jonas had been working in the cattle buildings located well beyond the main farm buildings so the easiest way for him to reach the main farmyard was along the back lane, the same lane which finally wound its way to the cottages and Jonas's home. The lane had been planned, when the old hall had been built centuries before as the route connecting the outlying farm now owned by the Dixons, the main now long gone hall and leading finally to the home farm and yard now used by Jonas. Deep in thought, as he approached Hall Farm, and still considering how to organise the removal, Jonas did not see Mrs Dixon and her son Edward in the small, iron rail topped walled garden in front of the big farmhouse until he was nearly upon it.

Instantly stopping walking just in time, he could see they were so engrossed in conversation that they had not seen his approach so he quickly dodged behind the barn he was just passing. The last thing he wanted was to be questioned about why he was going to the house farmyard, that could lead to further questions. Standing motionless hidden behind the corner of the stone barn he could hear them conversing in a very animated manner, their raised voices carrying on the light wind. 'You really are going to have to curb your spending, Edward, your father is most displeased, and wants to know what you spend so much money on. I hope you are not wasting money on the local or servant girls again, or on beer locally, I don't like you lowering yourself by mixing with the local men. If your father were ever to find you intoxicated he would not be pleased, and there could be consequences.'

'Now, Mother, you know I never waste money, but you have brought me up to expect a certain standard in life, and sometimes the local hostelry can be useful and amusing. Surely you wouldn't deny me a little entertainment, life in the country is very boring. You and Father really should consider moving to town, London is so entertaining. You deserve a more genteel way of life, Mother, you should mix in better society, my dear.' Was the son's return at which Jonas decided he shouldn't be seen to have heard this discussion so as he knew that by skirting the building he would come to a route into the farmyard from another direction that was what he did. Walking very slowly and carefully avoiding making any sound, Jonas crept along the barn side then through its small side door, across the dim near darkness of the interior, and out of the small access door cut into the large main doors then out into the yard.

Unaware that their words had been overheard, the mother and son became even more deeply involved in the subject of money when Edward asked, 'Have you broached the question of my new horse, to Father? I really must have one long before the season starts so that I can have him well schooled, I can't afford to look a fool, if the horse plays up.'

'Fool,' his mother replied. 'I am beginning to think I am the fool in this house. I work to make your father save money, but you spend it faster than he can save it, I don't know where this is all going to end. You talk about me moving in more genteel society, I struggle to have the money to keep you with all you say you need.'

The young man's thoughts raced as he looked at his mother's aging face. His eyes captured hers, with the gentle touch of a lover his hand reached out to stroke hers as it lay folded over her other at her waist. 'Dear Mother, you know I only want to make you proud of me, and to do that I must shine in society which costs money. I know you will never let me down, you always provide what I need. There might soon be a golden opportunity to have more money than you could ever have dreamed of, Mother.'

Edna Dixon eyed her son suspiciously. 'What mad scheme have you come up with now, Edward? I am not allowing you money for something like that last wild idea.'

Edward decided he had said enough for the moment, he needed to have a word with his father so. 'Oh no, Mother, this a very different proposition and one I am sure you are going to like.' After which he kissed her fleetingly on the lips, smiled as he turned and walked into the house. Mrs Dixon stood for a moment, the years falling away as she remembered holding a small curly haired baby who had stolen her heart and who she knew would always hold it captive. She sighed, admitting defeat as she entered the house, deliberating how to further save even more money.

Jonas knocked on the back kitchen door of the farmhouse, in order to ask where he would find Billy, but with no answer he knocked for a second time but still to no avail as it remained firmly closed. Sally or one of the other maids would usually answer the door but if they were not about he did not want to risk Mrs Dixon coming to open it as she would certainly question why he was there and he could not think of a possible answer, so he walked away to look around the yard. As Jonas's job at the farm involved working with the cattle and that meant his time was spent in the cattle sheds and far shippons he had little knowledge of the other general workings of the rest of the farm, other than occasionally calling at the house yard and farmhouse. Glancing further along beyond the domestic buildings to the range of yard farm buildings on the other side of the yard, he heard sounds of a clanging bucket coming from behind the door of a stable that he did know was sometimes used as a bullcalf pen for holding selling stock. He knocked now upon this door at the same time shouting 'Hello' to whoever was behind, only to have it also remain shut and his call unanswered. This was getting him nowhere, he thought, and so patience running out, Jonas knocked again, then turned the heavy iron ring latch handle and opened the door to find a muddy looking Billy lying full length in the dung and straw strewn calf pen. The noise Jonas had heard was the sound of the calf in the back of the pen eagerly licking out an empty bucket and by doing so knocking it against the pen's stone wall. First thinking that Billy was ill or injured he quickly bent down only to be met by a strong smell of foul whiskey. Instantly recoiling from the spirit stink he saw the red sleeping face of the big man, and in an instant the urge was too great and his hand struck the slumbering figure hard on the cheek, at the same time shouting at the motionless body, 'Wake up, yer drunken soak, yer kettled.' The effect was little as Billy simply rolled over with a grunt, now face down in the filth on the pen floor. Jonas now even

159

more incensed stamped outside to the yard trough, filled a waiting bucket and returned to empty the contents over Billy's head. The effect of the deluge of chilly water was instant as Billy immediately struggled to his feet and the calf cried out as the big heavy man fell against it, pushing it against the wall, before finally gaining his feet. As he rose he saw Jonas standing waiting with the look of thunder on his face, and as he became upright with a look of sheer fear, he glanced fleetingly at Jonas then ran off in the direction of the main stables and the loft above. Jonas knew Billy slept above the stables, and regardless of his lack of authority to enter the stables and the workers accommodation above, being only a worker himself, indignation drove him to follow Billy. After clattering up the open wooden stairs Billy tried to close the loft door to keep Jonas out but the older man fuelled by anger was too quick for the still half asleep Billy and quickly stuck his clog in the doorway. Prevented from closing the door Billy headed for the furthest corner of the room, where the ceiling sloped to a low side wall, and bending low to lean against the wall slid down into a quaking heap. Jonas did not rein back his condemnation as he stood threateningly over the cringing Billy who received the full brunt of Jonas's tongue, finally threatening the young man with, 'An' if yer don'st start pullin' thysell tergether a'll be speakin' ter Mr Dixon. I wer responsible for bringing ye 'eer an it looks bad on me.' Poor wet Billy was contrite, enthusiastically claiming he would change his ways, but as Jonas left him having gained his full promise of his help with the flitting on the coming Sunday, he knew that the drink problem would not be ended that easily.

When Jonas arrived home a little later, Tom was waiting for him, having been sent by Mr Sowerbutts. 'To save his father- in-law the journey to the Sowerbutts Estate, to discuss the removal.'

And also being instructed in the course of his trip to Jonas's to call in town and get his hair cut and a buy a new jacket and trousers with money provided by way of a 'sub' on his future wages. It was a Tom with a much altered look who again had arrived unannounced outside Agnes' back door. The smile on her face was only outshone by the smile on Gracie's face when at a call from Agnes she came to meet her smiling husband. Gracie ran to throw her arms around Tom exclaiming at his wonderfully changed appearance, but sighing he immediately but gently pushed her away. For just a moment their eyes met, but it was enough so Gracie was satisfied that all was well. 'No, lass, I must be off, tell thee faather when he arrives home that I'll be go and wait for him up on't main road. I am not going te risk getting him i' trouble with't Dixons by waiting here.' Tom did not have long to wait for as soon as the message was relayed when Jonas came home, he turned about and headed for the road, curious to see the changed man that Agnes had so enthusiastically described.

'Very good on Mr Sowerbutts t' send ye Tom.'

'Aye, Mr Bailey, but rather think he was more concerned with getting me tidied up on the way here. I don't think he wanted any of his customers t' see me in the state I was in,' suggested Tom with wide smile.

'Aye, Tom thee could weel be reet, tha were a fer untidy mess.' Was the return with an equally wide smile. 'Reet well we'r set for Sunday morning, meet yer outside Shepperton's gate a' seven o'clock.'

Tom nodded agreeing to these instructions. 'Right, Mr Bailey sir, I 'ad better be off. Oh and I nearly forgot will ye tell Gracie, for I forgot to tell her in mi rush, that there is a grand little cottage for us at Mr Sowerbutts', I'm sleeping over the stables there for now.' At which he turned to make his way back to Mr

161

Sowerbutts'.

True to his promise a very quiet and subdued Billy arrived at the Baileys' door on Sunday morning, his duties at Hall Farm carried out in double quick time he had been told by Jonas not to let anyone know where he was going or even that he was going anywhere in case Dixon or Shepperton got wind of what was afoot, the big man stood waiting, his cap screwed in his hands, for he was expecting further chastisement. But Jonas had other concerns so quickly nodded at Billy and told him to get up on the cart so they could get moving. Billy, thinking back on what had happened, had duly accepted how the timely arrival of Jonas had probably saved him from discovery by one of the other farm workers or even Mr Dixon himself. Understanding his lucky escape he swore to work very had for Jonas this day, and also in future to refuse Mr Edward's invitations to visit the whiskey spinner where they had been drinking the night before the morning Jonas had found him. Whenever the young Dixon invited Billy out Billy always refused, as he had promised Tom to do after the snowy night when Tom and Jonas had rescued him, but a little persuasion was all it took and Billy was won over and heading for trouble again. Jonas listened to the big man's promises uttered haltingly but without prompting as they rode along on the cart, glad that the lad saw the wrong in what he was doing, but doubting their full execution said, 'Well very good, lad, you just remember that but let's just now settle for getting the job in hand done today.'

'Aye, Mr Bailey, sir.' Was the quick reply, as he settled himself on the cart seat.

Travelling along the narrow rutted road towards Windyfell, Jonas had the chance to consider how they were going to approach old Shepperton who he was quite sure was going to object to the removal of the Briggs's goods even, thought Jonas, he is capable of claiming them to be his or forfeit in lieu of work. His concern was greater because Tom, when he had spoken to him the day before, elated by his new place and the cottage which came with it, did not seem to foresee the difficulties they might be faced with. Tom seemed to have purposely already put the terrible time behind him, just wanting to forget, finding himself now in such a good position. All weel an' good, thought Jonas but it has not gone by magic, it all has to be sorted out, cleaned up and finished. Well anyway, thought Jonas as they approached the even rougher muddy track and saw Tom standing by the broken gatepost leading to Windyfell, we are about to find out how it will end before very long. Jonas nodded at Tom. 'Reet, lad, hop on and we'll be off to do battle.'

Just as Jonas had surmised, Shepperton was waiting in the yard, obviously having heard their approach, and guessing that they had to come back to empty the cottage, he was standing hands on hips with his usual belligerent look upon his face. 'Thy's not 'aving stuff outa 'cottage. Thy owes me that in lost labour, Tom Briggs. So yer can bugger off.'

Calmly Jonas slowly stepped down from the cart motioning to the other two to stay where they were before they had a chance to follow his lead. 'Now,' he said very quietly but firmly, ' Mr Shepperton, yer know thy has 'ad yer money's worth outa this lad, we don't need any bother, and from what a' understan' yer ain't paid the lad any wages any how,' offered Jonas in a conciliatory tone.

Shepperton's tone also changed now almost to a whine. 'Surely thy ders't thy wont ter leave mi, Tom? We were getting on grand like, an yer misses were helping mi wi' house, meking a reet grand job on it. A' wer banna pay her thee knows. She were

163

meking such a reet grand job at cleaning up. A need ye both, how am I gunn'ta manage?' Jonas and Tom looked knowingly at each other at this ploy.

Jonas replied, 'Tha should a thought a' that afore, man, it's ter late now, they're gone elsewhere an' not comin' back,' returned Jonas deciding that the conversation had gone on long enough, at which he signalled to Billy to jump down from the cart.

As Billy landed with a noisy thud and clatter on the muddy yard cobbles, Shepperton took one look at the size of the big man, turned, swore profusely, followed by a sharply uttered, 'Bah, good riddance.' Then turned quickly crossed the yard and entered the farmhouse slamming the door behind him. The cottage had not been disturbed, which had been one of Jonas's concerns as he thought Shepperton might have done damage to the Briggs's furniture when they did not return, but all seemed intact so all three set about packing up the contents. As the three walked to and from the cart with furniture and the general contents of the cottage, Shepperton was to be seen moving about to watch them from several of the house windows. Once he opened the house door to shout across the yard, 'Mek sure tha teks nowt o' mine. Or a'll bi cumming ter get it.' But he never left the house again until they were driving from the yard.

The cart was soon loaded with pillows and blankets wedged between the wooden furniture, and ropes tied in place to avoid any loss of goods on the rough stony rutted lane. With Tom and Billy barely balanced perching on the cart sides, their feet resting on the cart's ridged frame sides, Jonas set off. Just as they passed between the broken leaning stone gatepost and its upright partner there was a shout and Tom looked back to see Shepperton standing at the yard entrance brandishing a shotgun in their direction as in a harsh tone just discernible at the distance he threatened them, 'Ner set foot o' me land again ar a'll use this on thee!' Now the job was done and thinking and finally allowing himself to understand it was finally over and he was very lucky to be out of it, Tom offered up a silent prayer of thanks along with a fervent wish never to see the old man or his farm again.

CHAPTER 18

The journey to Mr Sowerbutts' home was for the most part without problems except for two stops to adjust and secure the high piled load for even the ropes were failing to prevent the slipping of one piece of furniture against another, and Jonas did not want Agnes to find any scratches to incite criticism. The first time they had to stop was the first opportunity Tom had to speak to Jonas alone. 'I don't know proper how te thank ye, Mr Bailey. I alus seem te need yer help. Alus in trouble or meking a mess or summat.'

Jonas looked at the younger man's troubled face. 'Lad, we are put on this eer earth te elp one another, all 'a ask is yer look after our Gracie. Now let's be on our way, ther's werk te be doin'.'

Soon Tom's new place of work and home came into sight. As they passed between two very tall and very upright carved stone gateposts Jonas was fascinated to see atop one a carved horse's head and atop the other a carved bull's head. Hung from the posts and presently open invitingly wide, tall wrought iron gates each with a letter S inside an iron circle at their centre. Beyond the gates the smooth gravel drive was edged with a line of stone boulders. Jonas was very impressed so when a beaming Mr Sowerbutts came striding from the house to greet them he hurriedly jumped down from the cart, almost forgetting to tie the reins as he did so, and rushed towards him hand outstretched. 'By ek, Albert this lot's a sight t'b' proud on. Them theer gates are a fer bonny sight an' no mistek.'

'Well thank you, Jonas, I like them. I seek to convey, to all who enter upon my estate, what wonderful beasts I offer for sale. Do I not?' He quickly turned his attention to his new employee. 'Now, Tom, let's not dally, let's see about filling your cottage with your good lady's goods so that you can then go to collect her and your family from your mother-in-law's house, in order for them to settle into their new home.'

So with Mr Sowerbutts issuing instructions to all, the cottage was soon filled with Tom and Gracie's furniture and goods at which point Tom and Jonas were directed, 'To immediately take theirselves home to collect Mrs Briggs and her children. Tom, your good lady needs to be brought so she may unpack and instruct you to accordingly place her goods about and around her new abode. Ladies have I believe their own special touch when it comes to a house and home, my mother most certainly did and she was the most noble of ladies.' At which the two men were duly dispatched.

During the journey home, during which all three men tired after their exertions were for the most part silent, but Jonas could not resist. 'By 'ek that mon can't half tek it upon hisel' to organise folk.' At which point Tom discovered he had a sudden cough in order to disguise his amusement, Billy oblivious continued humming a cheery tune.

Albert Sowerbutts was a naturally generous man, partly perhaps due to never having had to struggle financially having been left the estate and business by his father, so he believed that he should share his good fortune with those who helped him make it, and that now included Tom and his family. They were soon settled into the cosy cottage located just a little way from the main house. Gracie stood with tears in her eyes when she saw the outside of the stone cottage and wept unashamedly when she saw the inside. The door and windows were painted cream and the glass of the windows clean and intact. Inside was just perfect, as she told her mother when she walked over for a visit a few days later, a real range with an oven like her mother's and a hot water tank at the side, and the white sink in the back kitchen even had a tap, a tap for water. Mr Sowerbutts believed in being modern. Gracie, when she had first entered the cottage, refused to sit down but instead kept wandering about their new home exclaiming every time she found a new delight, then at Mr Sowerbutt's encouragement, instructing the men where she wanted her furniture placing, while silently noting that it all needed more polishing to do justice to its new home. The walls even had wallpaper in the sitting room, and the two bedrooms, with flowers on it. A fact that Gracie later also later relayed to her Mother. 'Wallpaper i't sitting room, that's what Mr Sowerbutts calls it, my sitting room. I have a sitting room, Mam, with a proper fireplace and Mr Sowerbutts sez as he 'as some spare chairs we can 'ave for it.'

Mr Sowerbutts, they learnt, had never married, having never found 'quite the right lady' as he readily informed all who asked. 'A Lady such as his mother was what he had sought but never found, for his mother had been perfection in all things.' But he had his domestic needs catered for by 'Wilson, his man'. Arthur Wilson was a small timid man with thin flat hair and a habit of looking down when spoken to. Always eager to please in his own quiet way he happily turned his hand to all from cooking to laundry but refused to venture far from the house for fear of the outdoors. Tom learned from Mr Sowerbutts that Wilson's mother had never allowed out him to play with other children so his introvert nature had developed and at her death Albert's father had taken him in, and he had remained happily with the family ever since. This information Tom relayed to Gracie who was silent for a moment's consideration and then declared she was sure she would be able to help Wilson in some way or other to show their gratitude to Mr Sowerbutts. Wilson spoke little and when he did it was very quietly. He was inclined to walk very slowly always with eyes lowered only raising his gaze when he thought no one was looking. There was only one other worker at Fairacres, Sowerbutts' establishment, and he was also a very quiet man of few words, having been brought up in the workhouse he seemed to value his privacy greatly as a man who had seldom known such. Conscious of his tallness he tended to walk and stand with a stoop. He rarely ever smiled and had never been known to laugh, but Jack Heapy did the work of two men for he was Mr Sowerbutts' cattle man, and very proud of being in that position.

The arrival of the Briggs family changed many things at Fairacres. Firstly it changed Jack who had never seen happy children before, and he actually smiled at their antics and then still smiled as he worked. At the bidding of Mr Sowerbutts, the day after they arrived, Wilson braved the outdoors and visited Gracie in her cottage to see all was to her liking and within minutes Wilson and Gracie were friends, Wilson even raising his eyes to smile at a pleased Gracie. The meeting ended with Wilson returning to the house considering how he could further help the 'lovely lady' and with Gracie now vowing to be of help to both Wilson and Mr Sowerbutts in any way she could, to in some way thank them for what Gracie came to call their 'deliverance'.

Tom soon settled into the routine of the farm, quickly understanding how Mr Sowerbutts bought in the new stock to be improved before offering them for sale to new owners, and this included horses who often had to be well trained or retrained

169

before being considered suitable for sale, Mr Sowerbutts proudly never sold 'substandard beasts'. Tom loved the horses and it showed in the results so much so that Mr Sowerbutts exclaimed on entering the stables one morning, 'My my, Tom, it was a very good day when I employed you. You have got my requirements and the requirements of my wonderful beasts "to a tee", have you not?'

At which Tom replied, 'I hope so, sir, I am trying my very best.' Just managing to control the urge to add 'am I not?'

As Mr Sowerbutts moved away to other matters Tom returned to the horse he was schooling, leading the animal out, checking its shoes and that the bit was settled in its mouth before putting it through its paces, the animal confident and keen, the man happy and fulfilled. 'D'yer know, Roman, a' think thee and me al just a'ta go fer a trial ride up t' moor road an' see how yer do.' Moments later horse and rider left the gates of Fairacres and with the wind rushing past soon reached the quarry road. The wind was sharp this high its bite chilly as Tom had left without a warm jacket, the sudden feeling of cold on stopping brought a realisation of how change could happen so soon. Tom rode a little further, unable to resist, for he knew that just over a nearby wall he would be able to see Windyfell in the distance. He reined the horse to a halt and from his elevated position on the animal he could see the farm in the distance, but this far away it was only a group of buildings. The horse was becoming restless, a foot scraping at the loose stones of the road. 'Right ho, Roman, yer reet, time we went home, and I stopped tormentin' mi'sel, all that's in past, the future 'al bring what it must, surely it must bi better than what as gone.'

Gracie had just finished feeding the children at midday and had settled them down for a sleep, when reaching the bottom of

170

the stairs there was a loud insistent knocking at the front door. Quickly opening the door before the continued noise woke the children she was about to speak when all words were lost in an instant as there standing outside her door was an obviously impatient Edward Dixon. His eyes opened wide, his eyebrows raising, and then his mouth twisted in a sneering smile for he was evidently as surprised to see Gracie as she to see him. 'Well, well, if it isn't the little bird that got away. Last I heard you and your thug of a husband were on your way to the workhouse. I hardly expected to find you here. I was looking for Mr Sowerbutts' horseman as he and his employer come recommended as the source of a good hunter.'

Gracie was at a loss what to say but she just wanted rid of the man away from her house and although she really didn't want to tell him that the person he was looking for was Tom, she could see no other option, so quaking inside at the effort of calm speech she slowly answered, ' It is my husband you're looking for but he's not here at the moment, try the main house, Mr Sowerbutts should be in.'

'Really, well I never, landed on your feet haven't you both, well, I don't think I want to buy an animal that has had the hand of Tom Briggs upon it. I shall have to have a word with this Mr Sowerbutts about the standard of his staff.' At which he turned sharply on his heel, to make a point of turning his back on Gracie, and headed for the big house further down the drive. Gracie, relieved as she was to see him go, was distraught, she couldn't leave the children, she had no idea where Tom had headed after she saw him leave the yard on a horse, and she dreaded what Edward Dixon was going to say to Mr Sowerbutts. Gracie did not have long to wait for the second knock came on her door after what seemed only minutes. Gracie, her hands painfully clasped at her waist, waited for the worst when she saw Mr Sowerbutts standing outside her door, but the blue eyes twinkled as usual in the round cheery face as he happily informed her that he had, 'Sent the cocky young Mr Dixon on his way, hopefully never to set foot on my land again. Did I not? Told him he'd find a far better mount when he returned to London. London horses being far superior to those of Lancashire.' Gracie felt near to fainting as she comprehended what she had just heard. Then Mr Sowerbutts continued, 'Before I ever employed your good husband your father had fully explained what had gone before, and actually I had heard other stories from other sources relating to Mr Edward Dixon and his antics so the picture was quite clear. Never fear, dear lady, I know the value of your husband, do I not? Anyway I wouldn't want to submit one of my good horses to the kind of nasty treatment it would receive at the hands of such a man as Dixon.' At which he briefly bowed, rolled the tip of one side of his mustache and walked briskly back to his own house.

Tom returned to his cottage that night a satisfied and happy man, happily unaware of what had gone on during his absence, for to have his efforts complimented and to walk through the door of the cottage to see his wife sitting beside a warm fire whose flames were bathing the room in a soft golden glow, he was content beyond words. On nearing the hearth a tear formed in his eye as he saw the two small children asleep, one on either of his wife's shoulders, and her lovely face peaceful as she dozed. Quietly he placed a hand on either child for safety, as he spoke softly to the sleeping woman, 'Gracie love, are yer asleep?'

Instantly the bright eyes opened wide, and he saw he need not have feared as she grasped the children to her. 'We 'ave bin waiting for yer, lad.' Tom made no mention of Edward Dixon so Gracie could only assume that he had no knowledge of the man's visit so she had no intention of informing him, and she was now quite confident that Mr Sowerbutts would not be doing so either.

The year progressed and life at Fairacres was good for the Briggs family, Gracie often helping Wilson with baking and cooking in ways he was unacquainted with, but to his great appreciation. His hitherto unknown happy delight was obvious one day when he eagerly informed Gracie that, 'Mr Sowerbutts had complimented him on his recently improved meals.' Tom revelled in the knowledge his labours were appreciated and his knowledge of animals widened, Gracie blossomed in her third pregnancy and his children grew by the day it seemed.

Two happy years had passed with Gracie bringing two more girls into the world. Tom often found himself looking in wonder at his beautiful still raven haired wife as she fussed the blooming children or he simply cast his gaze around at the cottage or generally at his surroundings and he sighed satisfied in total disbelief at his good fortune.

Mr Sowerbutts' business was booming so much so that he had decided an assistant to Tom was required. When he broached the subject to Tom, there was a worrying, heart stopping moment as Tom thought initially that he was being dismissed until it was revealed by Mr Sowerbutts that his plan was for Tom and family to move into a smallholding that he owned, which was located a little way up the road nearer the village, so freeing the cottage for another man and family. 'You and your family will be most comfortable in the house at Daisy Croft, will you not, for it is a wonderful little farmhouse. You and your wife will be able to have a cow, for your own milk for the children and I have gathered your wife is a very good lady with the dairy, as I have seen her help Wilson when he was over busy, so you might be able to treat your employer to some Daisy Croft butter perhaps, might you not? You, Tom, will of course carry on in my employ, but will now become my steward and foreman and as befits such status will have a better abode, will you not?'

The picture now being made clear, along with Mr Sowerbutts' good intentions, Tom was elated beyond description, his head in a delighted spin he stole a few minutes of Mr Sowerbutts' time to relay the the joyful news to a soon ecstatic Gracie. 'Tom, I couldn't b' prouder if yer wer a lord, an we wer go'in ter live in a castle.' Was Gracie's reaction to the news, then she quietly added, 'Although I shall be very sorry to leave our cottage.'

Agnes and Jonas were equally pleased when quickly informed, complimenting Tom on his achievements much to the delight of a proud Gracie. 'Lad, yer 'ave showd yer metal, well done.' Was the pronouncement from a beaming Jonas. 'A knew yer wer a grand lad, an' 'ad it in ye, from the first moment a saw ye.'

Agnes looked in admiration at her daughter. 'What a lovely dress, Gracie. Is it new?'

'Aye, Mam, bought ready made, Tom said as I had to have one to show what a good job he has. Not boasting like, said a' were worth it.'

'Well it looks reet grand lass, he's a good lad.'

An added bonus of the move to Daisy Croft was it was closer to the home of Jonas and Agnes which allowed the couple more frequent visits to their daughter and her growing family. Happy that Gracie was settled, Agnes felt more confident while on a visit to confide her concerns about Jonas's health to her daughter. 'Thee faather is wostening of late, his chest is worse and he looks s' tired often, even in a morning o'late. After thee and Tom left, he ner took on any help. "Ner fund anybody like Tom," he said.

Our Dora and Sarah try help 'im but he doesn't like it, sez ther' ony fit fer weavin' an' housework, no bent fer animals like.'

Tom who had just walked in and heard the conversation glanced with an embarrassed look at Gracie before saying, 'I wish a could help Mrs Bailey, but I darens't set foot on yer place.'

'Ney, Tom, we know that, we'll manage, a just thought yer should know. Anyhow 'a must be off now, a need te bi meking summat fer tay,' replied the ever solid Agnes.

CHAPTER 19

'Jonas is not the only one with a bad chest,' muttered Agnes to herself as she puffed her way home, but quietly reassuring herself that it was all simply down to a recent chill, and her chest would clear up soon and she'd be back to normal in a few days, then philosophically thought, even if her knees would never be any better. Glad to be home she had prepared a pot of sliced potatoes and onions with a knob or two of precious butter, pushed it into the oven and just settled herself into a chair at the fireside when the back door opened very slowly to reveal a deathly pale Jonas. Instantly sensing something was amiss she rose to meet him only to see him stagger, but instantly recover, then slowly walk to his chair by the fireside and silently sit to gaze into the flickering flames. 'Jonas, what's wrong, lad, thy'r early home,' murmured Agnes quietly, thinking he was in pain, as she placed a hand on his shoulder.

The reply was slow and low, defeat in every syllable, 'It's finished, lass, gone, the lot, we've lost it, t' farm, aye and t' house. He just stood there and said he had sold the lot, sold my farm. Sold our house. We'll be homeless, we're fer the workhouse. No farmer will tek on an owd wreck like me, they'll think a'll a' n'work I' mi. How could he wi'out a hint, wi'out a warning? Never an inkling, lass, shows just how much we mean to him.'

Agnes was a moment taking in this sudden shocking onslaught trying to make sense of what her husband was saying, but recovered her wits sufficiently to demand, 'Jonas Bailey what are yer telling me, what d' yer mean?' As she spoke she moved to face the still trembling man to grab the shaking hands so as to still their sharp frantic movements. Jonas's voice broke with emotion as he further explained, 'Dixon's sold 'lot ter the Water Board. I remember seein' some fancy dressed strangers looking "round up there" few weeks ago, but thought nowt of it. A thought they were visiting young Dixon. Aye and m'be a wer reet. He's probably the one who's encouraged his faather, convinced 'im like. Cus he 'as ner had in'trest i' farmin.'

Agnes considered her husband for a moment before offering a reply. 'Now, Jonas please don't tek on so. We will sort this out together, you an' me like as we alus 'ave.'

Jonas looked at this wife, grateful for her cheerful confidence but knowing it was useless to hope. 'Nay, lass, the best we can hope for is te find somewhere te live, an' we've only got two weeks te do that. Th'animals 'll ave ter go, an' that definite, and straightway too. What are we go'in ter tell lasses, when they cum 'ome?'

'Truth, Jonas, as we alus ave.' Was the firm reply. Agnes moved to the kitchen range. 'Now, no messing we carry on as normal fer now, a've med summat to eat an' it's in the oven. We are banna need our strength. Sit by t' fire fer now until lassies cum 'ome, an' get warm ye'll feel better.'

Like in all family disasters, comfort is drawn from each other, and as later the couples' older daughters came home to be informed of the situation although the problem was not diminished, it was shared and in that sharing there was comfort. Jonas was persuaded that it was not his fault, that he was not to blame for the actions of the Dixons and on Dora adding the information that she had heard that the Water Board were out to buy all the land thereabout and build another new reservoir for they were short of water in Burnley and other near towns, Agnes turned to her husband. 'Theer, lad, it's not one bit thy's fault. If th're buying it all the're not goin' t'leave Dixons an' our bit alone.' The family began to console themselves with the knowledge that the farm's loss was inevitable, and they were not the only ones losing home and living. 'We'll survive, Jonas lad,' comforted Agnes, but even as she spoke the words, her mind was in a whirl searching for suggestions for their future for where to live and how to make a living. Sarah, ever practical, announced that, 'No one is banna starve while me an' Dora have our wages from 'mill, an' bosses are now planning adding a new shed te mill as trade is s' good.'

Dora put her hastily discarded shawl once more around her shoulders, offering to go and tell the news to Gracie and Tom, before they were informed by neighbours. 'For ye know bad news travels fast.' Were her parting words as she left the house.

Once Dora had left to walk down to Gracie's house, Jonas stirred himself, for the animals needed attention no matter what befell, so feeling his age and creaking bones much more than he had earlier in the day, he despondently trudged across the yard, then through the gate into the field and his waiting cows. Agnes watched him as he left and then moved to the window to follow his progress. She had never seen him so 'flat', Jonas was always the one to sort out any problems but this time he seemed defeated. 'He's aged ten year t'day, Sarah. It's knocked' life outta thee father, lass,' she muttered in a low sad voice to her daughter for she was sorely worried. Tea that night was a very quiet and sombre meal, Tom and Gracie had offered any help they could give but all saw that they could not turn the tide on change.

Later that evening as Agnes was waiting for Jonas to come in from his last check on the outside and the animals before they went to bed, standing by the back door waiting to hear his returning footsteps she was starting to be concerned after he had been gone twice the usual time. Opening the door and walking to the end of the house she shouted across the yard, 'Jonas, you there, where are yer.' But the silence was only broken by the low mooing of a beast. Concern finally overcoming her reluctance to have him think she was worried, she returned to the house, lit one of the storm lamps hung by the back door and, pulling a thicker shawl around her shoulders after putting on her old outside clogs left just inside the door, she crossed to the buildings on the far side of the yard.

Even as she walked towards the shippon she felt a strange stillness and noticed that although there was a shaft of light coming from the shippon window there were no sounds coming from any of the buildings.

She found him, sitting on a stool in the shippon, looking for all the world like he was about to reach for a milk bucket which was strange at this time of night, but then she realised he was leaning motionless against the wooden side of the stall, his eyes closed as in sleep but the slump of his body told her otherwise. 'Jonas lad, ar' thee asleep? Jonas lad cum on now wake up.' But as she spoke the words she knew in her heart there would be no answer. She reached forward, stroked the already chilling cheek and then straightened his cap which had slipped over to one side. Agnes stood silently for several minutes gazing at the man with whom she had shared so many years of hope, laughter and tears. Then she turned and released the halter of the cow waiting patiently next to her motionless husband and ushered it backwards out of the standing and along the shippon to a vacant stall. She returned to Jonas and again gently stroked his cold cheek, reluctant to leave him it being the acknowledgement that he was gone. She sat down on the spare milking stool that had been Tom's and gazed at the motionless man. 'Hey, lad, ah rather think tha'd had enough, ye wer tierd wen't tha, and now this; it wer all t'much.' Sitting there, the minutes passing, the silence only broken by the jangle of a cow halter, and in the darkness outside the cry of a hunting owl, the memories flowed and she smiled as she remembered. 'We've bin together a long while, lad. It's bin a good life.' Then with one last glance and sad fleeting smile Agnes left her husband to walk slowly back across the yard and return to the house. 'Dora, Sarah can yer cum back downstairs.' She shouted up the stairs. 'I need yer both outside.' Brought the girls down worried by the sharp broken voice of their usually cheerful mother. 'Lasses I have sad news te' tell yer. Thee father 'as passed away. A fun'd im outside i'nt shippon.' The two young women stood silently for several moments, until the shock registered into reality. Then both spoke suddenly, their natural reaction to try to comfort their mother with words and actions as they both stepped forward to touch the older woman. 'Now, go an' get dressed we 'ave a lot to do,' urged the practical Agnes.

As she waited for the two young women to dress and come down again, she plumped down on Jonas's chair as if unthinkingly to have contact with the last time she saw him alive. 'Ee, Nellie I could do wi you right now, lass. Help mi get thru this,' Agnes uttered under her breath, then turned as she heard her daughters arrive downstairs. 'Dora 'a need yer to go ter Gracie's an' get Tom, ney on second thought, wake up Elsie an' tek her wi' yer and you an' Elsie stay wi Gracie ter night. That's best. Childer'ner understand watt's goin' on.'

When Dora had left for Gracie's, Agnes motioned for her older daughter to sit in the chair opposite. 'Sarah we have a fair task i front on us, but we will get through never fear,' she told her.

Sarah nodded. 'Aye, Mam, we'll see it done don't worry. When Tom arrives a'll help 'im carry Faather in. We'll need a blanket.'

'Ee lass a'll fetch one, ye always were the strong en.' Agnes praised her daughter, pleased at her strength and support.

Tom soon arrived, leaving home immediately, Dora had explained what had happened not waiting for many details being anxious to get to Agnes's to help in any way he could, regardless of the fact that he should not go near the farm. Agnes and Sarah accompanied him to the shippon, the blanket over Sarah's arm. As they crossed the yard Tom expressed his concern about being on Dixon land, Agnes waved away his worries. 'Lad it ain't te'meke any difference now, we'll soon be off the place anyhow and a'll bi' telling Mr Great Dixon that a' need ye te help us, an' that's that. In the end the blanket was just wrapped around Jonas and Tom carried him in his arms, both Tom and Agnes shocked at the little weight of what had once been such a big solid man.

Mr Dixon, when informed later the next day, was all a show of concern, and offered any help but this was politely but firmly refused by an unconvinced Agnes. She wanted her own and certainly not the help of him and his kind as she firmly informed him that, 'We will be gone as yer wanted, as soon I can see him properly buried. An' a'll thank you if yer will allow Tom Briggs ter help wi animals and such, for the lasses and me will struggle wi out a man's help an' I don't think Jonas would 'ave wanted anybody else.'

This request was not to the landlord's liking but thinking quickly he agreed, telling himself that his son was away and his wife would never know, and anyway, if not, the clearing of the farm could take months, and that would not be to the liking of the Water Board and their waiting ready money. 'They wanted everyone and every thing off as soon as possible,' they had informed him only the day before.

'Why had the damn man to go and die?' he muttered to himself.

Mr Sowerbutts, as usual true to his generous good ways, allowed Tom any time he needed to arrange for the sorting and disposal of the animals and equipment, and in the end buying most of the stock and equipment himself to ease the process for he knew that Gracie and her mother Agnes would be comforted by the thought that Jonas's animals were sought after. In passing he remarked to Gracie that, 'Jonas Bailey knew how to pick an animal.' Knowing that this would make Agnes proud when this information was relayed to her as surely it would be. Tom found himself unable to sell Jonas's carthorse for he knew how much Jonas had thought of the animal, so it was moved to a new home at Daisy Croft, an action which moved a grateful Gracie to tears when she saw the old horse walking into their yard.

'Aw, Tom lad,' she softly murmured. 'Yer such a good lad, my love.'

The funeral was expected to be a quiet affair with only family in attendance, and one extra relation from Jonas's native Yorkshire. The arrival of this rather pompous individual, amused Tom who was surprised to find that Jonas like himself had hailed from east of the border. Sarah assuming the role of family head had written a letter to the Yorkshire relations informing them of Jonas's death, so quite rightly they had sent a representative who came in the form of Daniel Dickenson, a man who was very conscious of his position in life, and liked other people to also know of it, for he owned a grocers shop. 'Not just an ordinary grocers shop,' he quickly informed the family in his best well spoken pompous manner, 'but a very superior grocers shop selling superior and foreign goods to very well to do superior customers.'

Agnes for one was not impressed by Mr Dickenson with his fancy horse and trap and his high handed manner fancy clothes and top hat. 'For if he thought he could come and take over the funeral arrangements he was quite wrong,' she soon told her daughters. She was having none of it and soon informed him that she had sorted it all out and, 'That was that, but he was most welcome and to stay for the funeral tea after.'

He arrived several days before the day of the funeral, and he had fully introduced himself after his unannounced appearance at Agnes's door, she panicked thinking he would expect to be 'put up' but he had no such intention. 'I have arranged for a room at the local hostelry. It seems reasonably clean and they assure me that they have a very good cook, so we shall see,' he informed a very relieved Agnes whose only thought was 'Heaven help them.'

Agnes had planned a very small family funeral for she had not counted on how high the respect with which Jonas was held by his farming friends and neighbours and not just ones close by had been. Farmers arrived from miles away who Jonas had either dealt with for animals or feed or had met at sales and shows. Agnes was so shocked but quietly pleased when she saw the size of the crowd outside the church, and then, typically, she started panicking about how to provide food and drink. 'For all these people who must have thought highly of my Jonas, your faather. He would have been very proud to see such a congregation,' she whispered to Dora, but just at that point Mr Sowerbutts arrived and motioning to Sarah to join him for a word further down the churchyard informed her that his man Wilson was presently in the Bailey's barn setting up folding tables with pork pies, ham, bread and cheese, tea and light ale for those who would partake.

183

Mr Sowerbutts it seemed had come to realise while travelling around the area that Jonas was not to be allowed to go to his rest without due tribute.

Jonas arrived on the back of his own flat back cart, it being draped all in black cloth with a very smartly attired Tom driving, and his beloved carthorse proudly pulling the vehicle wearing fluttering black ribbons on his harness. The Sunday best dressed Tom and five neighbours, who had quietly and good naturedly argued for the right, carried Jonas into church between the rows of attentive men, followed by a very tearful but proud Agnes and family.

The last hymn sung, the burial party proceeded to the rear of the church to the open grave, and there, the graveyard crowded as seldom seen, Jonas was laid to rest, under the shade of a large ivy clad oak tree, by the side of the churchyard wall. Sarah touched her mother's arm. 'Now, Mam, we have to get home to offer that food an' drink to all these heer folk, for Mr Sowerbutts has organised it all wi' the help of Wilson and our Gracie, she's bin at it since 'early hours sez Mr Sowerbutts.'

Agnes walked through the barn doorway, looked at the crowd waiting for her and stopped, her eyes blurred with tears, but Mr Sowerbutts quickly stepping forward took her hand. 'Dear Lady, do come and sit at the table, you will have a very proud Jonas looking down on you, will you not?'

Sitting at the makeshift table Agnes was able to consider the kindness of Mr Sowerbutts and the efforts of Wilson, the mention of Gracie having been a party to organising the funeral tea, explained why she had been unable to see her daughter when she arrived at the church but on leaving had seen her and Tom standing at the back to the side of the doors. I have been a lucky woman, she silently thought to herself, never 'ad the sons Jonas so wanted, but mi husband and family could not 'ave been better. Life will go on no matter what, which just reminds mi, I must ask our Dora to nip int' house and draw back t' curtains, seeing as Sarah is insisting we 'ave to spend t' neet at her new house. They need to be pulled back straight after' funeral or folk will think ill of me, oh hy and she must check that the bread and ham and cakes a' 'ad med were brought out here to be eaten or tek em te' cottage fer us. Waste not want not. At which she went in search of Dora.

CHAPTER 20

Tom stood patiently in the kitchen by the back door of his mother-in-law's old home as she gathered up the last of the baskets and bundles, which contained what she had called 'the last of her worldly goods'. Afraid of seeming to interfere but desperate to help, he reached out a hand to lift a large bundle contained in an old sheet which had been firmly knotted at the top to hold it together. Agnes turned and looked at the bundle as if Tom's action had suddenly brought it to her attention. 'D'yer know, Tom, that bundle is like my life, some stuff in it came wi' me and Jonas when we cum 'ere, then the's stuff a' used when we was young when babies was born, and then theers stuff I 'ave just now stripped off of mi bed.' Tom hesitated unsure whether to carry the bundle out to the waiting cart, or wait for Agnes to say. Instead of moving towards the door she suddenly sat down on one of the remaining chairs as if weary of the whole matter. 'It was for the best for the lad, his heart was broke yer know, he'd never 'ave been 'appy agen. When I foun' him it seemed reet tht it should end in that theer shippon, he would ner a bin 'appy anywhere else tha' knows. Right then, cum on let's get this stuff on't cart, Our Sarah will 'ave the kettle on by now, in that new cottage of hers, it's gone half a' hour since she went on. Got gas it 'as for leet and a gas ring for boilin' even, how's that?' At which she bustled out of the door without looking back, out of the house which had been her home for over thirty years.

Tom carried the last bundle to the cart then returned to the house, where quickly mounting the stairs, he checked both rooms to make sure nothing had been forgotten. 'By heck, Mrs Bailey, thee musn't have left a speck o' dust o' these 'ere floors,' he told the empty rooms as he saw how clean they were. On once more leaving through the kitchen he glanced around, shrugged at the emotions and memories chasing through his head and went outside considering if he should check the buildings, then thought better of it as he saw the cart loaded high with furniture with a rolled mattress atop and a waiting Agnes. She was sitting on the cart seat clutching a large basket piled high with food wrapped in cloths. 'A'll cum back later on mi own,' he muttered to himself as he stepped up to the seat at the same time wondering how Agnes had managed to climb up to that high seat without any help. He flicked the reins and the cart moved off. Tom glanced at his passenger to see she was sitting very stiff backed and looking straight forward, her hands on the basket handle white at the tightness of her grip on it. Fearing to upset the woman for whom he had such great respect, he followed her lead and rode on in silence, the only sound the horses' hooves on the stone road and the creak of the harness.

Suddenly Agnes turned to Tom and asked, 'Tom, can we mek a quick stop at' grave on' way? Mr Throughton said 'stone would be put up this morning an' 'ad like ter see it.'

'Aye sure, 'ad like ter see it myself.' Was the instant reply from Tom after which the journey was continued once more in the same thoughtful silence.

Tom, stopped the cart outside the iron church gate, jumped down and quickly moved round the vehicle to help his less than agile mother-in-law to the ground, thinking that the descent might be more dangerous than the climb up, but not before glancing down the far side of the church to the area of the graveyard where Jonas's plot was situated. He was relieved when he could see the new bright clean stone point towering above Its neighbours on the far side of the churchyard. The two slowly walked the grass path towards the grave, Tom impressed by the stone's height and magnificence. Agnes sighed contentedly on seeing that it was as grand as Mr Throughton had promised, with a pointed top and carved leaves and flowers, and then she saw the lettering and a smile lit her face. Tom's immediate concern at this strange reaction was soon calmed when she cheerfully announced, 'Well,Mr Throughton, thy's done t' lad proud, thy's promoted him ter gentry an' living i' th' Hall. The lad'll be pleased, bless 'im. Money from his cattle paid for it yer know, seem'd only reet.' The woman, now silent, gazed around the peaceful green and upright stone scattered scene for a few moments, then spoke again. 'Now, Jonas lad, you rest content a'll be back to visit yer termorrer.' At which she turned to walk back to the cart. Tom reread the wording, then saw the omission of the words 'Farm Cottages', smiled to himself, then quickly turned to catch up with Agnes who with a sudden spring in her step had just disappeared round the corner of the church.

Sarah turned to watch her mother as she lifted a large brown pot from the fireside oven. 'It's a lot easier than t'other up at farm, it being higher, int'it, Mother?' she proclaimed proudly.

'Aye 'tis 'an no aguing,' agreed Agnes, silently thinking, aye better but not t' same.

Sarah was very proud of this cottage, for it was rented in her name she now being the sole wage earner. Dora had stunned all when she announced that she was going back to Yorkshire with the half-cousin Daniel Dickenson who had come to attend the funeral. He was considerably older than her but had offered to marry her and take care of her daughter Elsie as his own. It seemed that Mr Dickenson, who was unmarried, thought that a wife would be very useful on social occasions, for as he informed them in his usual high handed manner, with the growth of his business his social standing was rising and with that came invitations to events and the like and a wife would complete his appearance. 'On the way home we will spend two days in Manchester to allow me to choose new clothes for you and the child, your present appearance will not do at all. When we arrive home in Yorkshire I will engage a teacher to correct your and the child's mode of speech before you go out into society, and we will inform all concerned that the child was the result of a young marriage which ended when the father was killed in a farm accident soon after her birth.' At which Dora, although speechless for several moments after Mr Dickenson's announcement, it being a great opportunity but delivered in a quite uncomplimentary manner, had then on quick consideration decided that she was very lucky to receive such an offer and had quickly agreed.

So Sarah and Agnes were just the two in the cottage and were they agreed very comfortable, and the mill where Sarah worked was 'only a stone's throw away' as she informed all. Agnes as she heard her eldest daughter enthusiastically explaining their happiness at their new home to Gracie and Tom proudly thought, Aye, Jonas, yer passed on yer organising ways.

The cottage was nearly new having only had one previous tenant for a short length of time who as Agnes said had, 'Not been in it long enough to do any harm and put his stamp on it.' For he had been a tackler at the mill who soon after he moved in had been offered a better job Blackburn way. Their new home was in one of the new rows of houses being built alongside the new and developing mills of the area. To Sarah's delight each cottage had its own backyard with a backgate which would bolt for privacy, but Agnes had an initial fear and concern and that was the privy in the yard and each cottage had its own.

'Non of your owd fashioned sharing,' boasted a proud Sarah. Agnes's concern was the 'New fangled privy'. for it was a tumbler and she was of the opinion that 'Something could fall down that terrible hole' which took away the waste.

The builders had installed the sewer which ran along the length of the cottages under the privies. 'Mam, it's the modern way, no emptying tubs. The Twentieth century comes in a few years and we have to move with times.'

'Aye, that's as might be but I heerd tell of a lass who sent a babby down one. Who' drank summat and then sat on it waiting, an' it come but it got stuck in the swivel bit an' she had to own up. A reet t'do it weere.'

'Probably all a tale, Mam, folks don't like change.' Was the quick reply from Sarah. Agnes looked at her so earnest daughter, standing hands on hips in her new and fashionable clothes bought ready made from the Co-op drapers shop and sighed, but she was proud for she saw that Sarah was a part of the future.

Agnes moved to sit by the fire, in Jonas's old favourite rocking chair that had come from the old house. Moved a cushion into her aching back and settled to gaze into the fire and remember, but she also told herself to be 'Ruddy careful on that privy not to drop owt down that theer hole'.

Tom and Gracie and the again newly increased family were well settled in the little farmhouse at Daisy Croft, Tom leaving early each morning for Fairacres, with Gracie happily at home to see to family and their own stock, and now with a cow for milk sometimes able to make her own butter which was a great luxury compared to the usual dripping to spread on bread. Mr

Sowerbutts had received the block of butter he had hinted for and Gracie had delighted in the giving of it to him. The little farmhouse at Daisy Croft was beyond anything that Tom and Gracie ever hoped to live in. They had their own little farmyard and small yard and buildings and an acre of land where the cow lived and grazed along with several hens. Tom was even considering buying a couple of pigs. Life was once more comfortable and safe like it had been before they had to leave the cottage at Beckersley Hall farm, even better, but again in the quiet of night, Tom worried. He tried to dismiss this anxiety but it persisted. 'Just a daft old worrier I am,' He told himself. He could not find any reason to confide in Gracie and he was sure that she had no concerns so it was just him and the night.

Tom, suddenly woken by loud insistent knocking at the farmhouse door, almost falling out of bed in his haste, crossed quickly to the window. The casement stuck for a moment swollen by the recent heavy rain, then gave way to fly suddenly sideways. Almost losing his balance, shouting 'hello' even as he thrust his head through the opened space, Tom looked down to see Arthur Wilson standing below. 'Arthur, what's 'matter, lad it's barely getting up time.' And by the light of the storm lamp he was carrying, Tom could see his distraught face.

Then the man's tearful voice carried faintly up to the window. 'Oh, Tom it's 'Master, Mr Sowerbutts a' thinks as 'is dead, please cum.'

Tom's emotions flooded wildly about his head, but in a calm voice he shouted down, 'Reet, Arthur a'll be reet down.'

Then he turned to the bed to see a confused Gracie, roused from sleep at the voices. 'Tom what's up? Who's thee shoutin' at?'

'It's Mr Sowerbutts, Gracie, Arthur's down below a'm going

down now.' At which he grabbed his trousers and shirt from the bed foot and, struggled in his haste taking twice the time it should to don them, all the while trying to explain to a sleepy Gracie that Arthur Wilson had been knocking at the door and was at present standing outside in a very upset state and that he thought Mr Sowerbutts was dead.

Gracie lost no time in getting herself out of bed, dressed as quickly as possible and hurried down the stairs to see what Arthur had to say. Arthur was in the kitchen by the time Gracie arrived downstairs, sitting in a chair by the fireside. Gracie instinctively moved to the hearth and stirred the banked down fire which immediately blazed and helped light the room better than the single lamp that Tom had lit. She could see that Arthur was trembling, his hands shaking as he wiped his eyes. 'Now calm down, Arthur, what makes thee think Mr Sowerbutts is dead?' Her voice gentle, she dragged a stool close to and sat next to the distraught little man.

Arthur gulped, seemed to calm a little then all in a rush explained, 'A' weer awake, a' don't sleep such thy knows an it weer just a bit since and a' heerd this terrible bump an' bang come reet from his bedroom. A' went ter' door and knocked and called Mr Sowerbutts but theer weer no answer. A' knocked agin an' all weer quiet so a' went in an' theer he weer on't floor. I couldn't lift im h'e ter big. He wouldn't answer so a come fer thee. Did 'a do reet',Tom?'

Tom's mind was racing for as Arthur had been talking he had been thinking and his thoughts were worrying. He saw their lives being torn apart again, then immediately calmed himself for he could be jumping to all the wrong ideas. 'Aye, Arthur ye did reet to come for me. Now Arthur cum on let's go and see what's 'appened. A'll not get the cart, we'll be quicker walking, that's if

192

thee can manage all'way back.'

'Aye Tom a'll be fine a've had a little rest now.'

At a quick pace they soon reached the home of Mr Sowerbutts, arriving to find the front house door open as Arthur had left it in his hurry. Tom climbed the stairs, just stopping to light a lamp left at the foot of the stairs, thinking as he did so that he was taking a lot upon himself in the private home of his employer, but he could see no alternative. As he reached the head of the stairs he realised that Arthur had not followed up. 'Arthur, are yer cumming up?'

'Oh, Tom can a stay down here, a don't like it?' Was the faint reply.

'All reet, Arthur, a'll soon be down. De ye think as ye could go fer Doctor, that's best?'

The next reply was almost eager for Arthur wanted to get out of the house. 'Reet a'll go now.' And then Tom heard the front door close noisily as he left.

Tom was himself uneasy but thought it his duty to enter the bedroom, for Arthur had said it was the first door on the landing, and attend to his employer. Mr Sowerbutts had fallen on his side so Tom could easily place a hand on his forehead, he wasn't sure how to tell if a person was dead but there was no movement from the old man and his head felt very chilled. Deciding that he had best not move him he went back down stairs and outside to stand and wait in the approaching daylight. The Doctor seemed to arrive very quickly, patients of Mr Sowerbutts' standing were not to be kept waiting. He quickly disappeared into the house and soon arrived back outside to the two waiting men with a very solemn expression on his face. 'Aye you're right, lads, Mr Sowerbutts is dead. I think he knew that this could happen so a couple of years ago he told me the name of his local solicitor, very organised to the end was Mr Sowerbutts so I will send a messenger to him. I will arrange for Mr Sowerbutts to be moved to the undertakers. Tom as you are the most senior so you are in charge, I think it best you inform the other workers and carry on as normal until the solicitor arrives.'

Tom just wanted to go home to Gracie, sit down and think. It's all gone wrong again, kept screaming through his head, but instead he did as the Doctor had bid him and set about organising the other workers. How to let Gracie know was his first concern so he sent Arthur back to Daisy Croft to stay with the children, and to ask Gracie if she would come to him. Gracie by the time she arrived had thought as she walked and like Tom she was worried. 'Tom, a'm reet sorry about Mr Sowerbutts but what is te' 'ah happen to us now we could soon be out of job and house.' Because this was the conclusion she had come to on the journey to Fairacres.

Tom was tempted to lie and then decided the truth was best. 'Gracie a' don't know, we'll have te wait an' see.' At which the two parted, Gracie to home and Tom to his duties, still over awed by his sudden elevation to manager, but determined to do his best for Mr Sowerbutts.

The solicitor arrived later that morning along with his clerk who was carrying a large leather bag. Shouting to Tom, who had thought it best to stay around the yard, to attend to his trap and horse he disappeared into Mr Sowerbutts' house. He and the clerk appeared again about two hours later the leather bag obviously well filled, presumably with many papers, by the way the clerk was struggling to carry it.

He signalled to Tom to come over for instructions. 'I understand from the worthy Doctor that you Mr Briggs are the most senior and very responsible so I leave you in charge. I

194

should be back in two days and when I arrive I expect you to assemble the workers in the house kitchen to hear what instructions Mr Sowerbutts has left.' Harry Taylor who now lived in Tom's old cottage had brought round the solicitor's trap so then he quickly settled himself onto the vehicle's seat, urged his clerk to 'Hurry up man' and the trap disappeared down the drive.

True to his word the legal gentleman arrived mid morning on the second day along with the very well dressed solicitor from Manchester. Both gentlemen quickly disappeared into the house, indicating to Tom that he should follow. Arthur Watson had not wanted to stay in the house, and had been living with Jack Heapy over the stables, so no one had entered the house after Arthur had quickly cleaned any mess in the house or kitchen and collected his belongings. He had not really wanted to do any of this but Tom knowing his fear had asked Gracie to help him, her offer being very gratefully accepted. This leaving of the house seemed to meet with the approval of the Manchester solicitor who proceeded to arrange his papers on the large kitchen table, pull a chair close, and then told Tom to assemble the workers, but first he had to push all the other chairs under the table in case any workers thought to try to sit down.

Mr Berisford, as the Manchester gentleman announced was his name, informed the gathered men that Mr Sowerbutts' will would be read in Manchester, and was none of their concern other than for matters which did affect them. 'I will now inform you of those said matters. Tom Briggs you are left the sum of a hundred guineas, Arthur Wilson you are left the sum of a hundred guineas and instructed to buy a small cottage, Jack Heapy you are left the sum of a hundred guineas and instructed to buy a small cottage, Harry Taylor you are left the sum of fifty guineas. You all have been left a letter of reference for any prospective employer. Mr

Higgins, Mr Sowerbutts' local solicitor. I will now hand out the aforementioned money and letters. You are all to be paid full wages for as long as you are required to help the auctioneers to set up the property, stock and goods, and assist with the auction sale. Mr Higgins will be in attendance for the auction after which you are all to leave the premises. I would add that at leaving you must only take with you what is your own property, even if they are items which have been omitted from the auction. I will inform you that Mr Sowerbutts will be transported to Manchester for burial.' After he had finished speaking the room was in total silence, until Tom cleared his throat and informed the men that they could leave the house.

Arriving home, having left some very disturbed men at Fairacres, Tom walked into the kitchen at Daisy Croft, his mind in turmoil. He crossed to the fire and sat down slowly in the ladder back chair at the hearth side. Gracie, leaving the sink where she was washing pots, her face having a very serious expression, she came to sit in the chair opposite her silent husband. 'Well, Tom, what has that legal man said?'

Tom looked at his wife and just wondered where to start, then decided to make it simple for it had to be said. 'Lass, Mr Sowerbutts has left us a hundred guineas in his will but we are out of home and job, every thing has to be sold.'

Gracie made a quick intake of breath, then said in a great rush, 'No, not agin, we are homeless agin?'

'Aye, lass, but this time we aren't pennyless, thanks t' Mr Sowerbutts. He could not help us any more but he's left us money and a reference to help us all get work, an' a' don't think as how that solicitor were reet 'appy about it, but he couldn't alter it.' The next half hour was spent in Tom explaining and telling and Gracie listening wordless except for the occasional gasp or nod.

Mr Sowerbutts was duly moved to Manchester to be installed in the family tomb for it seemed, as they were informed by a rather piqued Doctor who had been paid and dismissed very quickly by the local solicitor, Mr Sowerbutts' father had been the younger son of a very wealthy family and now he was returned to it as it seemed had been his father and mother. Tom and the Doctor both smiled when the Doctor told him that the local solicitor had been equally summarily discharged of any great authority but had been informed by the Manchester solicitor, that he was required to supervise the auction proceedings. 'So what will you do now, Tom?' asked the Doctor.

'Find a new place, sir.'

'I think I might be able to help you there, lad. There will be no cottage but you have the money to buy one, the good Mr Sowerbutts saw to that.'

Tom looked up at this. 'Really, sir?'

'Yes the carrier on Burnley Road is looking for a new horse man cum driver. He is an acquaintance of mine and a decent man, you could do worse. Tell him I sent you.'

'Oh thank you, sir, a'll get away early today and go te' see 'im, they can't sack me fer doing that now can they?'

'No, lad, true that time has gone. Good luck.'

Tom feeling like a great weight had been lifted from him smiled at the Doctor and once more uttered, 'Thank you, sir.' As they parted.

CHAPTER 21

The carrier seemed a good man at first meeting and when Tom informed him that he was Mr Sowerbutts' horse man and had been sent by the Doctor the job was his. It seemed that Mr Arkroyd had heard of Tom's skill with horses. 'Aye, lad, yer reputation comes before ye, heard of ye being called a great horse man, an' that's summat.' Tom, quite taken aback by this compliment blushed, fortunately the carrier did not notice Tom's embarrassment, but continued, 'So if it suits ye all we have te' do is settle thee wages and hours and the job is sorted.'

It was a very relieved and happy Tom who with a light step made his way home to Daisy Croft. Entering the kitchen being in a very different frame of mind from when he left, he remained standing just inside the back door guessing Gracie would have heard him arrive. He heard her coming as she closed the little sitting room door, waited for her to enter the kitchen then with a big smile quickly placed his hands on either side of her waist, lifted her slightly from the floor and spun them both around. Dismay on her face, Gracie placed both hands on his chest. 'Tom Briggs have ye taken leave o' yer senses? Put mi down.'

'Nay, lass 'a 'ave the best news, a've got a job, an' a good en, horse man and driver for Mr Arkroyd the carrier on Burnley Road. Said as he 'ad heard tell 'a was a great horse man, how's that, thee husband's a great horse man?'

'Aw, Tom that's just wonderful, 'an te be told ye 'r a great horse man, mi dad would 'a bin proud an 'a know Mam will be, an so am I. Now all we have te do is find a home.'

'Aye, a'l start looking termorrow, a house or cottage we 'ave the money thanks to Mr Sowerbutts, bless him.'

The day was set for the auction, advertised on signs and in newspapers, the auctioneer's staff came to issue instructions on how the men had to set out everything on the estate. Even Gracie's help was requested to help sort out the contents of the house into boxes, piles and bundles. Everything from Mr Sowerbutts' own trap to the last brush and bucket in the yard was given a number by the auctioneer's staff. The day of the auction arrived, the auctioneer's voice ringing out from early in the morning. The crowds arrived early for the animal stock was sold first so that it could be removed soon to new homes, so lessening any chance of distress. Leading the last horse named Whistler, into the makeshift selling ring of straw bundles, Tom brushed a tear from his eye for it had been a favourite of his master, then as he listened to the rising price the pride rose in him as he watched the horse stand proud and another bid was forthcoming. Not a single animal was unsold. The house and estate were all sold together, including Tom's old cottage, for a splendid price followed by the same buyer securing a lot of the goods and chattels. It seemed someone wanted the place as it was, which pleased Tom. He was sure Mr Sowerbutts would be watching with that familiar smile and a twist of his mustache.

Having found a brush which had escaped the auction, Tom was sweeping the yard when the solicitor who had remained in the house for the day, emerged along with auctioneer. Obviously finished adding their figures, they both seemed pleased with the day's work. The solicitor purposefully crossed the yard to Tom, 'Now, my man, Tom Briggs isn't it?'

'Aye, sir, a good day, sir.'

'That's as might be but not your business to discuss, I'll thank you.'

'Sorry, sir.'

'Right, Briggs, now see all the workers leave the premises, empty handed please. You have checked that all animals and goods have been removed, except items bought by the purchaser of the estate?'

Tom unimpressed by the man's rudeness simply nodded but at the scowl he received relented and answered, 'Aye, sir.'

The solicitor seemed satisfied that he had rightly put this upstart in his place so carried on, 'In this bag is a chain and padlock, when you leave, and make sure you are last, wrap the chain to secure the gates and insert the lock to make it safe. Then leave the key with the Doctor, he is acting as my representative in my absence. You and the other workers will be able to collect any wages from him in two days' time, my clerk will be calculating them as we speak.'

This was obviously the end of the conversation for he turned and walked to his waiting trap, climbed aboard, checked the auctioneer was safely and comfortably alongside on the seat, flicked the reins and disappeared down the drive. Mr Higgins it seemed had, in the absence of his Manchester superior, regained some of his original arrogance.

Tom knocked on the Doctor's door, as he stood waiting he lifted his weight from foot to foot for they ached, it had been a hard and tiring day and his head hurt with all the noise and goings on. The Doctor opened the door standing back invitingly to allow Tom to enter. 'Hello Tom, been a busy day, come in?'

'Aye, sir. But 'a won't cum in thanks 'a think 'a need to go home for a sit down.'

'Aye, lad, I dare say it has been hard work'.

'Here's the key and 'a am fer sorry 'a havn't bin to thank ye fer t' job at carrier's before now but 'ave been reet busy.'

'Not to worry, lad, congratulations,' said the Doctor smiling.

'Well thanks agin, Doctor, a'll see thee in a couple of days fer me wages.'

'Right, Tom you be off to your good wife.'

The walk home was short but crowded with thoughts and memories. 'Mr Sowerbutts, 'a hope yer at peace,' he uttered quietly. 'A owe yer a lot, a think 'a might owe yer mi life, fer it wer not goin' well afor' 'a met thee. Bless ye.' At which he arrived home and prepared to retell the events of the day to Gracie.

Just as he had told the Doctor, Tom started his search for a new home the next day. His quest was soon fulfilled, as he found a cottage just on the edge of the village, so not far from Agnes and Sarah. When Gracie saw the cottage she was more than happy with it from the outside and when she saw the inside, which had been modernised by the owner before he had tried to sell it, she was delighted. The seller, a very smartly dressed middle aged man, explained that he was selling it because his mother had just died and she had lived there since she married and he had been brought up there, but he now lived in a house in Burnley where he was a mill manager. Being larger than the sort of terraced house that Sarah was renting, Gracie was dubious as to whether they could afford it. When they went upstairs to see the bedrooms, Mr Brown stayed downstairs, which gave Gracie the chance to quickly express her concerns. 'Tom are ye reet sure as we can afford this cottage> It's grand but it's a lot of money.'

'Gracie, we have the money from Mr Sowerbutts.'

'Are ye sure? It's reet grand, a white pot sink an' a better range than Sarah, it's just like the one at' cottage at Fairacres. An' it's clean, nothing broken.'

So the family had a new home, the cottage was called Ivy Cottage. The children were a bit confused at first and William the boy for a time very distraught at the loss of the cow which had to be sold for there were no buildings attached to the cottage but Tom quickly constructed a small hen cabin in the back yard so that they could keep the hens. Little Billy, after bidding a tearful farewell to the cow was somewhat consoled by being able to keep the hens and Gracie was pleased too for she had become used to having the luxury of her own eggs. The small cost of grain was better than buying eggs, for feeding the growing family was becoming more of a problem for as they grew they ate more and Gracie had no intention of them being hungry and skinny like many of the children around about.

Gracie was in the kitchen attempting to put all the pots and pans into the big cupboard, for she wanted to tidy up the kitchen mess from moving before setting about making tea for the children. It was two days since they had moved into the cottage and she had finished the priorities of making up the beds and clearing the build up of washing. She was very pleased with the washing boiler in the little wash house outside, Mr Brown had put in a new copper liner and rebuilt the fire hole, so the last of the washing was now blowing nicely on the line in the back garden. Just as she returned to the house, to start on the pots again, there was a knock on the door, at which she groaned. 'Not now,' she said under her breath, but the knock came again. She went to open the door to find Arthur Wilson and Jack Heapy standing outside. Reluctant to be rude to these friends she smiled and said, 'Cum on in, lads, what's to do?'

'How do, Gracie, we need a bit of advice like, lass.'

'Well if I can help.' Was her quick reply. The two men

standing front of her in front of her were obviously embarrassed by the looks on their faces and the shuffling of their feet. 'Why not sit thee sels down, lads, an' tell me what' problem is?' Gracie tried to put them at ease.

Both men looked at each other , then started to speak both at the same time, while moving to sit down on chairs arranged around the large kitchen table. Both became silent again, then Arthur spoke, 'It's like this, lass. Mr Sowerbutts left us both money for a cottage, but we doesn't want ter live alone like. If us were te buy a cottage together would folk think ill o' us?' And as he spoke his face became a rosy then bright red. 'Dors't thy know what a' mean? Two men live'in together like. I'd do the house and Jack 'as already got a job.'

Gracie hesitated, initially unsure what they were trying to say but the expectant and worried looks on their faces set her mind racing. Gracie suddenly 'twigged' what they were worried about, for Sally, always well informed about gossip, had once told her about two men who she had heard liked men better than women 'in a certain way' and could 'get in trouble for it'. Considering for a moment, desperate for an answer for them, for it was plain just what they were worried about being said, then the solution came. 'Lads nobody really knows ye do they, cus ye lived at Mr Sowerbutts? Did yer ever go out much, shops, church, or the ale houses or such?'

Both men looked aghast at either suggestion. 'Ney, lass, newt like that.' Was the ready answer from Jack.

'Well a' have an idea, give it out as' yer cousins like. Nobody will know it's not reet, an' say as Arthur can't walk much so stays at home. Well yer don't go out much Arthur do yer?'

This was greeted by enthusiastic nodding from Arthur.

'An' keep ter yerselves an' folk al' leave yer alone. An' Tom an' me al' say as yer are, an Jack's Mother died an he were sent t'e workhouse.'

The two men looked at each other, relief plain on their faces. 'D' yer reckon as it'll work, Gracie?' spoke up Jack.

'Aye just keep thy sen' to thy sen' an' it'l bi grand, an' a'll get Tom to spread around as yer cousins.'

'Oh, Gracie, thanks, yer a clever lass,' spoke up Jack, at which he stood to walk to the door, nudging Arthur to do the same.

'Ee tanks, lass,' added Arthur as they both disappeared out of the door.

Later when Gracie explained the meeting to Tom he was equally complimentary, quickly adding, 'But how'd yer come up wi that answer?'

'It just came inte' mi head, Tom. Thank goodness.'

'Well good fer you. They are two good lads.'

Mr Arkroyd paid his workers in the modern fashion every Friday but with ever increasing appetites of her growing family to feed Gracie often ran out of money before the next Friday. So when she heard that the mill where Sarah worked was taking on new trainee workers for the recently added shed, she saw an opportunity for herself, there was now no excuse for being at home to look after the cow and make butter. Agnes, at being informed of the idea, was not sure that she agreed. When Gracie broached the subject of her looking after the children Agnes offered several objections, but convinced by Gracie's strength of argument that the two older children could easily see to the younger ones, all Agnes had to do was supervise, feed them and be on hand, she weakened. So with the appeal of spending more time with her grandchildren she was almost won over. Then Gracie explained to her mother that she had been talking to a woman who she knew had several children, and who worked full time as a weaver and the woman had explained that often several women paid one woman to look after all their children. Gracie when she heard this was not sure that this was right for her children, and she thought her mother would probably agree for Agnes was of the opinion that some women 'dragged' their childer up rather than bringing them up properly, so she cleverly broached this alternative plan confident that Agnes would much prefer to look after the children, and she was right, Agnes was convinced. Still Agnes was sure that Gracie had no real idea of the noise, heat and hard standing work of the ten hour days of the weavers, but as ever she decided there was only one way for her to find out and anyway she might stick it.

CHAPTER 22

The mill was taking on the new weavers and general workers for another newly added shed but Gracie had no experience so could only start as a sweeper and fetcher but more weavers were urgently needed so she was soon set on next to an experienced weaver who could watch over and train her. 'There is so much te watch all a' once, an 'am meking mistakes and damages,' exclaimed Gracie in a nervous panic one morning.

'Now just calm th'sel, Gracie.' Was the advice from Peggy Walsh the older weaver who was training her. 'It's ony cus it's new tha'll soon be reet an neer feer they'll know what te expect, thy'er no worse than anybody else, lass. Fer a while all tha' weaves 'll bi cut up inter fents cutting out yer faults. They sort out 'best fents an' they'll land up on' market stalls. Don't ye feer they'll still mek money outa thee any road.'

So placated by this wisdom fuelled advice Gracie settled to the task. Agnes had been right to worry how Gracie would cope, especially with noise of the mill shed, for she was right, for on the first few days the constant hum and clattering came as a shock to the quiet Gracie who had never before heard how the whizing looms all together raised such a deafening sound which drowned out all speech. Her head throbbed and buzzed for weeks but gradually the sound receded and became tolerable with familiarity. Gracie was impressed to find that a lot of the older mill workers could lip read, often a necessity as many became quite deaf with the constant din. The advice from the old hand steadied Gracie and although her head still sometimes throbbed, the thought of the wage on the Friday stayed her resolve and she soon became used to the racket. Wise Peggy also had more advice to offer, on the subject of other weavers and their habits and antics. 'Keep thee head down, lass, ner gossip we' em, just pass a pleasant word like keep 'em 'appy but at a distance like. If they tek a dislike they can b' reet nasty bitches some of 'em. Oh ey an' if they offer ye a drink 'a tae refuse nicely like, daft buggers boil eggs o' top o' boiler then they use the wata fer brewing their tae, then the' get warts on ther tongs and lips, 'ave yer not seen some of em look a reet mess? Cus tha's a bonny lass the'll want t' get thee a wart, fer sheer bitchiness. Bring a billy can o' cowd tea an' heat it on't stream pipes.'

Gracie had her Mother's good sense to listen to the woman and keep out of trouble, for Peggy's warning only came just in time. Just after she arrived for work the following morning two of the older weavers approached her as she stood at her loom. 'How's tha doin, lass? Bet that owd bitch Peggy has bin telling tha not to mix wi' us. Thinks she's better than us.'

Gracie thought quickly, for she knew she had to be careful not to upset these women who were now standing hands on hips, heads and faces thrust towards her. 'No, she's n'ear said owt,' Gracie lied and the women seemed satisfied.

'Well she must have learnt after last time. Took a week fer her te get 'tar otta 'er 'air.' Gracie never spoke, just instinctively stood quietly and they seemed to lose interest in her when she gave no response or reaction. 'Bah yer just a wet. Come on, Lizzie, leave it.' Gracie sighed in relief and mumbled, under her breath, a quick thanks to Peggy, then got on with the day's work.

Quick to learn she soon became accustomed to the rhythm of the job and the faults in her cloth became less frequent as her confidence grew, and as Peggy had recommended, she kept her head and eyes down and all was quiet and she was left alone. Weeks, then months, passed and Gracie's weaving skills improved to leave her feeling proud as she looked at the cloth she was producing. She had become a very accomplished weaver and she basked in the knowledge that she wasn't just a woman earning a bit of money.

Returning home late one night to find one of the smaller children feverish, with a worried Tom and Agnes soon questioning the wisdom of her working, Gracie was pressed to cry, 'I'm not doin' this for fun yer know, we can't manage wi' out it, mi'money. I aint av'in my childder in secondand clothes.' Tom was tempted to argue but as he looked at his children and saw how much better fed and clothed they seemed than others in the neighbourhood, he realised it was futile to protest for Gracie would do all in her power to keep her brood that way. Thus ending his protests for much as he knew he could not change Gracie he also acknowledged that was why he loved her so.

A few days later driving past the local market stalls, as he made his way back to work after dropping off a delivery at the local provender mill, Tom's eye was caught by fluttering brightly coloured shawls draped high on a stall end. Tempted by their many shades he reined in the cart, tied the reins to the brake and stepped down and walked to the stall. On touching them the soft warm feel convinced him, he stood deliberating for several moments so much so that the stallholder sensing a possible sale came over towards him. 'Any lady would love one of those, sir, just t' thing to keep her warm on a chilly day, or a cool evening, lovely Yorkshire wool.' Was his opening gambit.

But it really wasn't necessary for Tom had already decided that the scarlet red one was perfect for Gracie, against her black hair. It'ad look lovely. Just the thing to keep her warm when goin' an cumin' home from' mill, 'am sure she often feels cowd, he thought. So money was handed over and the shawl was soon wrapped into a brown paper parcel and tied with string, with a loop to carry it by. Firmly clutching this treasure Tom headed back to the cart and carried on with his deliveries. Gracie's delight at the unexpected gift, her twirling and enthusiastic thanks a joy and relief to Tom, who had worried that she would chide him for wasting money.

Gracie had to admit to herself that working at the mill was not totally selfless because of the pride she felt in her work, the five o'clock rise for the six o'clock start was early but no earlier than she was used to and she enjoyed the change from the house, even though her jobs at home had often become a rushed and tiresome late night task. The cow had had to go but when it was dry between calves there was no milk anyway, so the loss was not too greatly felt and she still had the eggs except in midwinter when they went off lay. Also she enjoyed the company of other women which was often entertaining, for by quietly watching, she had found several friends among the quieter types. She was also reunited with her old friend Sally who used to work in the Dixon kitchen, and who was now also a weaver. Gracie was given her own loom close to that of Sally, leaving the training loom so Peggy could coach another trainee. Although chatting was impossible over the clatter of the machinery Gracie and Sally sometimes had opportunities to speak and reminisce. 'The Dixons are finally goin' down south to live before long, yer know, not good enough up ere fer em.' Sally informed Gracie one day at breakfast time break. 'Ther's only Daft Billy left an' Owd Ben the mug working ther' now. They kept 'em on ter see ter clearing up an' so Billy's a bit lost like, as ter what he's gunna do when the clearing's finished. He's been a moping a lot as well since the cattle went 'A' caught him sittin' in corner crying one day soft ap'ath says he don't know what he is banna do or wheer he'll live. D'yer think Tom might be after findin' im some work? He has a bit saved, a' know cus he showed it ter me, asked me ter marry him, silly beggar, an' when I laughed at him, he were reet mad.' On hearing this Gracie was saddened, poor Billy, he would be no match for the quick tongued Sally, and he really was going to be at a lost end without a job and home, and it just went to show, she thought, she hadn't been far wrong when she said to Sally that Billy would get the wrong idea.

As Gracie pulled on her new shawl before leaving the mill that night she drew it closer to her head and shoulders and glancing around enjoyed the admiring glances from Sally and the other girls. She had promised Sally she would ask Tom if they could do anything for Billy, Tom had always had a soft spot for the lad she knew and he really was going to be lost about what to do when the Dixons left, she was sure Tom would think of something.

CHAPTER 23

It was a few weeks later when Edward Dixon, home to help with the family removal, pulled on his brown check jacket, adjusted his newest grey felt hat to a fashionable angle, straightened the new fashion in neckties that he had taken to wearing, picked up his cane and left the house in search of Billy who he had warned to be ready for their final farewell trip to town. Billy still, when Mr Edward asked him, was torn between the remembered promise he had made to Jonas not to drink any more with Mr Edward, and his inclination to accompany his boss on what would be his last chance, for he knew that if he were alone entry to the houses where local whiskey was distilled would not be possible, they wouldn't let him in on his own. When he lost the connection with Mr Edward he felt sure that he would not be welcome in the whiskey spinners or the ale houses, and anyway, once the Dixons left he would have no more wages and even worse no home, and the thought left him fearful and afraid. He had spent many a quiet moment worrying about what he was going to do, but was no nearer to finding an answer and he became more frightened as the days went on. His memories of living in the workhouse when he was younger kept coming into his head to worry and torment him, and to make matters worse Tom didn't seem to have any time to spare for him any more, always working he was. All this spun round in his troubled mind so his decision to go with Edward Dixon was a foregone conclusion as the temptation was too great to deny, but he did remember to take his spade with him as an excuse for being out, in that he was looking for work. When Edward questioned him on its presence he quickly justified it by insisting that he might be able to show his skill and gain work. Edward scoffed at this idea but then considered that it might produce even further amusement as it had in the past. 'How are you at spinning it like a shillelagh, or you could carry it like a rifle, just like a bold and British soldier?' taunted Edward, knowing full well that plant the idea and the chances were Billy would do as he suggested after one drink and before the night was out.

The two men had almost reached the town when Edward's quick eyes spied Tom driving a cart approaching in the distance. The cart was loaded high with what seemed to be wooden boards, and Tom was concentrating, constantly checking that the high piled boards did not slip under the ropes, so he had not noticed Edward and Billy in the distance. Quickly Edward told Billy who it was approaching, at which Billy panicked and turned to run in the direction from which they had come. 'Stop, yer stupid idiot if yer run along the road the noise will make him notice you. Get yourself lost in the town for half an hour by going across the fields NOW and meet me later at Old Dan's.' His words accompanied by a quick poke in the ribs with his swagger stick to help Billy understand the urgency required, and a point of his arm and hand as to which direction to take. Billy did not need the push as he did not want Tom to see him out with Mr Edward so the big man quickly lumbered off into the field to the left leaving Edward to saunter along, and then to stand aside with a disdainful expression on his countenance as Tom aboard the cart passed by. Tom, finally noticing it was Edward Dixon in the road not wanting any trouble, rode past Edward Dixon determinedly keeping his eyes on the road and forward on the horse in front.

Billy, at a loss what to do with himself once he reached the outskirts of the town, and he was not quite sure how long half an hour was, found he had wandered into the market area of the town where the weekly market was still in progress, and just as Tom had been attracted by the bright shawl display so was Billy. The talkative stall holder once more saw his chance for a sale to a 'gentleman' and approached and easily convinced Billy, when he suggested that a 'lady friend' would most certainly appreciate such a garment. Billy encouraged by the man's assurance stroked the warm wool of a shawl whichh''then'snagged on his rough hands. Quickly moving his hands away fearful of the stallholder not liking him handling the shawl he asked the man, 'If a' buy this fer Sally d' yer think she'd marry me?' As he saw a chance to again try to convince Sally to marry him.

The stallholder was unsure how to answer such a precise question but unwilling to risk losing a sale assured Billy that, 'There was nothing better than a nice gift to convince a lady.' The counting of Billy's money took several minutes and although after emptying every pocket he was a farthing short, the stallholder wasn't going to lose a sale, so the purchase was completed. Billy did not fully understand what he was asking of Sally or the full implications of marriage, but he knew Tom was happy, and he was tired of being lonely, so he thought maybe this present might convince her. So this time it was Billy who walked happily away from the market carrying a brown paper string tied parcel containing a red shawl, and as he walked he was trying to think where he might find Sally, the quicker to give her his present and get her to agree to marry him.

The darkness of night had now fully arrived but Billy, still innocently unaware that the half hour had long passed, decided that no time being better than the present he would go and see if

213

he could find Sally and offer his prize. Coincidence often being the hand of fate, Sally was just coming out of the mill when Billy arrived outside the high mill yard wall. By the gas light on the inner yard wall he saw Sally walking across the mill yard and he stood outside the gates waiting for her to come through them. It was well past the finish time and everyone else had left but Sally had taken a fancy to a new tackler who had just been taken on the day before and she had been hanging around to try to speak to him, or at least get his attention, but the 'bloody busybody' overlooker as Sally called him under her breath just would not stop talking to the new man. Sally was normally in a rush to leave at finishing time, and now, feeling cold after standing about in the damp and darkening night she gave up her quest in disgust and so was unusually late leaving, just in time to be greeted by an excited Billy.

Billy, oblivious of the lucky timeliness of the meeting and equally unwitting of the now ill temper of Sally was not met with much friendliness. 'What are ye doin eer, Billy, an what are ye doin' cartin' that ruddy spade about wi yer? Get thesel 'ome, lad.' Poor Billy in his eagerness to show his gift to Sally, completely missed the bad tempered tone of Sally's comment and carried on fumbling with the string around the parcel, while at the same time still holding his spade under his arm pressing it to his side, almost dropping the contents of the parcel in his hurry. Sally who was just about to walk away noticed the flash of bright red in the light from the street lamp, as Billy, fumbling having partly unwrapped the gift, managed to save the parcel from falling to the flags, but in doing so allowed the shawl to escape from the brown paper. Her eyes gleamed as she saw the red wool, guessing the item inside was indeed another red shawl such as Gracie's, which she had silently so coveted. Her hands reached out almost

214

involuntarily grabbing the desired shawl, then holding its softness to her face, she smelt its sharp newness and quickly folded it afresh to drape around her shoulders. 'Aw, Billy, yer' a love, ta.'

Billy beamed back at the now smiling face, delighted at his success he was encouraged to pursue his cause. 'Now, Sally, will yer marry me now? Yer like it don't yer. A' can buy yer other stuff when 'a get work.' Sally looked at the broad smiling face, almost weakened for a moment, thought better of it, then burst out in harsh laughter. 'Ney, Billy yer really are daft, a'll ner marry yer, yerv' nowt up top. Don't yer know yer as daft as they say? Marry ye, never, ye daft bugger, but ta for the shawl, ta very much.' At which she admiringly stroked the soft wool wrapped across her chest, blew Billy a kiss and flounced off down the street.

The big man stood, his heart and mind beyond desolate as he stood outside the open metal mill gates for several minutes with the full harshness of Sally's words running around in his head. All the rejections, all the jokes at his expense, all the loneliness, all the no hope for the future, all accumulating in a spinning haze. So brushing away a tear he set off spade in hand to find Mr Edward at Old Dan's, at least Mr Edward would be glad to see him.

Edward Dixon had been drinking for about an hour when Billy walked through the door of the cottage owned by Dan Watson, so was sufficiently intoxicated so as to not notice the subdued mood of the new arrival. 'Now, Billy my friend, get this down yer, it'll do yer good. An you can buy the next two seeing as yer late.'

'Ow, Mr Edward sir, a've spent mi money on Sal but she still won't marry mi.'

'Well now Billy that's a sad thing, what you need is a few

glasses of Dan's best and you'll feel a lot better, you don't want to be burdening yourself with a wife.' Was the advice from Edward. 'Don't worry about the money I can deduct it from your wages.'

Billy had no idea what deduct was but Mr Edward had said not to worry about the money so had solved the money problem so he agreed. 'Thanks Mr Edward.'

Several hours later Billy was beyond arguing at the fifth drink that was pressed upon him for even though he knew he should be going home he saw no reason to attempt to behave any more, he was beyond caring. Edward unable to induce any more silliness from Billy was becoming bored and so had gone over to talk to a couple of the waterboard management men who had come in as obviously they had discovered the local whiskey supply. I'll buy 'em a drink, pays to keep them sweet, he thought as the deal was not fully completed yet.

Billy, after finding himself standing alone at he bar, had moved and seated himself on a stool in the corner by the fireplace, so leaning his spade against the wall at his side he began an inebriated brood on the evening's events. Sally had called him 'daft', well he knew he didn't understand everything but she wasn't married and he was sure he would soon get a job to have money to buy her things, everybody said he was the best digger ever. She was, he decided, only nice to him when he bought her things, but she had said he was daft and that she would never marry him. The only person who seemed to have time for him was Mr Edward and he was going away, he had told him so, so he was going to have nobody because even Tom seemed too busy to have time for him any more. The big man sat on the stool for a further few minutes, then picked up his spade and without a word to anyone left the cottage and trudged his way home to the

216

farm. As he drunkenly walked his way in the darkness he pondered his future and doing so suddenly understood that there was only him and Old Ben the mug left, all the other farm workers had been dismissed months ago it seemed like. The more he thought as he walked he mused through the drunken fog and saw that he and Ben were left to clear up, because that was what they had always done, he the heavy work and Ben the mugging that no one else wanted to do. So came the true realisation that soon when the clearing up had been done, they would not be wanted any more and he and Ben would be sent on their way and then they would be homeless. He finally reached the farmyard and although unsteady he climbed the wooden stairs to the loft and threw himself despondently on the narrow bed soon to fall hard asleep, his spade on the floor beside him.

The day after the drinking bout with Edward Dixon, Billy had a really bad headache and the memory of the conversation with Sally was continually running through his mind, she was, he decided, not very nice, and now he had no money, not even a penny left, better if he had not bought that shawl, it had been a waste of good money. Consequently he was very quiet when Old Ben had cheerily greeted him after seeing him walking across the yard later that morning, so much so that Ben had queried why he was in much a mood, and where had he been till now? The old man had been quite taken aback when Billy had suddenly rounded on him. 'Nowt d' do wi thee weer ave' bin, mind'in mi own business. Aye and' don'st yer see as wer both fer workhouse afor long, ye owd fool, there's newt t' be appy bout.' At which the older man walked off in a huff, knowing Billy was quite right.

Later that morning while loading some remaining hay from the now almost empty barn onto a cart, for it to be delivered to a farm lower down the valley, the two men were approached by a very smartly dressed Edward Dixon. Hat as always at an angle, he repeatedly slapped his riding crop on his beige twill breeches' leg as he walked toward the cart. Stopping a short distance from where they were working, Edward spoke, 'Right, men, when you have finished tonight report to the farm kitchen door to collect your wages. There is nothing much left to do and from now on it is up to the waterboard to sort out the place, they are now the owners of the farm. I was informed last night that the sale is complete. They have kindly said that you can sleep in the loft tonight if that suits you. Leave the site early tomorrow.' Billy and Ben both stood speechless, then Billy threw the two prong hay fork he was holding down onto the cobbles the metal prongs ringing on the cobbles and they then causing the fork to slide along the yard. Billy crossed the yard without looking back then walked on into the adjoining field and disappeared from view. Ben at a loss what to do carried on loading the cart, nobody had told him to stop.

After his initial burst of anger Billy had slowed his steps and wandered aimlessly about the fields for several hours and was starting to feel hungry, and as the only place he knew there might be food was the farm he trudged back and on arriving in the farmyard was greeted by silence. There was no answer at the kitchen door and after searching the other buildings around the yard found not a person, all was deserted. Frustrated and unsure what to do he sat on the side of the large stone water trough, scooped a drink of water in his hand, glanced around the silent yard as slowly a tear formed and then ran down his cheek. Soon the big man was sobbing quietly, and that was how Ben found him a little later. 'Ney, Billy thee mus't teek on so, thee an me wee'l find summat, see a got thee wages.' Was the old man's attempt to cheer Billy. Billy never said a word, simply took the money from Ben, pushed it into this trouser pocket, and after standing thinking for a moment, headed towards the stables and up to the loft. His spade was where he had left it that morning leaning against the loft wall, and he grabbed it suddenly gaining comfort from its familiar smooth feel in his hands. Returning to the yard he nodded at Ben but without a word started to walk away. 'Hey up, Billy cum back 'ere, what yer gunna do?'

'D'no but ani't stopping eer.' Was the sharp reply at which he left the worried Ben standing in the yard, and headed in the direction of the town.

CHAPTER 24

It was nearly finishing time and Gracie was tired, she was sometimes delayed by Sally wanting to chat as they donned shawls ready to leave, but tonight Gracie was eager to get away as she wanted to call at Ma Blackburn's shop on her way home, so she rushed off before Sally could catch her. Tilly Blackburn ran a grocers shop on Top Row, and she always kept her prices keen and offered cheaper prices on fresh goods and leftover bread that she sold off for the bakers next door after they had closed for the night. This attracted the late leaving mill workers always on the lookout for cheap food. Gracie knew she could get three loaves for the price of two and anything else that might be cheap that night. A pie would be nice fer childer, she thought. Quickly gathering her basket and new shawl, Gracie escaped before Sally could stop her. Sally had just got the extra job of returning empty shuttle bobbins to the overlooker's station at the rear of the shed so she was late, the last to be finishing.

It was the day after Billy had given Sally her shawl and when she found that Gracie had left before her she was disappointed at not being able to show off her own newly acquired garment. She decided to follow her to Ma Blackburn's where she thought she would probably call as she knew it was her usual habit on her way home. She was right for when Sally arrived outside the little cluttered low ceiling shop located at the top of the stone steps up to Top Row Gracie was already paying for her purchases. Sally saw her when she peered through the shop door glass, then she lifted the latch to open the door to enter the shop but paused standing poised in the doorway. 'Look what a've got,' boasted Sally to all in the shop as she did a little standing dance and showed off Billy's gift with a twirl. Standing by the counter, at the back of the shop, Gracie's eyes widened at the sight of what Sally was wearing, for she had an inkling of how much they cost and knew that Sally was always moaning she was broke.

'Oh Sally you've got one too, that's nice for you, aren't they warm?' was Gracie's cautious reply, wary of asking how she came by it.

'So yer see yer not ony one wi a grand shawl, that Daft Billy bought it fer mi silly bugger h'is still tryin ter get mi ter marry 'im but he's wasting 'is time.'

Ma Blackburn's voice shrilled, 'Shut that doere.' Which Sally then did, but not before her words had carried out though the door to anyone listening outside, although not the earlier words from Gracie who was too far inside the shop for her voice to carry out into the night.

Gracie stared at Sally at a loss what further to say to the other woman but her heart going out to poor Billy. Finally, her concern for Billy overcoming her reluctance, she spoke slowly, 'Sally yer shouldn't let him buy yer stuff and that shawl wer dear a' know.'

'Well thy's got one why can't I a' one anall?' Was Sally's terse reply.

'Because Billy don't understand, an anyway he can't 'ave much money an' ees gunna need all he 'as when he's thrown off the farm, it al be soon,' carried on the exasperated Gracie.

'Weel, that's not my problem. Weel, I didn't mek him buy it, and anyhow they wouldn't 'ave it back now. Anyhow he'd ony spend it on beer it's better on my back.' At which she flounced over to the display of jars of sweets which was arranged on a

221

shelf at the rear of the shop, leaving Gracie standing at a loss for further words.

Back at the mill the gates were again just being closed as Billy arrived outside looking for Sally, but the overlooker who was locking up suggested that he try Ma Blackburn's and thoughtfully reminded him that the steep path and bridge over the railway was the quickest route and would get him there sooner. The man was quite right about his directions, for as Billy reached the far end of the bridge, he saw Sally gradually appear coming up the steep stone steps from the road below, her face and blond hair peeping from under the shawl caught in the bluey green circle of light from the gas lamp at the head of the steps. He watched her as she stopped for a moment to peer into the shop and then open the door and stand just inside it, the light inside the shop showing her actions of showing off the shawl to those inside quite clearly. When he was close to the shop Billy hesitated, and stepped back into the shadows of the bridge canopy from where he stood watching seeing Sally posing to show off the shawl, then he heard her words carry out into the night as she spoke to Gracie. Confused and upset, the anger in him began to swell. How could she take the shawl but then say all those things. Then he remembered. 'She had said I was daft,' he repeated to himself over and over again. 'Said I had newt on top, but I had mi hat on.' But really why that mattered he did not understand.

What he did know was that he had no home to go to, nowhere to sleep after tonight and it would have all been all right if Sally had said she would marry him because when you were married you had a home, married people always had a home. Well he was going to make sure that if Sal would not marry him, she would marry no one else, he just had to work out how to stop her. He continued standing in the shadows, brooding, he twisted his hands continually around the wooden spade handle gaining some small comfort from its familiar smooth feel. A train approached, making the metal bridge vibrate and shaking him out of his musing. Yes, he decided he would wait and ask her again, she seemed so pleased with the shawl he was sure she would have changed her mind.

Standing in the shadow cast by the iron roof of the railway bridge Billy waited patiently. The sound of the bell attached to the door indicated someone was leaving the shop and Billy started forward but it was a young lad obviously sent for some late purchase. He stepped back once more into the shadows but as he did he once again through the open door heard Sally's voice for she had moved back towards Gracie, nearer the door as Gracie prepared to leave the shop. 'Gracie de yer think yer could ask Tom to tell Billy ter bloody well leave me alone he's starting te be a proper nuisance?' A shocked Gracie did not reply, she could not find the words, she just turned from Sally to the door.

Billy heard her words, 'No,' he muttered, he decided she wasn't going to change her mind. 'But if she won't marry me she ani't marrying anybody else I'll tell her that.'

As he waited for Sally to emerge what Billy did not know was that Gracie who was wearing her own red shawl was also in the shop and ready to leave. He was alerted again to the shop door opening by another tinkling of the sprung bell and then the light from the doorway slanted on the pavement flags. He saw the woman come out and start towards the steps down to the main road. It must be Sally because he could see the red of the shawl as she gripped it hard and tight under her chin against the chilling night air. Just as the woman had opened the door, Billy heard a another train approaching under the bridge, he opened his mouth to speak her name and just at that point the train passing under the bridge blew its horn. The woman never hesitated, Billy's words drowned by the sound of the train, but carried on walking towards the steps. Billy watched for a second then he stepped towards her, he lifted his hand to stop her but in his hand was the spade. As his hand reached out the spade then raised high into the air. He drew back his hand and with it the spade back up and behind his shoulder and then with all the desperation and despair in his fuddled mind he swung it at the head of the woman who had mocked him. The spade hit its mark with a sickening thud of accuracy, the power of the blow twisting the face and body of the woman towards Billy before she tumbled headfirst down the steep stone steps. His eyes, then his brain, registered the face, the wrong face. He had just hit Gracie, lovely Gracie, he had seen her face before she fell, but it should have been Sally coming out of the shop, why was it Gracie and not Sally. Billy stunned and confused stood as though frozen. For a moment there was a silence before Sally, who had dallied before leaving the shop but standing shocked still saw the steel gleam of the use polished spade as it arced through the air to find its target and screamed as she stood in the shop doorway. Then Billy cried out, the cry of a wounded creature, then a high pitched long 'No-o'. The desire to hid, to run away took hold. 'Must hide, run can't look.' He ran stumbling blindly just to get further away from what he had done. 'Run must run 'way then a can't see 'er.' His voice cracked in his throat as the same words were uttered again and again as he disappeared along the metal bridge his footsteps a clattering echo in the darkness, his spade clutched in his hands.

The scream and cries had brought people hurrying to see what was going on and what the swelling crowd at the bottom of the steps saw by the gas light was a crumpled Gracie lying in two dark spreading stains. The wound at her head was almost hidden by her dark hair and the shawl but blood was trickling onto the flags beneath her and her skirt was becoming dark sodden as the unborn child she was carrying lost its grip on life.

After the initial shock of the terrible sight they had found, all began to take action. A woman bending close cried, 'She's still breathing.'

A man amongst the group motioned to another and they quickly lifted from its hinges a lobbyway door. Ushering the now large crowd back they gently laid the injured Gracie onto the door and two other eager men helped lift the makeshift stretcher high. A woman realising who the injured woman was spoke, 'It's Grace Briggs, Gracie Bailey as was, she lives at Ivy Cottage on the main road, I'll fetch her mother.' At which she ran off in the direction of Sarah's cottage.

The four men headed in the direction of the cottage followed by several of the crowd. The remainder of the crowd were now shocked by the appearance at the bottom of the steps of an hysterical Sally shouting to all. 'It's all my bloody fault, it were Billy, Daft Billy he hit her wi' his spade. A' bet he thought Gracie were me. Ee were reet mad at me 'cause a' wouldn't wed him.' At this she started screaming again, then plumped down on the bottom of the stone steps sobbing loudly. The delay in Sally's arrival had been due to her shock at what had happened and the fact that she had realised that she was the intended target and should now be lying on the ground bleeding. She had stood leaning against the shop wall for several minutes until she had come to her senses and knew that she should be seeing if Gracie was 'all reet', but she wasn't and she had just arrived in time to see them carry her away. 'I' should bi me,' she muttered.

Sarah was stunned, her mind in turmoil as she turned from receiving the news at the door, to try to convey the same to her mother. 'Mother, Gracie's been badly hurt in an accident, it must be an accident Mabel Slater said.'

Agnes turned to her daughter. 'Aye it must be. I'll get mi shawl. Lets go an' see what's 'appen'd te lass.'

'Mabel said as they wer' teeking her home,' said Sarah.

'Weel that's ony reet. Let's be gone.'

A distraught Sarah reached Ivy Cottage ahead of the slower and equally troubled Agnes. The back door was open and Sarah saw the terrible sight of a blood stained Gracie lying on the door which had been placed on the big kitchen table. She also saw the streaks of blood on the green painted door and for a moment a wave of deep terrible sickness rose inside her then the strong Sarah regained control as she quickly turned to her mother, who had just arrived. 'Oh, Mam, a' think she's very bad.'

Agnes walked past the now motionless Sarah into the dimly lit cottage kitchen to face the worst sight she had ever seen. She placed her hand on the forehead of her prostrate daughter and felt the chill that was creeping over the broken body. Then glancing around the crowded room her concern was equally for the children and Tom. The children were huddled in the kitchen's furthest corner half under the stairs. The oldest girl stricken faced was standing clutching the baby and the only boy was arms around the other girls as they all stood huddled together, the occasional whimper coming from first one then another. Agnes looked at the crowd which had crushed into the room. 'I thank ye all fer yer concern an' help but ask ye t' leave us alone now.' Many amongst the crowd nodded in silent agreement and the room was cleared in a very few minutes.

Tom was standing at the end of the door his blooded hands placed either side of Gracie's head. 'Mother we need warm water to wash her face and hair, her lovely hair is full of blood and bits

226

from the flags where she fell. Shall a go ter get her nightdress for yer and then a' can carry her te bed?'

Agnes looked at her son-in-law at a loss what to say, strangely her brain registered that for the first time the lad had called her Mother. Looking at the fearful sight before her, the lamplight casting shadows and the sides of the room disappearing into the darkness, it seemed she was viewing it all from a distance and the sounds were fading. Then the inner strength of the woman surfaced as she turned to Sarah who had not moved since arriving. 'Sarah love, a think it best if yer tek t' childer te cottage fer t'neet. Just go quickly upstairs and get theer neet clothes and some cloths fer t' baby an' tek em all home now, gi em some porrige an' bread.'

Sarah now comforted with something to do quickly carried out her mother's instructions and she and the children hurriedly wrapped in various shawls and jackets left hand in hand for their aunt's cottage, the oldest girl who was last still clutching the baby turned at the door and cried out 'Mam' but Sarah quickly turned her and putting her arm around the child's shoulders directed her outside where the others were waiting.

Just as Sarah left, a distraught Sally almost stumbled through the open door. 'Oh, Mrs Bailey it wer Billy, I saw him from' shop door, a think it wer meant fer me. Oh what 'ave a done? I wouldn't marry 'im, an 'ee wer reet mad.'

Agnes, while trying to make sense of what Sally was saying, was at the same time stroking the hand of her daughter, her other hand on Tom's arm. 'Sally be quiet, do summat useful an' go fer Dr Malley.'

But Sally was so disturbed that the tirade carried on unabated. 'All't men 'ave gone looking fer 'im he ran off, but they can't fin' Constable, whos' likely drunk in Owd Dan's.'

Agnes could stand no more. 'Sally go an get Dr Malley, yer mouth al' get thee ther if not yer feet.'

Sally was suddenly quiet. 'Aye, Mrs Bailey.' And she was gone out of the door.

Alice Cornall, one of the nearby neighbours, now appeared at the doorway. Her voice low she asked, 'Agnes is ther owt a can do ter help?'

'Aye, Alice, thanks, can yer go ter Sarah's an fetch Mrs Bellow's sheets, jus tell er that she'll know what tha means?'

'Sure Agnes al be gone.' At which she turned and left for Sarah's cottage.

Alone with Tom, Agnes glanced at his stoney face. Her voice was a whisper as slowly she said, 'Tom, she's dead, she's gone, all we can do is what's reet, will yer let me d' that?' Tom looked at his mother-in-law not understanding. 'Tom, she needs ter b' washed, will thee get that theer neetdress?'

When, after several moments hesitation at which Agnes feared he really was not understanding, Tom slowly disappeared up the stairs, Agnes turned to look at the fire and saw with much relief that the embers were still red, she quickly added some sticks from the bucket at the fireside and as they flared added coal. There was water in the kettle so she moved the hob over the heat. She then turned to her daughter lying on the door. A sob escaped her lips, lips that were becoming sore and swollen from the harsh biting she was inflicting on them. Silently she formed the words, 'Oh mi lass, mi lovely lass, God wi' welcome yer.'

Tom descended the stairs slowly, as he had ascended like an old man, he handed the nightdress to Agnes, turned and moved to a chair at the fireside. 'Tom de yer understand what a 'ave te do, yer do don't yer? She needs te b' washed an dressed decent, an I'm not 'avin that ther dirty Maggie Hill do'in' it. She's mi own lass.'

Tom looked uncomprehendingly at his mother-in-law for several moments and then harsh reality and understanding dawned, he turned his face to the fire. Agnes stood silently for a moment, she knew that she should not touch or move Gracie until the doctor arrived but Sally had to find him and if he was not at home it could be a long while and anyway his house was about half a mile away. Avoiding looking at the silent man by the fire, Agnes eased herself down onto a stand chair at the side of the table grateful for the weight off her legs. The mantle clock chimed the hour breaking the near silence of the room for nobody noticed the clock's tick, at which Agnes glanced at first the clock then her son-in-law but he had not moved he was as if in a trance. Many more minutes passed and even the steady stoic Agnes was beginning to shake with shock when there was a knock on the door and the doctor entered. Dr Malley was well in middle age and normally past being shocked but even he drew back at the sight of the damage to Gracie's head. There was little need for much examination that was plain for the doctor to see. 'She is dead, Mrs Bailey. What happened, Mrs Bailey, do you know?' he queried gently.

Agnes struggled to find the words to explain how her daughter had died. Died. Yes she was dead. Her child, her Gracie, her lovely Gracie. The words chased around in her head as the doctor waited patiently. Finally Agnes managed to convey a brief account of the accident for she was still sure it was an accident, as she had been told. The doctor quickly crossed the room to sit in the vacant chair at the other side of the fireplace to speak to the silent Tom. 'Hello, Tom, I am sorry but your wife is dead, and with it being sudden there will have to be an inquest. They might insist that her body has to be on view.'

But before the doctor could say anything further Tom raised his eyes and quietly said, 'No, the only time she leaves this house is to go to her grave. I need to look after her.' Then he turned his face once more to gaze into the fire's flames. The doctor's heart went out to the man opposite, who the last time he saw him was so full of optimism, he did not deserve this.

The doctor stood, walked over to Agnes and glancing at Gracie said, 'I'll see what I can do about the inquest, to make it as easy as possible. I'll send you the paper you need from me. If you have some brandy or some such it might help the lad, but nothing will really.' Then left without another word.

Agnes remained seated her head now calm her heart crying, sobbing, no screaming in her chest. Just then there was another knock at the door and Alice Cornall entered carrying the linen sheets. Agnes, grateful for the interruption, motioned with her head to Tom at the fireside. Alice instantly understood the situation and in a low voice said, 'Sorry a've bin a while, Agnes, a've bin helping Sarah wi' childer, they're all upset,fer they don't understan.' She then asked, 'Will yer let mi help yer, Agnes, wi' lass 'ad be proud ter.'

Agnes nodded her grateful thanks, not speaking for fear her voice would break. Then the two women silently and gently began their task. Finally, the door removed, the table being of enough length to support Gracie's body, a prized sheet was maneouvred gently under a Gracie now dressed in the clean white nightdress, an empty lace pillowcase under her padded head and the second sheet gently laid over her. Alice was strangely grateful that Gracie's beautiful face was perfect beneath the now smooth cloud of flowing black hair. She had wiped her daughter's face so gently as memories of doing so to the small child who had brought so much joy crowded her head. Agnes sighed, crossed to the stone sink and emptied the red coloured water from the enamel bowl she was holding, then rinsed it out with the remainder of the water in the now nearly cold kettle. Alice quickly looked at Tom and whispered to Agnes, 'What do we do now?'

'Yer go, Alice, 'a think as we ave ter leave 'em alone. The doctor said give him brandy or summat but I have none, he don't understand folk like us a newt like that. A' doubt he'd have owt a' offered. A'll cum back first leet ter'morn, ther's newt ter be done wi 'im ter nite.' Agnes now looked at Tom for again he had not moved or spoken while the two women had attended to Gracie. 'Tom, Gracie is reet now, a'll be away t'see how childer are.' But there was no reply from the motionless man. Glancing around the room Agnes then saw Gracie's basket and shawl that someone had obviously picked up and brought to the cottage. Her shopping was still in the basket and Agnes saw the loaves still in their paper wrapping. She tried again. 'Tom a' am gun' te teke this loaf fer childer, they'll bi hungry.' But still no reply so picking up the bread and with with one last glance towards the fire she left the cottage.

Alone in the now quiet room Tom crossed to his wife. He stood beside the table, his hands cupped the cold face and he then bent and kissed the now cold lips. 'Gracie my heart is broken.' The soft words floating on the silence. He sat on the stand chair as Agnes had and holding Gracie's hand settled his head against her cold body. 'A' shan't leave thee, lass, ner fear,' he whispered. 'God bless.'

He was still sitting there when Agnes arrived back the following morning. She felt the tears coming at the sorrowful sight, but told herself she had to be strong for the lad was going to be no help that was plain. 'Tom, lad, wake up, theer are things te bi done.' He looked up at his mother-in-law like he was truly in a trance, no sign of recognition or understanding. 'The'll at te go te undertekers, Tom.'

Still no word of comprehension, then. 'Nay thee go, Mother. A'll a'ta stay wi Gracie.' Agnes looked at the stricken face.

'So this is how its' te'be,' she acknowledged to herself. 'Aw well so be it.' At which she picked up her shawl, wrapped it around her shoulders and took herself off to the undertakers. As she told Sarah later, 'He's a broken man, a lost soul, heart broken, we'll have our work cut out 'cause there will be no help or effort from him.'

She was right, barely eating, he sat beside his wife until the undertakers arrived with her coffin, but he refused to allow them to place the lid. 'Not 'til we are ready t' carry her t'grave.' Then he sat down bedside her once more.

The search for Billy went on all night, even though weary men knew they would have to turn up for work the next day they continued, but to no effect. Nobody had seen him since he ran away from the shop and over the railway bridge. In the end they found his body easily, they knew where it was and where to drag when a waterworks man found his treasured spade abandoned on the bank of the new reservoir the next morning. The rescue boat was brought from the other higher reservoir, manned and pushed onto the water. The grappling hook thrown in and dragged as the second man rowed away from the bank. A result was quick in coming. The hook soon caught what they were searching for. The great weight of drowned Billy was it seemed unwilling to be lifted into the boat for twice it defied them by slipping back out when half in and almost sunk the small boat in the process, men in the boat hanging on to the sides as the boat rocked wildly. So they settled for dragging Billy's body to the reservoir edge where it took four men to pull him from the water and heave him onto a hand cart. The local Constable for once now sober and tidy took charge and ordered the men to take the body to the police station. Then he contrived to be there before them by rushing ahead in order to direct them to place Billy in the cell on the bench. The officer had never been faced with such a situation before and although he knew the man was dead he was a murderer and this seemed the best place until he was instructed otherwise. The further instructions soon came with the arrival of a sergeant from Manchester who wasted no time in organising the further transportation of Billy's remains to the mortuary at Strangeways Gaol. When word got round that the cart had arrived to collect Billy's body a crowd collected outside the police station. It took four policemen to carry the stretcher and as they passed through the pressing crowd not a word was heard until they were lifting up the tail board of the cart when a woman's voice shouted 'Murderer' at which the word became a chant until the sergeant shouted silence as he gained his seat beside the driver, then the cart moved off.

CHAPTER 25

Tom never did remember much about the weeks after Gracie died, just a series of pictures that periodically came back into his head. The one where the children were standing huddled at the back of the room under the stairs, the oldest her arms holding the baby close to her chest, as they carried Gracie into the kitchen. Mrs Bailey and another woman washing away the blood and dressing Gracie as though for going to bed, which was right, he thought, as she was asleep. The doctor who told him Gracie had to be taken away and telling him in no way was she leaving her home to be displayed to all and sundry. Then the doctor coming back to say she could stay with Tom after all. Himself, for he would let no other, carrying Gracie through to the little parlour when the joiner and his lad brought the wooden coffin. There he placed his wife in the padded box, and finally the tears coursed down the crumpled face. The tears became sobs as he still remained standing beside the coffin. He stood motionless his gaze never moving from Gracie's white lifeless face looking for all the world like a beautiful wax mask as they finally covered the coffin with the wooden lid, just before they carried her out to the hearse. The vision of the blood smeared green lobby door, that somebody finally took away, kept creeping into his mind like a reminder of the harsh reality of it all. Then standing with the children, Agnes and Sarah and a quickly summoned Dora, all around the black heaped soil at the grave side. Dora not looking like herself at all for she wore fancy clothes and now she spoke like a lady, and despite his protests she would insist in buying the childer new clothes. Tom did not like the charity but as Mother had said, for now he always found himself calling Agnes Mother, Gracie would have been so proud to see them all so well dressed. The unwanted callers offering condolences at the cottage door. Tom barely managing to be polite, he just wanted them to leave him alone. The women, for there was more than one, even a very well dressed one, who offered homes temporary or permanent to the children. All were turned away with a 'Ta but we'll manage weel enough, we stay together, my wife will not have it otherways.'

Agnes banged once hard on the door then walked straight into the kitchen of the farmhouse. 'Tom Briggs, this has gone on long enough,' she almost shouted at the man slumped in the chair beside the cold hearth. 'For Gracie's sake yer 'ave ter sort th'sel out. Aye fer Gracie and fer th' childer, fer Gracie's childer. That's what she 'ad want yer te do, lad.' Tom looked at his mother-in-law, then turned away without rising from the chair, and without a word. 'Two weeks, Tom, and not a hand turn of work or care fer the childer. Look at mi lad. It's got to stop. Now!, 'am not runnin' this eer ouse fer ever. An' Mr Arkroyd is worried to death about yer, an he can't keep thee job open fer ever, lad. Will yer not consider Mrs Worthington's offer? She called on me again yesterday, she sez she'll bring up the two middle uns, Martha and Vera, her 'usband bein mill manager she's well off- they's de well wi her. She said they could cum home t' visit like.'

'No, an' a'll thank yer not ter mention it agin, they stay together.' Was the firm reply.

Agnes was not to be put off. 'It can't carry on, Tom, yer 'ave ter shake up. Parish a'll tek 'em from ye if they think thy's not lookin' atter 'em. The childer need te cum 'ome. Tom, thee are sitting ther' in same clothes tha' wore fer fun'rel and thy's neer got a beard on thee chin, an' the place is a disgrace. Thee childer need thee.' Was the last final plea.

The man rose, turned away from the agitated woman towards the door, and as he walked out of the house uttered one word, 'Why?' Agnes swore at his retreating back, not a woman to swear but she was beyond normal words. Then she went home, the childer would need their tea; somebody had to look after them.

Almost stumbling, Tom headed at a run towards the graveyard, to where Gracie was for he needed her help, he needed her. He did not want to carry on, he didn't know how to carry on, and Mother just kept nagging at him. There was the old oak tree just inside the wall of the graveyard so near that it sheltered her grave, and it was to this that Tom headed to lean against its strength. Its familiar rough hardness comforted him as it had for many hours in the last two weeks. He slid to the ground, his back still propped against the rough bark, the pain comforting as it scratched his back. He sat staring at the arch top stone at the grave head, mindlessly reading the words chiselled into it. 'Well, lass, at least ye have the company of thee faather, Gracie, two good souls together.' There was no desire in him to return to the house so, when he finally rose his body stiff and cold from the hard ground, he headed out towards the fells, perhaps there would be peace there, and as he gained altitude his mind calmed and his footsteps became surer. He wasn't sure how long he had been walking but it must have been a while because the light was fading. He had not walked with any destination in mind, so he was quite surprised when he became aware of where he was. The sound of the stream caught his attention then he saw the hawthorn tree on the water's edge. 'Still here, then, Old friend,' he murmured to himself not expecting any answer from the tree. Suddenly weary, he stumbled, regaining his footing, he climbed a little further, then sat down suddenly against a moss covered boulder. Again feeling he needed support, gaining comfort from a solid thing, he leant against its cold hardness.

He awoke suddenly, now very cold, for he had slept for many hours, the first time a true sleep since they had carried Gracie in though the house door. At first at a loss as to where he was, then total clear recall and memories flooded back, and a sob choked his throat and the hopelessness cloud descended. Tom now slowly became aware of the darkness, which at first had eluded him because of the brightness of the moon. It was bouncing its cold light on the surface of the pond which made him remember another time when he was in the same place. He was not shocked to be here, it seemed right. He closed his eyes to try to visualise her face, but somehow it would not come to him and he became desperate to see it. He sat for long minutes hands pressed to either side of his forehead all the while whispering her name, but she would not come to him. 'Gracie, Gracie, Gracie.' Her name called so softly and so many times. Desolate he opened his eyes and in that same well remembered white gleam he now saw them in the distance. They were there, the slim barefoot girl with dark tousled curls wearing a white dress and the big dog both walking towards the water. They reached the pit and stopped to remain motionless at the water's edge. The dog turned to gaze at the girl who stroked her hand over its head. For many moments they remained, the girl no not just a girl it was Gracie, gazing into the water and the dog gazing at the girl. Now the girl started to skip and twirl as the dog still sat patiently watching. The twirling stopped suddenly as if Gracie had sensed something and she looked directly towards him, then she started to walk towards him. Still struck motionless as he had been at first sight of them, just as he had many years ago, but his heart was racing. Delight

237

and joy now lit his face. This was no dream, they had come back to him. Then tentatively he held out a hand to them as they approached but they seemed not to see him, and they passed unseeing silently by him. He tried to make a step towards them, but his feet would not move. 'Gracie,' he tried to say, but his voice had no sound. They did not turn or look back. 'Must follow,' he told himself, as he then tried again to call out but his tongue and mouth were too dry to make sounds. Desperate he tried to follow but still his feet would not move. Then they were gone, gone into the moonlight, but no, no not gone that was her voice, he clearly heard well remembered words whispered softly on the breeze. 'Cum on, lad, it's time to go home.'